THE DISCLOSURE PROTOCOL

Dean Crawford

© 2018 Dean Crawford
Published: 1st May 2018
Publisher: Fictum Ltd
The right of Dean Crawford to be identified as author of this Work has been asserted by him in accordance with sections 77 and 78 of the Copyright, Designs and Patents Act 1988.
All rights reserved.

www.deancrawfordbooks.com

I

Carron Bridge, Scotland

'I'm not goin' onto the moors.'

Tyler Nicks was not someone who would normally have shown fear, but standing on the edge of miles of uninhabited moorland in the dead of night, he figured that the guys could cut him a break. The growled reply blew that illusion right out of the water.

'Don't go yellow on us Tyler.' Bill Shankley, known to his friends simply as "Shank", sneered at Tyler, his features visible now in the faint glow from several torches held by their accomplices. 'This was your idea, remember?'

Shank was a local trouble maker whom Tyler had run into a few times in school. Tyler was the bigger but younger of the two, but what Shank lost in stature he more than made up for with a near-psychotic aggression. Shank was much feared, not so much because of his willingness to fight as much as the fear of what he might do in such a fight. Tyler reckoned Shank would be found dead within a few years with a knife in his guts, such was his reckless abandon.

'Yeah, that was before the lights got worse,' Tyler replied, trying to conceal the genuine fear that he felt creeping through his bones.

They were standing to the west of a fire break that ran alongside Muir Mill, a lonely spot a few miles out of Bonnybridge. Beyond were the open moors and hills, a tapestry of lonely tracks and remote hiking paths. To the south the nearest town was a few miles away, to the west the Carron Valley Reservoir and nothing but miles of moors, hills and forests.

'The lights was what got us here,' Shank reminded him. 'Are we gonna check this out or are you gonna head home to your mummy?'

A ripple of sniggers from their companions, none of whom were more than fifteen years of age, stiffened Tyler's resolve. He gripped his flashlight tighter in his hand, noting that despite his mocking Shank was making no attempt to take the lead. Tyler had noticed that about some people, how they were able to manipulate others into taking their risks for them and then mocking them if they failed. He wouldn't let Shank get the better of him.

'It's this way.'

Tyler led the way across the firebreak and into the woodland, following a natural gulley that would lead them west up the steep hillside. On the brow of the mountains was a clearing that afforded spectacular views to the west, but it was also where the lights had been seen.

Tyler knew that lots of folk came from across the country from England, Wales and even from abroad to try to spot the lights. Most of them were UFO nuts, the kind of people who believed that the government was run by alien reptiles or some such, and who paraded around with cameras and wild-eyed expressions. The locals called them "Mulders" for some reason, although Tyler wasn't sure what a Mulder was. Something to do with a television programme or something.

'That way.'

Shank spotted the old hiking trail and Tyler followed it up toward the peaks invisible against the deep blackness of the night. This far from major towns, there was absolutely no ambient light whatsoever and the heavy cloud cover made it seem as though they were walking a narrow path with nothing but deep space on all sides. It was only when Tyler reached the brow of the hills and turned to catch his breath that he spotted the glittering lights of Falkirk in the distance. A few headlights on distant country roads drifted like white beacons in the deep blackness, and he was surprised that the ever-present wind that normally buffeted the tops of the hillsides was missing, the air still and silent.

The other three joined him and Shank wiped sweat from his brow and glanced over his shoulder at the view without interest. 'Now what?'

'Now, we wait,' Tyler replied.

The lights had been seen for several nights in a row now, enough that the sightings had appeared in the local Gazette under various headlines; *Strange lights haunt the moors. What are the lights that we see over the mountains? UFOs or natural phenomena? Is Scotland being visited by beings from another world?*

'How long do we have to wait?'

Another thing about Shank was his lack of patience. Tyler went from being nervous about coming up here to annoyed that he'd even mentioned his plan to Shank at all.

'How the hell should I know? If you don't want to be here, go someplace else, okay?'

Shank muttered something unintelligible and then sat down on a damp rock and got his cell phone out. The screen glowed in the darkness and lit his face with a ghoulish light as he began playing some sort of game. Tyler left his own cell phone where it was in his pocket, knowing that the light would spoil his night vision if he let the glare hit his face.

Whereas Shank and the others had been brought up in Falkirk, Tyler had been raised on a farm and had spent most of his life outdoors. It was for that reason that he was surprised at his own reluctance to come out here at night, and the moment he started thinking about it, the worse it got. Why did he feel so concerned? The hillside was silent but for their own presence, and Murphy's Law suggested that all they would get for their efforts tonight was damp arses and a scolding for being out so late without telling anyone where they were and…

'What's that?'

'What's what?' Tyler asked.

One of the lads was pointing out into the darkness, towards Falkirk. The distant town was little more than a glow reflected off the low clouds and obscured by distance, but Tyler quickly caught sight of a flickering glow a couple of miles away, out on the moors.

'Looks like a camp fire,' he replied. 'Probably some of the tourists looking for the lights too.'

'Bloody waste of time,' Shank uttered. 'At least they had the sense to start a fire.'

Tyler tutted but said nothing. They sat down on the heather and tried to make themselves comfortable, but Tyler felt twitchy and unsettled. Again, he wondered why he was feeling so odd, and then it hit him as suddenly as though he had been struck. The wind.

Tyler looked up at the clouds and watched them scudding along in the darkness above them. A twenty-knot wind, easy. Yet he could feel nothing on his face, the dense grasses around them utterly still and silent. He looked around at Shank and the others, all of them oblivious to the discrepancy.

'Where's the wind?' he asked out loud.

'What now?'

Tyler pointed up at the sky. 'Where's the wind, it should be blowing a gale up here.'

The boys looked up at the clouds, and it was as if as one they all began to suddenly feel the concern that was haunting Tyler, as though finally realising that they really should not be here at all. Shank stood up and jammed his cell phone in his pocket, masking his unease with impatience.

'Sod this, I've had enough. I'm going home.'

The others made to leave, getting up off the heather, and Tyler opened his mouth to speak when there was a burst of light so bright that Tyler felt as though he had been hit with something physical. He heard himself cry out, heard the shouts of alarm from the others as they all toppled over in the sudden, blinding brightness.

The hairs on Tyler's arms and neck rose up beneath his thick winter jacket and the air hummed as though alive, but it felt as though he was under water and could not move freely. His arms felt heavy and lethargic and all sound seemed dull and muted. He tried to shield his eyes against the fearsome orb of white light blazing into his eyes but it was so powerful that even when he closed them he could still see a vivid red glow.

'What's happening?!' Shank yelled in horror, and tried to scramble away from the light.

Tyler reached out to stop him, worried that they would be in greater danger if they split up, and then suddenly the light vanished and they were plunged into a deep blackness. The intense humming vanished and Tyler heard their breathing in the darkness, panicked and uneasy, and then he heard something else.

The wind was back, rumbling across the lonely mountains as it always had. He looked up in confusion across the hilltop, saw the gleaming lights of Falkirk far to the east. The flickering camp fires they had seen earlier had disappeared, as though the tourists had suddenly left without warning.

'What the hell was that?' Shank uttered.

The fury that it seemed had been permanently etched into Shank's features had been replaced by open panic, his eyes wide and wild. Tyler couldn't get his thoughts in order but he knew that they had been virtually right beneath the light, or whatever it had been. He was trying to think about whether they should get off the mountain and back home when the youngest boy in the group threw an arm out and pointed across the hillside.

'There's someone there.'

Tyler felt a cold dread run like ice through his veins as he turned and saw a figure moving unsteadily across the hilltop, dimly illuminated by the glow from their flashlights. Tyler recognised the figure as a man, although somewhat short and walking as though he might be injured in some way. He wondered if one of the tourists had been on the hillside and had been injured when the light struck.

'Are you okay?'

The man looked up at them as he approached, but he did not reply. As he moved close enough to be seen clearly in the flashlight beams, Tyler realised that there was something not quite right about him. At first, he couldn't put his finger on it but gradually he began noticing things that didn't make any sense. The man looked to be about thirty years old, and yet he was a good three inches shorter than Tyler. He wore a thin beard, and his jaw was wide and his eyes somewhat sunken, his skin a little pale and dirty. On the wind, Tyler got a whiff of intense body odour from the man, and Shank coughed a little as he too smelled the man's scent.

Tyler looked the man up and down. He was wearing a loose tunic of some sort, made from woven wool and open at the neck, and his pants were long and tied up at the ankle beneath oddly shaped boots. The flashlight beams converged on the man as he came to stand before them, and he looked at the flashlights in apparent terror as he threw his arms up and staggered away from them.

'Thoust oone as baernett hr aecan and binnan eower thy han?!' the man uttered.

Tyler hesitated. The man's voice was not of a local tone, and the dialect was something that he didn't recognise but sounded oddly familiar. The man must be one of the odd-ball tourists who had gotten lost on the mountain, or maybe even a homeless vagrant.

'Where are you from, pal?' Shank asked, some of his confusion and terror now having abated as he stood up off the heather and confronted the man.

The man looked at him in confusion and shook his head, staring around himself in the darkness with his arms still shielding his face from the flashlights. 'Yonder yfel?'

Tyler began to feel a superstitious awe creep through his body as he watched the man. He was strangely smaller than he should have been and there was something both alien and familiar about the way he was speaking that reminded Tyler of his great grandmother. Before she had passed away she had occasionally drifted off into some kind of reminiscience, perhaps because she was suffering from Alzheimers. On those occasions she had stopped speaking English and reverted to her childhood language, Gaelic.

'Co as a that hu?' Tyler asked the man where he was from, using what he could recall of the language.

The man looked at him but shook his head, confused and agitated. Shank laughed suddenly.

'I reckon this one's had too many happy biscuits! Hey fella, how about you share some of them with us?'

Shank walked toward the man, but Tyler tried to stop him. 'Shank, get away from him.'

'What's he gonna do, kick me in the shins?' Shank chuckled as he shone his flashlight straight at the man's face. 'Look at him, he's a couple of stones short of a wall. Hey, where are you from?'

The man backed away and cast a fearful gaze at the flashlight beams pointing at him.

'Waegn swelan cwide ofbeatan mey!'

The man's tone had changed from fear to panic.

'Shank, leave him be!' Tyler yelled.

Shank laughed, advancing on the man, and all at once the stranger yanked a short-bladed knife from beneath his tunic, the dull metal blade flashing wickedly in the flashlight beams. Shank let out a yelp of panic and tried to scramble away, but the man was far too fast. The blade flickered as he swiped and Tyler felt his gut churn over as Shank's cry for help was snatched from his throat along with a spray of blood as the blade sliced through flesh.

Shank's flashlight fell from his hand and he toppled onto his back on the heather, choking on his own blood as Tyler and the other boys whirled and fled screaming down the hillside in the darkness, their voices echoing out into the wilderness on the lonely winds.

***

II

Larbert Police Station, near Falkirk

'What the bloody hell is going on up there?'

Detective Sergeant Andy McLoughlin was not the sort to be easily alarmed, but for the first time in years his heart was beating hard inside his chest and he knew that something major had gone down. The police helicopter was hovering over the moors to the east of the town, ambulances were out in force and the public were screaming down the phones at him to get officers out to Carron Bridge as fast as he could.

'We're not sure,' his desk duty officer, Jenkins, replied, one hand covering a phone. 'Reports are that one youth is dead and two more severely injured. We have one man in custody but all hell's broken loose up there.'

Time seemed to stand still for Andy as he heard the words that he knew were about to turn his world upside-down. One youth dead. Murder was not something that happened much in this community, the local crime sprees limited to shoplifting and the occasional vandalism. Out in the villages, crime was almost unheard of because the low population density meant that everyone knew, well, *everyone*. A farmer couldn't sneeze out there without someone else knowing about it within an hour.

'I'm taking a unit out. You say one's in custody?'

'An unidentified male was tracked down by a local farmer,' came Jenkin's reply. 'There's a patrol car on site holding him and waiting for a van to bring him in. No identifying marks, no fingerprint record showing up after the field test. Believed to be under the influence of drugs.'

Drugs. If there was one thing that had brought crime even up here it was drugs. When people couldn't get them or couldn't afford to buy them, their desperation was such that otherwise sane and law-abiding folks would turn overnight into prolific offenders to feed their growing addiction. Andy hated drugs perhaps more than anything else on the streets.

'OK, have the van bring him straight here. I'll take over when they arrive.'

Andy made his way to the interview room and set up the tape recorder and also the CCTV camera that would record the interview. There was nothing left to chance, no way that a person charged with an offence could make up stories of abuse at the hands of police – everything was recorded as proof of what had taken place. Satisfied that everything was in order, Andy headed back out to the front of the station in time to see the police van pull in.

The man that his officers pulled out of the back looked as though he'd been living in the wild for some time. Andy felt his concerns increase as the man was hauled out of the van by two police officers who clearly had a tough time controlling him. The man was dressed in meagre clothing, thin cloth or wool of some kind, his hair lank and his build slightly smaller than Andy would have expected. His voice was rough and his language indecipherable, and he was apparently fighting for his life.

'He's been tasered once but he won't calm down!' an officer yelled at Andy.

Drugs could do that to a man, make them supernaturally strong, if only for a while. Coupled with genuine fear or a warped psychology, they could be capable of anything. Andy's first instinct was that this man was a European immigrant who had been left behind and was surviving on basic instinct, and that might mean that his fear was genuine. As the officers struggled to control the man, Andy stepped forward and grabbed the captive by his shoulders and pushed him backwards to pin him against the van.

The man was six inches shorter than Andy but he was tremendously strong. Wild, pale blue eyes glared up at him, spittle flying from his lips as he garbled something unintelligible. Andy held him in place, and then gradually began to release the pressure with each expulsion of breath. An old psychological trick he'd learned in the army, it was a way of calming someone down when they're unable to escape and are panicking. The man sensed the gradual release of pressure and some of the feral panic in his eyes abated as he looked at Andy again.

Andy kept releasing the pressure on the man's shoulders, and nodded to his officers to back away from their captive for a moment. They reluctantly stood back, hands on Tasers in case he tried to make a break for it or attack their sergeant. Andy looked down at the bedraggled man and spoke in a soft, calm voice.

'Okay, now, what's your name?'

'Towhon bydel eow?' the man echoed back, his voice inflected with something that sounded both alien and similar.

'Do you have a name?' Andy tried again.

The man frowned and shook his head, confused. He looked around, apparently afraid of everything around him. His eyes cast over the van, the ground at their feet, the uniform that Andy wore and the Tasers with great fear, going back and forth as though the entire world were threatening him.

'Can you speak English?'

The man frowned, his eyes as vacant as if Andy had spoken Japanese. Andy knew that he was getting nowhere and turned to one of the officers.

'What do we know?'

'Four kids up on the hills outside of town, went to see what all those strange lights that have been appearing were about. They claim they saw one, then this gentleman appears nearby. They couldn't understand each other, then he pulls a knife on them and started swinging. One dead, two injured and all survivors in a state of shock.'

Andy nodded, and then with one hand he guided the strange little man away from the vehicle and toward the station. The man resisted slightly, staring at the lights glowing above the entrance and the brilliantly lit interior.

'It's okay,' Andy said softly, convinced now that he was dealing with someone who was suffering from some unspeakable psychological illness, perhaps a catastrophic mental breakdown. 'It's just lights.'

Andy held the door open for the captive, the two police officers following him close behind and wary of anything the stranger might attempt.

'Get him a coffee and a blanket,' Andy said. 'Interview room one.'

Although some might have considered it odd that such things might be provided to a suspected killer, the fact was that Andy already knew that this was no ordinary homicide. Not only was there a juvenile dead and several more assaulted, including police officers, this man was clearly disturbed and may not have been able to control his own actions. The fact that he could not be identified and appeared more scared of the police than they were of him suggested that they did not yet have the full story, and despite the evidence their new suspect had to remain innocent until *proven* guilty.

Andy led the man at a shuffle into the interview room as a WPC provided him with a blanket and a cup of coffee. The man accepted the blanket willingly, but he merely sniffed at the coffee and recoiled from it.

'Beth, do we have any Community Officers who speak Gaelic or anything like that? Maybe even eastern European languages, Polish or whatever?'

The WPC shook her head. 'I know a few people who speak Gaelic but they're not local. It'll take them a while to get here. As for Eastern European, ask anyone in Stirling, they're everywhere these days. I'll call them and see what they can do.'

Andy nodded as she left, while Officer Jenkins remaining in the interview room with the suspect as the door closed. Andy sat down opposite the captive and looked him in the eye.

'English,' Andy pointed at himself. 'Do you speak English?'

The man stared at him, mystified. Andy pointed at him.

'Are you English? Polish? Where are you from?'

The man stared for a moment longer, and then pointed at the Taser armed officer nearby.

'Wamful.'

'What?'

'Wholic,' the man said.

Andy wondered what the hell the man was saying, but then the suspect pointed to his own tunic.

'Cotte,' he said.

'Coat!' Andy echoed in surprise. 'Coat.'

The man gave a slight shrug but nodded. Andy finally felt a sense of relief. There was a language barrier here but as long as they could understand each other in a basic sense then a translator could be found to bridge that gap, and he would be able to find out what had really happened up on that hillside.

The man pointed to his pants. 'Howse.'

Andy frowned uncertainly. The man tried again and pointed to his shoes, which were ankle high and made of what looked like crude leather.

'Buyte.'

Andy began to get an uneasy feeling about the man. 'Boot,' he replied, tapping his own foot.

'Buyte,' the man nodded, and smiled for the first time, apparently now as relieved as Andy was. 'Buyte. Canne eow asecgan me aer and there yfel?'

Andy sat in silence for a moment. He knew that he was being asked a question by the tone and inflection of the sentence and the expression on the man's face, which was now in earnest and hungry for answers. The trouble was, he didn't know what the hell he was being asked.

'We're getting nowhere here,' he said finally.

The officer alongside him stepped forward. 'Sir, if I may – I've got an app for that.'

'You've got a what?'

Officer Jenkins produced a cell phone from his pocket, the screen glowing with light as he opened it. The captive recoiled as Jenkins set the cell phone down on the table, apparently both afraid and mesmerised by the device. Andy watched him carefully as Jenkins selected an app from the screen.

'What's that?' Andy asked.

'Voice translation app,' Jenkins replied. 'I picked one up the other day for a few quid, because of our troubles with understanding the Polish folks in town.'

Andy saw Jenkins switch the app on, and then he looked at the captive before them.

'Speak,' Jenkins said, and motioned with his hands to encourage the man to say something.

'Yfel raeran hnot underniman,' the man said, frowning at Andy.

To his surprise the cell phone beeped, and Jenkins picked it up. Andy saw him stare at the screen for a moment in confusion and then his face paled and his jaw slowly fell open.

'What?' Andy asked. 'Does it recognise his language?'

Jenkins nodded slowly, and forced his voice to work.

'It says that he's speaking English.'

'But he can't be,' Andy protested, 'we can't understand a word he's saying.'

Jenkins held out the cell phone to Andy, replying as he did so.

'The app can't identify the precise language, but it's saying he's speaking Middle English.'

Andy saw the screen and gaped in amazement. The captive's words were there before him on the screen;

Yfel raeran hnot underniman.

And beneath them in plain English was the apparent translation from what the app described as Middle English.

I do not understand.

Andy looked up at the man before them, barely able to comprehend what he was being asked to believe.

'What precisely, is "Middle English"?' he asked the officer, knowing the answer already but unable to come to terms with it.

'Medieval,' the officer replied. 'He's speaking a language that's several hundred years old.'

***

III

'He's got to be some kind of reenactor or something, one of those history buffs,' Andy said as he stood outside the interview room with the officer a minute later. 'He's hiding behind his knowledge of some ancient language. Maybe he's a fantasist or something?'

Jenkins shook his head.

'I don't know. The kids' witness statements check out, they're not lying about what happened, and this guy hasn't shown up on any database we have. No fingerprints, no name and address, no identifying documents, nothing.'

Andy rubbed his temples as he tried to figure out what that really meant.

'It only tells us that he doesn't have a criminal record in this country and that he doesn't have any identifying documents. I'd bet a weeks' wages that a search of that hillside in the morning will reveal his paperwork. He's probably tossed it after the murder and is hiding behind some cock and bull language gag.'

Jenkins said nothing. His silence said it all to Andy.

'You're not buying into this are you? You really think this guy appeared in a flash of light out of the bloody Dark Ages?'

'You've seen his clothes, his appearance, the language,' Jenkins said. 'Something's going on here Andy. That guy may not be able to speak right but you can tell by looking at him that he's spooked by everything he sees. Even light bulbs scare the hell out of him! That's not something you see everyday and all the boys' reports say that he only became aggressive when he was provoked. Prior to that he seemed as lost and afraid as he does now.'

Andy knew that Jenkins was right. So far, everything pointed to something almost supernatural, but a lifetime of experience had taught him that anything that appears supernatural is in fact perfectly natural but merely *unfamiliar*.

'There's no way that this guy appeared out of a ball of light from King Arthur's round bloody table and ended up in Scotland with a knife to a boy's throat. I want every available officer to start questioning all the local residents in the morning, especially anyone running a bed and breakfast with foreign guests present. We need to find out who this guy is and either charge him or let him go. If we don't have a story sorted in the next twenty-three hours, we're going to have a real cold case on our hands.'

'Righto,' Jenkins said. 'I'll gather the lads and organise something.'

As Jenkins turned to leave, Andy reached for his own cell phone. 'What was the name of that app again?'

By the time he got back into the room, the man was sitting with the coffee in his hands and sniffing it cautiously. He was still cuffed but able to move a bit and Andy was no longer concerned about the man suddenly leaping up and attacking anyone. Andy shut the door and sat down again, the suspect looking at him expectantly.

Andy spoke into the cell phone, but this time he spoke a series of words very slowly and clearly in English, then turned the cell phone toward the captive and played back the words in translated Middle English. The screen showed his words; *"What is your name?"*. The monotone drone of the automated voice sounded as alien in tone as the words themselves.

'Giefan and me eower nem—nan.'

The man yelped in amazement, looking from the phone to Andy and back, and Andy felt a shiver of superstitious awe creep down his spine as the man tapped his chest and nodded vigorously.

'Seemon,' he said. 'Seemon.'

'Simon,' Andy gasped, and then reminded himself that this man was more than likely playing games with him. Andy spoke again into the phone and it translated his words: *"Where are you from?"*.

'Aer an there maeo eower hand?'

Simon's face melted into an expression of awestruck delight, and Andy was shocked to see tears stream down the man's cheeks and dampen his scraggy beard.

'Comncoc,' he replied. 'Yfel alibban to Comncoc.'

'Cumnock,' Andy breathed as he recognised the name of the town in East Ayreshire, not far from where they now sat. He looked down at the phone screen.

I live in Comncoc.

Andy spoke again into the cell phone, keeping his voice and words as clear and simple as he could.

'How did you get here?'

The phone droned its translation: *'Aet—hwega eow raecan her?'*

Simon's joy mutated into fear and his eyes darted up to the ceiling. Slowly, he raised his hand and pointed up.

'Yfellic lydre deoflu overtake me awegeade.'

Andy looked down at the cell phone screen and his blood ran cold through his veins.

The bad demons took me away, into the sky.

'Bad demons?' Andy echoed, the phone translating for him once again.
Simon nodded, clutching the blanket close about his shoulders once again.
'He winnan mid sin sceine, ge onfon oos awegeade uhtsanglic niht.'

They come with their lights, and take us away at night.

Andy could feel the hairs on the back of his arms stand up. He was watching the man before him and he could see absolutely none of the tell-tale signs of a liar or someone attempting to deceive. Simon was afraid, startled by the simplest pieces of modern technology and clearly had no idea what a cup of coffee was for. Currently, he was clasping the paper cup in his hands and using it to warm them.

Gently, Andy reached out and took the cup. Then, he sipped from it. Simon watched him in silent fascination for a moment, then Andy set the cup down again between them.

'Coffee,' he said as he pointed at it.

The cell phone remained silent, and Andy figured that such a thing had not existed for medieval folk, hence no such translation existed for it.

'Warm drink,' he tried again.

'Clyppan wring,' the phone chirped.

Simon looked again at the coffee, and then he gently picked it up and took a tentative sip. Andy watched as Simon screwed his nose up a little at the taste, but then he took some more and within seconds was sipping every few seconds, a look of wonder on his face.

Andy began to wonder if Jenkins was not right after all. As insane as it seemed, everything about this guy pointed to something other than deception. He looked to be about twenty to twenty-five years of age, but he was built more like a young teenager, as though he had been deprived of proper nutrition when growing up. Andy had once visited HMS Victory in Portsmouth harbour in England, the 18th Century warship the former flagship of the Royal Navy under Admiral Nelson and famous for the victory at the Battle of Trafalgar. He recalled being amazed at how low he had to stoop to get through the various doorways and bulkheads, the doors built for men much smaller than they were now.

Andy picked up the plastic evidence bag containing the knife and looked at it. The blade was metal all right, but aged and stained with dirt and what looked like old blood, as well as the fresher stains from the victim on the hillside. The handle was crudely carved from wood, the blade set within it and held in place by tightly bound woven string that itself looked coarse and different to the kind of thing one could buy in a convenience store.

'Danc doo cnihtcild de rihtes?'

Andy looked up and saw Simon glance at the blade and then up at him. He looked at the phone screen.

Will the boy be all right?

Andy closed his eyes for a moment. This couldn't be happening. He shook his head slowly.

'The boy died.'

'Dod cnihtcild deagung.'
Simon sighed and shook his head, his eyes full of sorrow.
'Se oferweorpan me mid hin bryne.'

He attacked me with his light.

Andy swallowed. He knew when he was out of his depth. Either this guy was totally insane and had lost touch with all sense of reality, or he was sitting in front of a man who was about five hundred years out of his own time and couldn't deal with even the most basic of modern technology. Either way, he was a danger to the public and to himself, and somehow Andy knew that being locked up in a prison cell wasn't the answer here. He did not doubt that this man had killed a fourteen-year-old boy. What he did now doubt was that the attack had been in any way malicious.

'Stay here,' Andy said.

'Bidan her,' the phone chirped merrily.

Simon nodded, sitting with his hands clasped around the cup and a hopeful look in his eye. Andy hurried to the front desk in time to see Jenkins running back towards him.

'We're gonna need help with this one,' Andy said. 'This is way out of our league and…'

'I know,' Jenkins replied, panicked and with his face flushed. 'They're already here.'

'Who's here?'

Jenkins jabbed a thumb over his shoulder.

'The army,' he said. 'They've cordoned off the town and they're coming here for that guy.'

***

IV

Andy dashed through the station with Jenkins following even as he heard heavy vehicles pulling up outside, shouts coming from barked orders as troops deployed around the town. A deep, thumping noise echoed through the station, one that Andy recognised from his army days as the huge double-rotors of a Chinook heavy-lift helicopter.

Andy entered the interview room and saw Simon on his feet with his back pressed against the far wall, his eyes searching the ceiling for the source of the sound as the Chinook thundered overhead outside.

'It's okay,' Andy said, and then added. 'Stay calm.'

'*Stapol stille,*' droned the cell phone.

Simon watched as Andy clambered up onto a chair and opened up the side of the camera that had recorded the interview. Carefully, he plugged a USB cable into the camera and then shoved the other end into his cell phone. He watched as the data downloaded, and then his phone chirped and he unplugged the phone and closed the side of the camera.

He had no idea what the hell was going on here, but he wasn't stupid. Whatever had happened on that hillside was serious enough to have the army come down here and raid their station. Likewise, he knew that there would be no stone left unturned and that if he had no evidence of what had happened then he would be ridiculed openly in order to help cover up the events of the night. The same thing had happened in the past, when police officers had submitted genuine sightings of paranormal events and been forced out of their jobs by agencies keen to play down such bizarre experiences. Bonnybridge and the surrounding areas were known hotspots for UFO activity, and he wouldn't allow the army to silence his officers about any of this.

Andy turned to Simon and beckoned for him to follow, once again struck by how short he was and by the medieval look of his clothing. Simon followed willingly, having established some level of trust now in Andy. They hurried out of the interview room, Jenkins following them.

'You can't get him out, they're everywhere out there.'

'Keep the army at bay,' Andy instructed. 'I'll put Simon here in the cells for safety's sake.'

'What the hell do they want? This is a civil case, nothing to do with the military.'

'That's what bothers me,' Andy replied as he led Simon to a cell door and gestured for him to enter it.

Simon hesitated, uncertain. Andy spoke into his phone as he tapped the walls of the cell with his knuckles.

'Safe room. Strong.'

'Nyt—wieroe rymet.'

Simon took a breath and slowly walked into the cell, Andy closing and locking the door behind him. The army would have to ask very nicely to get him out of there, and they'd need a tank to get inside without the key.

Satisfied that Simon could not be taken without his consent, Andy turned and walked to the front desk just as a figure dressed in combat fatigues burst in with four armed soldiers alongside him. Andy recognised an officer, or a *Rupert*, as they were known to the troops. Chin held high, an air of superiority palpable around him, the officer spoke with clipped tones.

'Captain Chatsworth, British Army! We're here for the man you brought in from the hills.'

No questions, no mistakes, they were after Simon for some reason.

'The gentleman is in custody, captain,' Andy replied, 'and is being detained for questioning.'

'We'll take it from here,' Chatsworth barked. 'You can release him into our custody.'

'This is a civil case and a murder investigation,' Andy said. 'You have no jurisdiction and no business here.'

The officer peered down at Andy, his men behind him with their SA-80 rifles clutched close at port-arms, ready to deploy at a moment's notice.

'You'll do as you're told. This is army territory now and you answer to me.'

'I answered to people like you for fifteen years,' Andy replied. 'Didn't get me very far.'

Andy couldn't resist the opportunity to rile an officer without fear of reprisal. Captain Chatsworth looked as though he was going to spontaneously combust and opened his mouth to deliver the neutron bomb retort that Andy fully expected, and would hugely enjoy, when another voice from outside cut him off.

'There's something out here!'

'Something out *where*?' Chatsworth barked over his shoulder, his eyes fixed on Andy.

'In the sky!'

Andy and the officer exchanged a glance and then without another word Chatsworth whirled and marched out of the station. Unable to resist his own curiosity, Andy followed them outside and looked up into the darkened skies above the station.

The clouds were low and sullen, just visible drifting with the wind over the mountain peaks. Andy was briefly stunned to see that there were multiple vehicles parked around the station; three-tonners each holding forty troops, jeeps and the Chinook still thundering through the night somewhere close by. That the army would deploy such resources in search of one lonely and confused man stunned

Andy, but then he turned and he realised that it might not be Simon that they were seeking after all.

Amid the clouds tumbling overhead, Andy saw a diffuse patch of light stationary in the night sky. He could see the clouds in detail as they scudded past it, illuminated by the light of a fearsome white glow that they partially concealed. It was hovering directly above the hills barely a mile from where they stood.

'What the hell is that?' Andy uttered.

Chatsworth's reply was as stern as his orders.

'None of your business. We require the occupant you captured.'

Andy blinked. 'Occupant?'

'Don't play games with me!' the officer snapped. 'My men will blow the station apart if we have to in order to…'

'We only have one guy in custody,' Andy insisted. 'He's as confused as we are.'

Chatsworth stared at him, suddenly not so sure of himself.

'We received intelligence suggesting that an occupant of that object had been found out here on the hills.'

Occupant. That object. Andy's mind was racing and suddenly he realised what the army must be doing here and whom they thought Andy had in custody.

'His name's Simon,' Andy said, 'and he's…'

'It's moving!'

Andy turned and saw the light drift slightly to the right over the hills. Then it suddenly zipped right across the valley in the blink of an eye and froze in motion directly above their heads. Andy heard a rush of gasps and expletives from the soldiers around him as they craned their necks to look up into the clouds, the glow filling the sky above them as though a full moon were hiding just within the cloud base.

The clouds scudded by, the men watching in amazement, and then a small break in the clouds afforded them a brief glimpse of the source of the light and Andy felt his guts convulse with something akin to primal fear.

There was a black, vaguely boomerang shaped object concealed within the clouds that was both metallic, bright and yet as dark as night at the same time. The hairs on his head tingled and he felt an unseen energy pulsating from the object, heard police and army radio transmissions vanish with a crackling sound as the air fell still all around them. The engines on the army trucks coughed and fell silent, headlamps and flashlights blinked out and it seemed as though time itself suddenly stood still.

He could see glowing lights around the craft's rim and two more points, red and green, underneath it. What scared him so was the fact that it was clearly solid and yet was also partially translucent, as though it were made from nothing more substantial than a mirage, and yet he could see the tumbling clouds spiralling past its edges in swirling vortexes, curling off the edges of something that was both there and not there at the same time. Andy could see vague reflections of what looked like metallic black panels on the underside, the lights from distant Falkirk glinting against the hull.

'What *is* that?!' someone managed to utter.

Before anyone could reply there was a blinding flash of light from the object and then suddenly it vanished and plunged them all back into absolute darkness. The charged atmosphere faded away on the breeze that reappeared around them, and he heard the vehicle's engines cough into life as the lights in the station and the headlamp beams flickered back into existence.

Nobody said anything for what felt like an age, but then Chatsworth turned to Andy.

'You don't understand, officer,' he said in a far more compliant tone. 'We'd *really* like to speak to the man you have in custody.'

Andy, his eyes still searching the clouds above them, nodded, all thoughts of resistance completely blown away by what he had witnessed. Now he wanted to talk to Simon again too, and one of the man's replies during questioning sent a shiver of fear down his spine.

The bad demons took me away.

Andy hurried into the station, Chatsworth following with his men as Andy led them to the cells and fumbled with his keys.

'We put Simon in here for safety's sake, although I don't think that he's going to cause you any problems. We've been using a cell phone's translator function to speak to him.'

'Translator?' the officer asked.

'He only speaks medieval English,' Andy explained, and immediately realised that he no longer questioned anything about Simon's story. After what had just happened, how could he?

Andy opened the cell door and walked in with his cell phone in his hand.

'Simon, there are some people here to…'

Andy stopped in the centre of the cell and stared in disbelief at what he saw before him.

The cell was entirely empty, and Simon was nowhere to be seen.

'Is this some kind of joke?' Chatsworth rumbled.

Jenkins came to Andy's aid. 'No, we put him in here right before you arrived. He couldn't have got out!'

Chatsworth trembled with restrained rage and he turned to Andy.

'I want everything you have on this guy, every last scrap of evidence, and then we will leave and none of you will speak of any of this again to anybody, ever, is that understood?!'

Andy nodded and hurried out of the cell, heading for the interview room to retrieve the CCTV footage of the interview. Right now, it was the only evidence they had to prove they'd ever had anyone in custody, and he had no idea how he was going to explain any of this to his superior in the morning. There was one thing that he was sure of though; he would be keeping quiet about his copy of the interview with Simon now residing on his cell phone.

***

V

Central Intelligence Agency, Langley, Virginia

General Scott "Mac" Mackenzie was not a happy man.

He walked through the corridors of the CIA with a folder under one arm and a cloud over his head that simply would not go away. Ever since he had been taken off active duty and re-assigned to the Foreign Intelligence Desk at the CIA he had felt that he'd been sidelined.

At fifty-two years old, Mackenzie still ran ten kilometres every morning and could bench press enough weight to put men half his age to shame. He had served his entire career with distinction with the 101st Airborne, the famed "Screaming Eagles", and had believed that he would serve as a field officer for the remainder of his career when, quite out of the blue, he was pulled from front line operations in Iraq and seconded as a liason to the CIA's FID. No explanation, no brief other than to handle whatever paperwork came through. Mackenzie would have simply liked to know what he'd done wrong to be assigned a desk job that had numbed his brain for the past nine months, but none of his fellow officers knew a damned thing about it.

The FID office was small, and he had no secretary. Buried in a part of the building where there was little foot traffic, Mackenzie had considered resigning from the army more than once during his tenure here, something that would have been unthinkable to him prior to the assignment. He knew that he'd been put out to pasture, but he couldn't bring himself to face it and instead carried out his duties with the same vigour with which he had charged enemy machine gun nests in Afghanistan. He was a stubborn and implacable old man, just like his father had been, and he wasn't about to let the pen pushers in the Pentagon send him down without a fight.

As he walked in to his office and tossed the folder onto his desk, he saw that another folder was already there. It was unmarked save for a small stamp that Mackenzie picked up and read.

COSMIC
Rep #: 417315/a

He knew that COSMIC was an oft-used term for high level classification within the agency, and indeed across the US intelligence network. The fact that it had been left unattended on his desk was therefore somewhat unusual: such files normally were only distributed after a briefing and emphasis on keeping them out of sight.

THE DISCLOSURE PROTOCOL   Dean Crawford

Mackenzie's curiosity peaked, he closed his office door and sat down at his desk, making himself comfortable before he opened the folder and retrieved from within it a file and several high-quality photographs. There was an image of a man and a woman; the man in his late thirties to perhaps early forties, with shaggy brown hair and a wide jaw, the woman in her early thirties and of Hispanic origin, long dark hair and brown eyes. Along with the images were several fitness reports attained from where he knew not, and another image of a man who looked to be in his late seventies, with white hair and a cunning gleam in his eyes. All of the images were easily identifiable as surveillance shots, as none of the people in them appeared to be aware that they were being photographed.

Mackenzie set the images of the people to one side and then looked at the next, and last image, in the folder. For a moment he was not sure what he was looking at, and then he realised and he froze in his chair. Either someone down the hall was planning the biggest wind-up in agency history, or Mackenzie was looking at something he was sure he shouldn't have been.

The image was hazy and indistinct, but it showed some form of craft traversing a blue sky flecked with scattered cumulus cloud. The craft was angular, shaped like a boomerang with straight edges, and it seemed to have lights at each end. However, the image was of something that was semi-transparent, as though someone had taken a photograph out of a window of the sky, and a reflection in the glass from something in the room behind them had made it into the shot. Mackenzie could see trees near the bottom of the image, and an airliner at altitude trailing vapour, giving some indication of scale.

Along with the image was a report and he leafed through it quickly. The report contained more images, each the same as the one in his hand but adjusted for Infra-Red, Ultra-Violet and other frequencies beyond the optical spectrum. At the end of the report, a few lines caught his attention.

The Unidentified Aerial Phenomena is confirmed as solid, present and is not the result of image manipulation.
Assessment by triangulation and field measurements indicates a wingspan of approximately six hundred feet.
The UAP made no noise, and vanished at high velocity after being observed for over one minute.
It is imperative that we find out what the UAP is, who is acquiring these images of it, and how.

Mackenzie set the report down and stared at the image for a long time. Like everyone on planet earth, he had heard of the UFO phenomenon and he had seen documentaries on television about what might be behind them. However, he had never personally bought into the conspiracy theories surrounding supposed captured flying disks at Roswell or alien autopsies. Such stories were confined to the fringes of reality, where imaginations ran riot in the minds of people with nothing better to do with their days than reimagine the past in a format that conformed to their fantasies. But, this? This was different. This was not some crackpot report suggesting that earth was being visited by beings from another world. This was an image captured by an unknown agency, depicting something that clearly was not of this world, and openly admitting that it had no idea what it was looking at.

Unidentified Aerial Phenomena was a phrase used within the intelligence community as a label applied to what were previously referred to as UFOs. The original term was out-dated and had too many negative connotations to be taken seriously, and so UAP was used instead as it attracted less attention and was more likely to garner serious study. The fact that the report was on his desk meant that someone wanted him to look into things, and he leafed through the papers in the file until he found the brief attached to the project.

FAO: General Scott Mackenzie
From: ARIES

If you are reading this, then please take it as evidence that I have either retired or passed away and am in effect passing on the baton of this research to the Foreign Intelligence Desk at the CIA. Although our respective agencies have often failed to see eye to eye, I sought a man in whom I felt the necessary qualities to carry through the work were in abundance; fortitude, an open mind and a true devotion to country. I hope that my trust is well placed.

I worked for two decades at the head of a Defense Intelligence Agency funded operation known as ARIES, a Black Budget task force designed to investigate phenomena that were beyond human understanding and written off as fantasy by other agencies. Sadly, world–events and a change in government brought ARIES funding to a close and much of its assets were seized or destroyed, more in fear of the truth and a need for control of that truth than anything else. Hence, I pass our work on to you at the CIA in the hopes that where I have failed, you will succeed.

The two operatives in the images I have supplied worked for me. They are civilians with unique skills who were invaluable to me throughout my service at ARIES. If you can find them, they can brief you in detail. I can recommend no two agents more highly than they.

Finally, the exotic imagery you now possess does not belong to our government. Someone, somewhere, has taken the study of UAPs to a point beyond anything we were able to achieve. The images were sent to a civilian organisation known as MUFON, the Mutual UFO Network, and later to me for safe keeping. I do not know who took them, only that there are now half a dozen such images and that the perpetrator appears to be suggesting that they will go public with them if our government does not agree to their terms.

As the liason officer for the FID it is almost certain that you will be tasked officially by the government with handling this case within days of receiving this folder. Their motives will be unclear. The only person you can trust now is yourself, Scott. There are people out there who will, and have, killed to obtain this information and that contained within other projects within the remit of ARIES.

Watch your back, and tell nobody about this file,
Yours,
Douglas Ian Jarvis

Mackenzie sat back in his chair and stared at the letter for some time, then at the image of the old man. Jarvis. He'd heard the name from time to time, a former Marine Captain if he recalled correctly, who'd made some waves up at the Pentagon. Retired, then disappeared off the face of the planet.

Mackenzie glanced at the images of the two agents whom Jarvis had recommended so highly. One was a former United States Marine turned journalist, turned private investigator and bail bondsman. The other, a former D.C. police officer who had gone into business with the former Marine and forged a healthy career working for the DIA before everything had gone south.

Beside the pictures was an ARIES case history for the pair, and as Mackenzie read it so his eyes widened and his awareness of what ARIES had been up to the past few years opened up his mind. Could any of this have been possible? He knew right away that there was only one way for him to be sure, and that meant he would have to locate the pair of them and find out for himself. The only trouble was that their whereabouts had been unknown for almost a year. He only had their names to go on.

Ethan Warner, and Nicola Lopez.

Mackenzie felt compelled to pursue the details and get ahead of the game, just in case Jarvis was right and he was about to get a knock on his office door. But at the same time he knew nothing about who was controlling the case, and for that matter he had no idea who had dropped this thing on his desk. He had another stack of paperwork to get through, and he didn't want to risk becoming even more of an outcast by working on spooky projects that might further tarnish his name. Mackenzie replaced the contents of the file in the folder and slipped it into his desk drawer. He didn't care what Jarvis thought. He knew he wasn't about to get a knock on his door about this.

As he closed the desk drawer with the folder in it, there was a knock at his door. Mackenzie raised a superstitious eyebrow.

'Enter.'

The door opened and Deputy Direction CIA Edward McCain walked in.

'You got a moment, Scott?' he asked. 'We need to talk.'

McCain was a Vietnam veteran who had risen through the ranks upon his return from Asia, leaving the military for a command post at Langley. A soldier at heart and a man more than cynical of the Washington mill, Mackenzie liked him because he had experienced life on the front line in a dirty war and yet still retained his humanity. His grizzled looks and rough voice completed the image of the battle-hardened soldier.

'Sure,' Mackenzie replied. 'What's up?'

McCain sat down opposite, his expression somewhat furtive, uncomfortable.

'Scott, I need you to look into something for me if you can, on your own time.'

Mackenzie nodded willingly for the DDCIA to continue, but inside his mind did a backflip. Having the DDCIA ask you to do something off the books was not a common occurance, to say the least, even if they were old friends.

'Name it.'

'I need you to look into an event that took place yesterday in Scotland, England. We're picking up a lot of chatter about it and have guys on the ground from Special Ops but the Brits are keeping us in the dark right now.'

'Sure, what kind of event was it? Terrorist related, espionage, political?'

McCain shifted in his seat as though he was sitting on needles.

'A bit of all three,' he suggested, and then produced an image of something and laid it on the desk between them.

Mackenzie looked down at it and his heart skipped a beat. A black sky filled with sullen clouds, pierced by a fierce white light emanating from a boomerang-shaped object partially concealed in the cloud base.

'You ever seen anything like that before?' McCain asked him.

Mackenzie shook his head. 'Russian? Chinese?'

'None of the above, we're pretty sure about that,' McCain replied.

'What do we know about it so far?'

'I'll give you the file details as soon as you're ready,' McCain said, apparently relieved that Mackenzie was taking him seriously. 'You'll get everything we know about this phenomenon. CIA wants a handle on this as soon as you can. This image was taken at the scene and sent to CIA, FBI and DIA last night from Scotland, England. No media coverage, no intelligence leaks, no nothing, yet someone shows up at the right place and time and takes this shot. It's not the first, Scott. Someone's up to something and we need to know how they're doing it. The Director doesn't want to muddy the waters with a paper trail that says we're looking into UFO sightings again, we both know how that looks to the public. So, would you be willing to shoot off and take a look at this for me? Paid leave, all expenses, just get it done and quietly report back to me.'

Mackenzie took a breath. If this wasn't the weirdest day that he'd ever experienced then he couldn't remember the other one. He picked up the image and nodded.

'Sure, I'll look into it. I know some people in the British military and intel' community. Let me make a few calls and I'll see what I can dig up.'

***

VI

Detective Sergeant Andy McLoughlin drove east out of Bonnybridge, heading home after his shift had ended. The sun was not yet up over the cloudy horizon, but then at five in the morning not many things were up. Right now, he was tired and wanted nothing more than to get into bed and catch up on some sleep.

The night had been a long one, and in the wake of the extraordinary events of the previous week everything else seemed to be something of an anti-climax. Both he and Jenkins had spoken in anxious whispers about what had occurred, about what it all meant, but they had not made any headway and the military sure as hell wasn't saying anything. Captain Chatsworth did not return any of Andy's calls, and the military denied any knowledge of a deployment of troops to Bonnybridge on the night in question. “We know nothing" and "it didn't happen" seemed to be the default position of the local military, and when he had used a Freedom of Information Act request for the radar data from a local Royal Air Force base, it had been denied, with the public relations officer reporting that nothing out of the ordinary had been seen that night either visually or on radar. Of course, "out of the ordinary" was something that held its own context depending on the opinions and experiences of the viewer – maybe such sightings were not uncommon for military observers in air control towers, and thus not deemed "out of the ordinary".

Andy had finally found out about an organisation called the Mutual UFO Network, or MUFON, and had decided to send them a copy of Simon's interview on condition that it was not distributed in any way. MUFON had agreed, and had soon gathered corroborating evidence from Bonnybridge witnesses who had seen the bright lights and the military presence on the night of the event. However, without any hard evidence the event was just that, and an interview with a strangely-dressed man with an archaic dialect was interesting but not proof of a major alien event and military cover-up.

Within days, Andy realised that he had absolutely nothing and that the event would be consigned to his memory as a remarkable, but unrecorded event.

Andy drove to his home and pulled up outside. The street was silent, houses dark and the streetlights still casting pools of yellow light amid the blackness. It had recently rained and Andy could feel the chill of the night in the air as he stepped out of his car and locked it. He hurried to his front door and opened it, then stepped inside, eager to shut out the cold.

A hand clamped around his face in an instant and he was yanked over backwards. Strong arms grabbed him, pinning him down as the front door was closed and plastic restraints were fastened around his ankles and wrists, his arms pulled tight behind his back.

Andy squirmed and twisted, but the men were too many and he was hoisted aloft and carried through his own home into the living room. A single chair was placed on a sheet of plastic that now covered the carpet on the floor. Andy was dumped onto the chair and swiftly bound in place with lengths of gaffer tape that strapped him around the chest and thighs.

Satisfied that he was securely bound, the men stood back from him as another took their place. Andy blinked, the man before him half in shadow in the pale light of dawn. His face was blotchy and his skin oddly white, pasty and unhealthy looking. Squat, with broad shoulders and a barrel chest, the man was dressed in a black suit that contrasted sharply with his skin. He stood with his hands clasped before him, appearing both calm and on the verge of action.

'Mister McCloughlin,' he said in heavily accented Russian, 'I do not wish to take up much of your time so I will be brief. Your wife and daughters are upstairs and they are safe. If you do that which I ask of you, they will remain safe. Do you understand?'

Andy wanted to leap up and batter the man to death with his bare hands but he nodded instead, fighting the urge to spit in his face.

'Good,' the Russian smiled, rather like a great white shark does just before biting into its prey. 'You witnessed an extraordinary event recently that involved the British Army. You will tell me all about it.'

Andy's mind raced. *Damn*, this thing had gotten far further than he would ever have believed possible in such a short space of time. Suddenly, despite the overt threat to himself and to his family's safety, he understood that this was not about money or extortion or crime but about governments warring for information.

The Russian sat down on Andy's dining room chair and folded his hands expectantly in his lap. Andy, careful to convey the absolute contempt he felt for the Russian as he spoke, detailed everything that had happened. He spoke of the killing on the moors, the discovery and interview with Simon, the UFO sighting and the disappearance of the man who had claimed to have come from medieval times.

The Russian listened quietly until Andy had finished, and then nodded sagely.

'I see,' he whispered softly after a few moments. 'And the footage that you sent to the civilians at MUFON?'

'The Army confiscated everything,' Andy replied. 'I kept the recording so that if information slipped out of my office and the army attemped to cover it up by slandering my officers, I would have proof to protect them.'

The Russian nodded slowly, watching Andy as though sizing him up.

'And yet you sent it to MUFON anyway,' he murmured.

'They're under strict orders not to broadcast it, to protect the careers of the officers involved,' Andy replied. 'It's only the interview, not the sighting of a UFO. There is nothing on that camera footage that could be described as sensational on that front.'

The Russian smiled, his eyes as black as night, his skin creasing like old cloth left out to dry in the sun.

'Not on your version,' he replied.

'What do you mean?'

The Russian glanced briefly over his shoulder, and one of his men came forward with a small laptop that he placed on the table beside Andy. The man pressed play, and Andy saw the footage from an observation camera in one of the police cells and Simon sitting within it, staring fearfully at the ceiling. Andy could hear the thundering Chinook outside the cells, could see Simon looking for the source of the sound.

The cell was otherwise still, and as Andy watched he realised that the footage was taken after he had left Simon to confront the army officers. Fascinated, he watched as Simon paced up and down, staring up at the ceiling, clearly afraid of the noise outside. Then, quite suddenly, the camera flared brilliant white, bright enough to illuminate the gloomy living room. Andy saw Simon shudder. He jerked to one side and then became bolt upright, his arms quivering by his sides as his eyes rolled up in their sockets as what looked like static electricity danced across his body. His jaw convulsed and his torso shook as though he was in the grip of some kind of seizure, and then the camera flared white again and the cell reappeared, utterly empty.

For a few moments there was nothing, and then Andy saw himself and Captain Chatsworth burst into the cell. The Russian leaned forward and switched off the footage, then leaned back and looked at Andy.

For a moment, Andy didn't know what to say.

'We didn't see that,' he finally blurted. 'We were outside the cells. How did you get this footage?'

'We have people in the Ministry of Defence,' the Russian replied with supreme confidence. 'Now, you will listen to me. I know that you are a former military man, a patriot, and that when I have gone you will seek to inform the authorities of this visit. I am here to inform you that doing so will be a very bad idea. Your contact at MUFON was not as forthcoming as you were and made it difficult for us to find out who witnessed these events, so that we could question them. That individual has since suffered an unfortunate accident and is in the morgue in Falkirk.'

Andy swallowed thickly, knowing somehow that the Russian was telling the truth as he went on.

'You will not speak of this. You will give us the copy you made of the footage that you possess. You will never again send it to any agency, anywhere on earth. We know where you live, and we think that you have a very beautiful family. It would be a terrible shame if they were to suffer an accident of their own, don't you think?'

Andy fought the urge to attempt to lash out at the Russian. He refused to appear intimidated, but he nodded while radiating silent rage. The Russian leaned back, and then reached into his pocket and produced a photograph. He laid it on the table between them and Andy's rage vanished as he saw perfect images of the

UFO that he and others had witnessed that fateful night. He could see optical images, infra-red, ultra-violet shots that revealed the vast object's shape that had largely been hidden in the clouds at the time, the blinding light obscuring it from view.

Andy noticed that the image had been taken from some distance away, perhaps on hills to the south. The Russian leaned forward again.

'These images were sent to the American CIA and other intelligence agencies by someone who was there, who knew that this was going to happen. They're threatening to go public with these images if the Americans do not disclose everything they supposedly know about the UFO phenomenon. Time is of the essence, Mister McCloughlin, as the Americans will be equally keen to speak to whoever was behind that camera. We want to know who that person is, and you're going to use every resource at your disposal to identify them before they left this area, understood?'

***

VII

Wild Beach, Cocos Islands

The silence was the best thing about West Island, and the one thing that Ethan Warner coveted the most. The islands were little known, two coral reefs that were hidden within literally hundreds of thousands of square miles of open ocean in the South Pacific.

The sky was almost always blue, and what little rainfall there was generally arrived in the evenings to cool the air. Most of the island's sparse population were European, many of them people who appreciated the silence just as much as Ethan did, along with the white-sand beaches and coral reefs that surrounded the tropical paradise. Forests of palms swayed in the ocean winds as he walked toward the island's south-eastern tip, just off Air Force Road.

Across a mile-wide lagoon and sand bar was Home Island, mostly home to native islanders. Beyond that, there wasn't another land mass until Christmas Island, a thousand kilometres to the east. Australia was even further away to the south east, and represented the governorship of the island. The English native language and the remoteness of the spot suited him perfectly, as it did Nicola Lopez, whom he could see reclining on the beach as he walked across the warm sand.

It had been almost a year since their alliance with Doug Jarvis and Rhys Garrett had come to an end. With the government no longer hunting them, believing them to be dead, and with the cabal of Majestic Twelve no more, their work had been done. The billions of dollars that had been taken from the cabal had largely been repatriated to the government via Garrett himself, the billionaire businessman organising both the return of the funds and ensuring the freedom of both Ethan and Nicola. Jarvis too had vanished, along with Aaron Mitchell, although Ethan had heard through the few contacts that he maintained in the outside world that Doug had since passed away. The loss of the old man was something of a blow to him, despite all the trouble that Jarvis had caused them as he juggled his loyalty to his country and government with his friendship with Ethan and Nicola. Despite Ethan's melancholy, that chapter of their lives was now over and, since Garrett had also ensured that *not quite* all of the money pilfered by Majestic Twelve had made it back into government coffers, both he and and Lopez were now wealthy enough not to have to worry about their futures any longer. A life on the beach sure beat hunting down bail runners on Chicago's south side for a living.

'Turned out nice again,' Lopez murmured as Ethan sat down alongside her. She didn't turn her head or open her eyes.

Ethan smiled wryly. She was lying on her back, wearing a nice little two-piece swim suit and a perfect tan. She had let her hair grow longer and now easily passed for one of the locals over on Home Island, though they rarely travelled there nowadays. West Island had a few shops and a small fishing industry that gave them everything that they needed, and it even had a small airport that provided scheduled flights to Australia and Sumatra twice a week. The little mall had Internet access and Ethan had a satellite link in their little home in Beacon Heights, on the island's west shore.

'We should probably do something more pro-active,' he said as he leaned back on his elbows in the sand and watched the rollers shining in the sunlight as they tumbled gently onto the sand nearby. 'This retirement thing is getting a little thin.'

Lopez nodded without opening her eyes.

'You're right,' she murmured. 'Let's go back to being paid peanuts for being shot at.'

She turned to look at him and he burst out laughing. 'Okay, I'll shut up.'

'Good.'

Ethan tucked his hands behind his head and lay back on the sand. Like Lopez, he ran around the island's circumference every other morning to keep his fitness up, and they had a little gym in the house to work out on, but apart from that they hadn't fired a gun between them in nine months. He didn't miss it. At least, not mostly. Sometimes it did feel as though the world was moving on and that they had been left behind in a sort of vacuum, trapped in time, forgotten. But then he would see the news reports about the world outside and he realised that they were missing nothing at all. They didn't use Facebook or Twitter, didn't use their e-mails very much and would likely keep it that way as, apart from contact with their families, neither Ethan or Lopez had any real desire to be found.

Ethan had used to watch the scheduled flights come in, bringing tourists from mainland Australia and usually a few natives from Sumatra, who had first arrived here when the islands had been discovered two centuries before. For a few months after they had first arrived he and Nicola had routinely observed the incoming passengers, staking out the tiny airport to ensure that nobody coming onto the island was looking for them. As the weeks had turned to months, they had finally relented, fairly sure that if anyone was to come looking for them, it wouldn't be to try to put a bullet in the back of their brains.

Therefore, Ethan was not too concerned when he glimpsed a tall man striding out onto Wild Beach in their general direction. It was only when he looked twice that alarm bells began to ring in his mind.

The man was wearing casual slacks and a loose shirt but his bearing was unmistakeably military. His chin was up and he walked with a purpose, a purpose that was bringing him directly toward them. Ethan kept his head facing toward the sky, cradled in his hands, but he kept his gaze swivelled toward the newcomer, hidden behind his sunglasses.

'Incoming,' he whispered to Lopez.

The man moved to within a couple of yards of them both and realised only at the last moment that Ethan was watching him.

'Ethan Warner?'

'Never heard of him,' Ethan replied.

The man smiled and glanced out at the ocean, the sunlight catching his greying hair.

'You're a long way from home, Marine. And this is the first time I've seen a former DC cop sunning herself on a beach.'

Ethan sighed at the same time as Lopez alongside him. The guy, whoever he was, knew enough not to be easily swayed but Ethan was in no mood for conversation.

'Beat it, pal,' he said without rancour. He wanted no arguments but he also was determined to convey the fact that the visitor was unwelcome here.

'You don't know why I'm here.'

'We don't care why you're here,' Lopez corrected him. 'Unless we've won a state lottery, there's nothing much that you can say that will interest us.'

The man shrugged. 'Jarvis sent me.'

Ethan remained silent and still for a moment. He knew that the old man was gone, and that made him wonder how this guy could have been sent anywhere by Jarvis. Either the man was a phony or Jarvis may have departed the mortal coil only after making one last parting shot.

'Jarvis is no more,' Ethan replied cautiously.

'I know,' came the reply. 'It's what he sent me that got me out here, looking for you two.'

'We're not for hire any more,' Lopez uttered.

'I'm not here to hire you.'

Ethan and Lopez both turned their heads at the same time. For a moment, Ethan wasn't sure whether to believe the guy or not. Lopez lifted her sunglasses from her eyes and peered at the man.

'Army,' she said, 'still serving judging by that haircut. You guys wouldn't come all the way out here looking for us without a damned good reason.'

'That's right,' the man smiled. Despite Ethan's reservations, the guy was hard not to like and had an easy manner. 'I need your advice.'

Ethan sat up as the man extended his hand.

'General Scott Mackenzie, Central Intelligence Agency.'

Ethan shook his hand cautiously. 'You're a spook?'

'I know,' Mackenzie said, 'I read your files and I know that you were at one point hunted by the agency. Those days are long over, I can promise you.'

'That's what the DIA said, right before your agents were chasing us across Asia, firing first and asking questions later,' Lopez shot back, ignoring the proferred hand. 'I don't trust spooks.'

'Nor do I,' Mackenzie said, not taking offence, 'I was drafted into the agency from my field post nine months ago. I wasn't happy about it then and I'm not happy about it now. However, this is an important case which is why I took personal leave and came all the way out here to find you both.'

Now Ethan really *was* interested. 'You're off the books?'

'Totally,' Mackenzie confirmed. 'This is between us and nobody else, because as far as I can make out nobody else can be trusted with this information and I don't have a team at the agency with the skills to investigate whatever the hell it is that's crossed my desk.'

Mackenzie seemed somewhat confused, as though he had been presented with something that he could not handle and wanted to palm off onto someone else.

'What have you got in that file?' Ethan asked.

'That's just the point,' Mackenzie said. 'I don't understand any of it myself and that's why I need the both of you to take a look and tell me what you think.'

Ethan glanced at the file. 'No strings.'

'None,' Mackenzie agreed. 'When I get back to Virginia I'll have to write an official report and reccomendations to the White House advising them on what to do about all of this, and right now I haven't written a single word.'

Ethan sensed somehow that the general was not baiting them and that he really was unsure of what he was holding on to.

'Where'd it come from, to have landed on your desk?' Lopez challenged, ever suspicious.

Mackenzie opened the file and replied as he handed the contents to Ethan.

'The United Kingdom,' he said. 'This is highly classified material, so it remains between us, understood?'

The beach was empty apart from themselves and as Ethan began reading the contents of the file so he felt the hairs on the back of his neck rise up.

***

VIII

'What's in it?'

Lopez, despite her caution, could not resist leaning over Ethan's shoulder as he read from the file, Mackenzie outlining the details as he did so.

'The incident occurred in Scotland, two weeks ago. Local police were in attendance and it's confirmed by multiple corroborating witness accounts that the event occurred precisely as was claimed.'

Ethan could see that the incident had attracted the attention of observers both civilian and military. The British Army had despatched an entire platoon of soldiers to the site within minutes of the sighting, and much of the evidence that remained at the site had been confiscated by the troops and spirited away.

'The incident was preceded by two weeks of sightings of strange lights out on open ground near the area of Bonnybridge, Scotland. The sightings are of interest because they have been corroborated with anomalous radar returns from a local Royal Air Force base. I managed to uncover documents reporting that the staff at the base thought that the radar systems were playing up and had them checked by specialists who said that the systems were operating normally.'

A fortnight before Mackenzie had shown up on the beach with them, Ethan read, a large number of witnesses had seen a brilliant light above a desolate beauty spot in Scotland. This light had been followed by a number of local electrical disturbances, and also by the appearance of a man named within the documents as "Simon". The individual concerned had surprised a group of teenage boys that had also witnessed the lights, but then for some reason had become spooked and attacked them. One boy had died and two others were severely injured before Simon was apprehended by local law enforcement and taken to a police station for questioning.

'Seems normal enough,' Lopez opined as Ethan turned the page.

'You'd think,' Mackenzie murmured. 'It's what happened next that really sends this whole case off the wall.'

Ethan read through the signed affidivits provided by the police officers who had interviewed the suspect, Simon. He heard Lopez gasp as she got to where he was in the report.

'Medieval?' she said, and looked at Ethan. 'You think that this could be related to the case we investigated in New Mexico all those years ago?'

'What happened in New Mexico?' Mackenzie asked.

'It's classified,' Lopez smiled sweetly at the general.

'You wanna tell me about it?' Mackenzie asked Ethan.

Ethan shook his head. Years before, as part of a Defense Intelligence Agency investigation, both Lopez and himself had been sent to investigate the rumoured existence of American Civil War soldiers hiding out in the wilderness, apparently immune to ageing. The investigation had uncovered spectacular discoveries within the world of fringe science, but the events Mackenzie's report referred to seemed to be something completely new.

'This isn't about cellular biology,' he replied. 'This is something different.'

'Something else,' Mackenzie agreed. 'All witnesses were required to sign the British Official Secrets Act to prevent them from sharing their stories with the media. The Brits have put a pretty tight lid on all of this.'

'Again,' Lopez asked, 'if they're keeping tight-lipped about what happened then how do you know about it?'

'We have people in the British intelligence service who help keep us informed,' Mackenzie smiled. 'Just as they do in ours. It's the way of things. I was able to talk to the army officer who handled the case, and he was smart enough to fill me in on a few details and hand over a copy of the interview. I don't think the Brits knew what to do with it any more than I do.'

'It says here,' Ethan said, 'that linguistic specialists examined CCTV footage of the interview and confirmed that this guy, Simon, was speaking middle English, a dialect not used for over four hundred years.'

'Either he was an expert putting on a very good show,' Mackenzie replied, 'or the unthinkable is true.'

'That's nuts,' Lopez said. 'You're saying this guy was from four hundred years ago?'

'I wouldn't have believed it either,' Mackenzie admitted, 'and right now I don't know what the hell to do about it. But the claim would have been dismissed if it weren't for what happened next, and in the days following the sighting.'

Ethan turned the page. During the interview the British Army had arrived, having been informed of an unknown radar return and bright lights in the vicinity. To Ethan, that smacked of a unit on stand-by in the area for just such an eventuality – the British Army was very professional but relatively small and would not have despatched troops so quickly to what was in effect a civilian matter.

Then, the light returned.

'He vanished from a locked cell?' Lopez read out loud from the report.

'Gone,' Mackenzie confirmed. 'Securely contained and with no means of escape. The police unit's commanding officer had personally put this Simon in the cell because he was concerned for the man's safety and sanity. For obvious reasons he considered Simon a danger to others and to himself. That was the last they saw of him. Simon's disappearance coincided with the return of the bright lights, which materialised directly over the spot in the building where Simon was being held.'

Ethan nodded slowly. 'An abduction event.'

'You believe in this sort of thing,' Mackenzie observed.

'Not usually,' Ethan replied, 'but we're aware of such reports. They cropped up from time to time in our investigations with the DIA. Most of the reports we studied were not contemporary though, but historical.'

'Historical? How old?' Mackenzie asked with a frown.

'Centuries,' Lopez replied, 'before the UFO phenomenon was created. They're the only cases without precedent and thus the most likely to be genuine.'

Ethan read on, and then he got to the lab reports.

'Is this for real?' he asked.

Mackenzie nodded. 'It's why I'm here.'

Ethan read through the reports from the labs to which a small sample of blood had been sent, blood belonging to Simon himself and taken as a precaution by the arresting officers. The police in the United Kingdom no longer had their own dedicated forensics laboratory due to budget cuts, so all such material was outsourced to civilian laboratories, allowing Mackenzie the chance to track the reports down. The pin-prick sample provided only enough material for a database match and DNA check, and what came back had required the signing of more Official Secrets Act documents.

'The DNA confirmed his age,' Lopez whispered.

'It did,' Mackenzie said. 'It suggested that, based on mitochondrial mutations that have occurred since, Simon could not have been born before the year 1298 or after the year 1463. The lab couldn't have been clearer. Simon was at least six hundred years old in terms of his mitochondrial DNA, although physically he appeared to be about twenty five years of age.'

Ethan sat back and looked at the lab reports. The British Police had commissioned three more independent tests on the blood, each coming back with the same results and requiring more careful gagging orders on those who had conducted the tests. Simon, whoever he had been, was a medieval man who had appeared briefly in twenty first century Scotland.

'This is insane,' Ethan said. 'None of it makes any sense. How far have the Brits got with this?'

'They're as up in the air as we are,' Mackenzie replied. 'They just don't have people with sufficient expertise to study this kind of event, and they're as loathe as we are to hand it over to civilian organisations who would likely muddy the waters with conspiracy theories and wild speculation. It's *possible*, however remotely, that there is a conventional explanation for Simon's appearance and vanishing.'

'You don't sound like you're convincing yourself,' Lopez said, 'much less us.'

Mackenzie nodded, and produced another smaller folder from which he retrieved a single photograph, printed on high-quality paper. He handed it to them with a sigh.

'I wish I could say otherwise, but this was taken at the same time as the events occurred and we don't know who the hell shot it.'

Ethan held the image up for himself and Lopez to see and they both gasped in shock at the same moment.

The image had been taken at night, and at the bottom of the shot was what Ethan presumed was the police station where the events in Scotland had taken place. He could see patrol vehicles and two large military trucks parked outside the station, and all around was blackness but for the top half of the image.

There, vivid against the night sky, was an object emitting a brilliant halo of kaleidoscopic light, flaring like multi-coloured sunrises. Ethan could see at once that it was metallic, solid and as large as a couple of houses. He could see the lights from the police station reflecting weakly off its hull, could see the object's own lights illuminating the road and the police station below it. Somehow, even in an age of digital manipulation where the camera could lie as quickly and as easily as the criminal, Ethan knew that he wasn't looking at a forgery. This, without a doubt, was the clearest and sharpest image of an unidentified flying object that he'd ever seen in his life.

'Is this actually real?' Lopez asked, suspicious of such a perfect image.

'It's real,' Mackenzie confirmed. 'I had it tested by every lab I could find, all under strict non-disclosure protocols. It's there, it's solid, and we don't know what the hell to do about it.'

***

XI

'I'm not sure what you want us to do about it either,' Ethan said as he handed the image back.

Mackenzie filed the photograph away as he replied.

'The government of the United States has two problems,' he began. 'The first is that the preponderance of high-quality image capturing technology in the hands of the public mean that equally high-quality images of Unidentified Aerial Phenomena are going to become the norm as time progresses. There is a well-documented program of denial of such things within the military and political sphere, but there is an equally well-documented acceptance of visitations by unknown craft among the general public.'

'We know the score,' Lopez said. 'Governments deny the presence of these things to prevent panic, while also trying to obtain them in order to benefit from the advanced technology they must contain.'

'I came to the right people,' Mackenzie grinned. 'That, in a nutshell, is the official line within the government and the CIA. Admit nothing, gather everything. They'll deny it to the ends of the earth of course, but we have dozens of official witnesses and former members who carried the secret for decades who are now on their deathbeds and willing to testify, in front of Congress and under oath, what they saw and what they were involved in. The cat's going to get out of the bag real soon and I've been charged with some way of controlling that process. The government accepts it's going to happen, they just want to keep a handle on it.'

Ethan nodded as he understood the general's predicament.

'So, they're going to release images like this to convince people?'

'No,' Mackenzie replied. 'This image is the second problem. It wasn't taken by the CIA.'

'You said it was shot in Scotland?' Lopez pointed out. 'I figured that the British Army must have taken it.'

'The British Army had only just rolled up,' Mackenzie said. 'Analysis shows that this image was captured using a high-powered zoom lens, meaning that whoever took it was some distance away. Further more, it came with a note.'

'A note?' Ethan echoed.

Mackenzie showed them the note, which was printed on plain paper.

You can't deceive the people forever. Full disclosure is inevitable. Reveal the truth now, or these will go public on every media outlet in the world.

'Are you kidding me?' Lopez said in delight. 'The CIA is being held to ransom?'

'In a manner of speaking,' Mackenzie said.

'How, though?' Ethan asked. 'It's a great shot, but it's just one picture and with all the others being faked out there it's not enough on its own to convince the people of the truth, that this planet has been visited by extra-terrestrial species for millenia.'

'It's not just one shot,' Mackenzie admitted as he handed Ethan a series of images. 'Whoever is behind this is snapping UFOs all over the United States and we have no idea how they're doing it.'

Ethan saw the penny drop in Lopez's eyes as she rolled them and laid back down on the sand.

'Here we go,' she uttered. 'Somebody has a toy that the CIA wants and it's gotten them all jealous. So now they want us to go find out who's behind it and steal their technology.'

Mackenzie shrugged.

'That is kind of what the CIA does, but in this case it's not the mission we have in mind. It would appear that somebody, somewhere, has developed the ability to predict when and where UFOs appear. We just want to know how they're doing it so that we can do the same and figure out what these things are.'

'Huh,' Lopez uttered from where she lay, 'and then presumably capture a few of them and reverse-engineer their technology for use in weapons.'

'I don't know,' Mackenzie replied. 'I don't make policy. All I know is that people are becoming ever more sophisticated in their ability to study these things, and we're playing catch up at the CIA. Our folks just don't have the expertise to figure these things out, and I've spent the last few days researching everything the Barn has worked on and trying to get up to speed on it all. We sent a team out to examine the Japan Air Lines UFO incident in 1986 and confiscated all of the material, but we still don't know what we're really dealing with decades later.'

'What happened in '86?' Ethan asked.

'The crew of JAL Flight 1628, a cargo Boeing 747, witnessed multiple UFOs at night over Eastern Alaska while en-route from Paris to Tokyo. The craft were caught on radar in close proximity to the 747, and when the lights of Fairbanks illuminated one of the craft the captain of the 747, who was a former fighter pilot with over ten thousand hours experience, described a craft that was twice the size of an aircraft carrier shadowing his airplane. A month or so later, an Alaska Airlines airplane reported a radar track in the same area that was confirmed by ground radar as moving at speeds of up to eighteen thousand miles per hour while climbing rapidly. A third sighting, of a disc shaped object shadowing an airplane, was reported in the same month by the crew of a US Air Force KC-135 tanker.'

Mackenzie looked out at the blue waves and horizon as he went on.

'The Federal Aviation Administration studied all of the events closely, but especially the JAL close encounter because there was so much hard evidence to back up the reports of the 747 crew. That was where the CIA got involved. The

Navy's Vice Admiral Engen visited the FAA headquarters and requested that the witnesses talk to nobody about the incident until they had been given official clearance to do so. The FBI, CIA and then-President Reagan's Scientific Study Team were present, and at the end of the meeting the CIA confiscated everything. It's only because of the presence of copies of the reports in the FAA Division Chief's office that the story got out into the public media at all. That event happened decades ago, and yet despite all the data we're still no closer to understanding what these things are. All the talk on the conspiracy theory websites and radio shows is blather about nothing. The biggest secret the CIA harbours is that nobody has a clue what these things are, and we have absolutely no way of stopping them. They manoeuvre with impunity through our airspace and appear unaffected by our sensors and weapons, and worse still they appear to be abducting ordinary citizens at will.'

Mackenzie produced another slim file that he handed to Ethan.

'Manhattan Island, November 1989. A woman named Linda Napolitano was abducted from her apartment building at three in the morning. She claimed to have been transported on a beam of light out of her apartment high above the city and taken aboard an alien craft. It would pass as nothing more than fantasy, had it not been witnessed by several people, one of whom was a statesman at the United Nations, Javier Perez de Cueller. His bodyguards claimed that the statesman was visibly shaken after witnessing the abduction of Linda Napolitano by three small beings, who took her into a large flying craft on a beam of light.' Mackenzie detailed the rest of the event as Ethan listened closely, suitably intrigued.

The report was detailed, including descriptions of the event by the bodyguards and a retired telephone operator named Janet Kimball, who had witnessed the entire event but had believed it to be a movie scene being filmed in the city. Although Javier Perez de Cueller had repeatedly been approached by investigators regarding the incident, the man who would later become the Peruvian President and Secretary General of the United Nations had refused to go public with his experience, simply remaining silent whenever confronted about it. That said, he had also never once denied that the incident had taken place.

'The whole report is highly credible,' Mackenzie said, 'and is just one of many that we have on file at the CIA. Many have been investigated by agents in the field but often we figure that most of those who believe themselves to have been taken remain silent on the issue.'

'Fear of ridicule,' Lopez murmured as she read through the report with Ethan. 'They don't want to draw attention to themselves.'

Ethan handed back the document. 'You're not here just for advice.'

Mackenzie sighed as he packed the information away in the files he carried with him.

'I don't know where to start with all of this. I have a case involving a medieval man somehow ending up in modern day Scotland who then vanishes without trace from a locked cell. I've got UFO sightings that simply cannot be dismissed, and

I've got cases of abductions where the mental and physical health of the victims is under tangible threat.'

'Which victims?' Lopez asked, concerned.

'The CIA has followed a few, isolated cases over the years where the testimony is so powerful that it cannot be denied. We know that something is happening, but we're powerless to prevent it. I can't talk to you about it here, even this far away from everyone else. It's just too sensitive. Is there somewhere we can go where nobody can *possibly* see or hear us?'

Ethan looked at Lopez, who shrugged.

'I guess it can't hurt to take a look.'

Ethan nodded and gestured to a nearby jetty, where several small powerboats were tied up.

'Wanna take a ride?'

***

X

The motor launch was little more than a dug-out canoe, one of the local designs that traversed the lagoons where fishermen plied their trade beneath the equatorial sun. Ethan guided the launch out into the centre of a lagoon just off the island's west coast, a sandbar visible beneath the gin clear water where the ocean passed between the two islands. Here, far from the coast, there was nothing but blue sky and water, fish and the lapping of the shallow water against the hull as he shut the engine off.

'This is about as far from Washington's eyes as you're ever likely to get,' Ethan said, 'so if there's something that you need to say then now's the time.'

Mackenzie sat on the bow and spoke quietly, as though even here he felt certain that unknown eyes were watching.

'Most people think that the US government possesses alien technology. We've all seen the documentaries I guess, at one time or another. The truth isn't quite so clear-cut. I was given the role I now have in order to try to understand the nature of these visitors, largely because while it's true that our government has access to alien technology, for the most part even our brightest minds don't have a clue what they're looking at.'

'Are you talking about Roswell?' Lopez asked.

To Ethan's surprise, Mackenzie nodded.

'From what I can gather Roswell was a real event and a flying craft was recovered from a ranch in New Mexico in 1947. However, what was recovered was something that seemed more like a drone than anything else. The craft had few controls, nothing that could be figured out as instrumentation, no electrical circuits, nothing. The thing was just like a lump of shaped metal that had dropped out of the sky. To this day, no engineer has been able to figure out how the thing worked.'

Ethan had never before considered that, although the US might have recovered alien craft, they might also have failed to understand them by now.

'But they've had this thing for decades, right?' Lopez argued. 'How could they not have understood it?'

'Because you're looking at this from a practical point of view,' Mackenzie explained. 'When you look at it from a military view point, the reason becomes clear. You don't drop your own technological secrets into your enemy's back yard.'

Ethan frowned.

'Enemy?' he echoed the general's choice of words. 'You think that they consider us to be an enemy?'

'Why else would you closely monitor a species?' Mackenzie asked. 'Why else would you take them, perform medical experiments on them and do so for hundreds of years?'

'Not to invade,' Lopez countered. 'If they're so clever then they wouldn't take that long to figure us out.'

'I agree,' Mackenzie said. 'That's why we figure that the object recovered in New Mexico was a drone of some sorts. We don't think that these things are the main show. We think that they're scouts, heading out across the universe in search of life. Simple, long-range scouts designed to find life and then report back later. They could even be autonomous, just like some of our own drones.'

Ethan thought about that for a moment. While it was standard military practice to reconnoitre a target prior to an assault, that was not the only reason for sending in drones to check out an area.

'They could be explorers,' he said. 'There's no reason to suspect them of being hostile. Even if they do interact with us from time to time, they could see us as nothing more than an obstacle to some other goal or purpose that they might have.'

'Again, I agree on all counts,' Mackenzie said. 'Which is why I need you both on this for me, and not just for me. We can't admit it publicly, but the CIA is watching an individual in Nevada right now and we'd like you to travel out there and meet with them.'

Ethan's senses came alive with suspicion and he saw clouds of distrust shadow Lopez's eyes as she glanced at him.

'We're out of the game,' Ethan repeated. 'We don't want to get involved in any more shadow-boxing with government agencies, especially off the books like this. We did that before and all it got us was nearly killed and none of the pension.'

'And yet you're here,' Mackenzie said as he spread his arms wide to encompass the entire island. 'And you're both wealthy. I know that you profited immensely from taking down the cabal known as Majestic Twelve. You're sitting here enjoying the quiet life but the work is far from complete. ARIES was only the beginning, the first attempt at understanding events in history and today that have defied conventional explanations. I'm giving you the chance to spearhead a new mission in...'

'You're giving us the chance to get embroiled in something that may end up in us getting killed if someone at the CIA decides we're expendable or we know too much,' Lopez interrupted. 'We're not going down that road again.'

'Then don't,' Mackenzie replied. 'Don't do it for me, for the CIA or even for your country. Do it for Sophie Taggart.'

'Who's Sophie Taggart?' Ethan asked.

Mackenzie handed Ethan a photograph, and Ethan's heart squeezed inside his chest as he saw the image of an angelic girl. The girl was smiling at the camera, but she seemed sad at the same time, as though the troubles of the world were weighing down on her shoulders.

'Seven-year-old Sophie Taggart is currently undergoing treatment for Post Traumatic Stress Disorder,' Mackenzie explained. 'Initially, physicians believed that she was the victim of parental abuse, but they quickly realised that wasn't the case when the parents requested cameras be put in their house to figure out what was happening to their daughter at night. She would wake up screaming, night terrors they called them, and became increasingly withdrawn at school and home.'

'What did the cameras see?' Lopez asked.

Mackenzie shifted uncomfortably on the bow of the boat, as though even talking about what was happening was difficult for him.

'This,' he said, and handed them another still image.

Ethan looked at the image and little insects of loathing scuttled beneath his skin. The image was of a darkened bedroom, and he could see what he presumed was Sophie's bed with her asleep in it. But it was what was beside the bed that made his skin crawl.

'They visit her,' Mackenzie said, 'and they take her away.'

The figure captured by the camera was perhaps four feet tall, with large and oval black eyes and strange, pale skin. Its bulbous head contained no visible nose or mouth, and its limbs were long and thin. Even more strangely, it appeared translucent.

'This is the only image we captured,' Mackenzie said, 'everything else is filled with white noise. This girl isn't lying, and whatever is happening to her is sending her slowly insane. I want you both to come back to the States, step in here and find out what the hell is going on, because this goes beyond our government and our country. This is about little children being abducted, and I want to know what these bastards are and what they're doing here.'

***

XI

Great Salt Lake Desert, Utah

'Stay quiet.'

The desert night was vast and black, as though they were standing within a whole universe of darkness. Kyle Trent knew that the canyons to either side of the track were blocking the distant lights of Dugway, giving the impression that they were alone in an endless darkness on the edge of Simpson Springs camping ground.

Few people came out here at night, and for good reason. Everyone had heard the stories. The nearby community of Dugway was home to around eight hundred people, and they were the only permanent residents for miles in every direction. What Kyle was doing was dangerous, he knew, but the thirst for knowledge had now grown more powerful than his concern for his own safety. His cameraman felt differently.

'This is insane.'

Greg Parfitt hauled a set of four cameras along the track, while Kyle shouldered the tripods and lenses.

'This is where the data led us,' Kyle snapped back. 'You knew that when we left. Quit complaining, we're almost in position.'

The track led up the side of a rugged hill, one of many littering the edges of the desert. Atop the hillside was the perfect vantage point that Kyle had selected, one with commanding views of the vast desert darkness sprawling before them. And within that darkness was over one thousand square miles of the most restricted and classified land and airspace in the continental United States, a place so secret that it made Area 51 look like Disneyland.

'Almost there.'

Kyle was huffing and puffing as he laboured up the steep slope and finally broke free onto the crest of the ridgeline. As he did so he saw the vast plains and distant mountains move into view, while the twinkling lights of Vernon glistened like jewels in black velvet to the east.

Greg hauled his load alongside Kyle and slumped in the darkness. Kyle was beginning to regret hiring his friend for this outing. Despite the promise of what was to come, Greg was already miserable, cold and tired. He had no idea what was about to happen and Kyle could tell by the look on his face that he was on the verge of going home.

'This will be worth it.'

'Yeah, right,' Greg mumbled.

Kyle glanced at his watch, the dial glowing faintly to avoid messing up his night vision. Kyle liked to think of himself as an explorer, a warrior for the truth. He was dressed in black camouflage gear with nigh-vision goggles tilted back and away from his eyes, and his skin was darkened by black camouflage cream. A belt at his waist held pouches containing survival gear, and with his hiking boots and bandana he looked every inch the elite soldier. In actual fact he had been nowhere near the military in his entire life. He told people that this was because he despised the reasons that America's government had sent its sons and daughters into war zones, to line the pockets of politicians and weapons companies. In truth, it was because Kyle was thin, didn't like the dark much and had been terrified of guns ever since he'd been mugged by two drug addicts for his pocket money when he was twelve years old. Although the gun was later found to have been a fake, the terrified Kyle could not have known it, so realistic was the look of the weapon.

Kyle ignored Greg's complaining, just as he had ignored the fact that despite his strict instructions Greg had turned up for their hike in jeans and sneakers, his only nod to camouflage a black bomber jacket. Clearly, he had not taken seriously Kyle's warnings that the people who guarded the facility out in the desert were known to operate with lethal force, or that they were operating within the base's boundary, an area strictly off limits to civilians.

'Come on, it's almost time.'

Greg dragged himself into motion again and began unpacking the cameras.

'Nothing's gonna happen, man.'

Kyle shook his head as he set up the tripods. He knew better, but even the images that he had shown Greg had not convinced his friend of anything other than Kyle's ability with a computer and his willingness to embellish the truth. Kyle rued the day he'd claimed to be joining the Navy SEALS as soon as he left high school, saying that he'd been accepted into the corps. He'd been shooting for impressing the girls, but instead the jocks had mocked him mercilessly for months. When the semester had come to an end, Kyle had been spotted stacking shelves in the local Walmart and the abuse that had followed had driven him even further into the life of seclusion that he had chosen for himself.

He would show them. Kyle had discovered the wonders of computer programming and the mysterious and vast world of the Internet at an age young enough to become a genius at it before he was out of his teens. That was the only reason he was now operating within the boundaries of a secretive military base without detection: he'd hacked two of the seismic sensors and one IR camera on the northern approach to the base. Now, he was on a mission that he was sure any Navy SEAL would have appreciated and admired: the search, always, for the truth, even under circumstances of great danger.

'Where do you want the IR camera?' Greg asked.

'Set it up looking west, I don't want the town of Vernon giving us false signals.'

Greg Parfitt was from Salt Lake City and worked in a local tech store. He was a necessary evil to Kyle's plan as, on his meagre salary from the convenience store he could not afford to buy or hire the computers and cameras necessary for this endeavour. Hell, it had cost him a months' salary just to make it to Scotland in time for the event he had photographed there, but that trip had secured his place in legend, at least in his own eyes. His parents had believed he was travelling to expand his horizons, and, suitably impressed by his determination had let him go. He had sent the images he had captured to the CIA with a threat that he would expose the truth if they did not release full disclosure to the public about the phenomenon that every human being on the planet was aware of and wanted answers to. Of course, he had neglected to let his parents know about that part of his journey, instead regaling them with tales of life in Edinburgh and the Highlands.

Greg had brought four cameras with him and two laptop computers. An optical lens was supported with two infra-red cameras and one ultra-violet. Each was capable of recording hours of high-resolution imagery at high magnifications thanks to the telephoto lenses that Kyle carried, all of which were being mounted upon tripod stands to record super-stable film. The two laptops controlled electrical motors affixed to each tripod, allowing the cameras to both turn smoothly and also to track objects in the sky using dedicated software coded by Kyle.

With the cameras set up and ready to record, Kyle turned his gaze to the west. In the far-off distance were a string of glistening lights that betrayed the presence of a super-secret U. S. Army facility known as the Dugway Proving Ground. Although most people had heard of places like Area 51 at Groom Lake, what they didn't realise was that the public fascination with such locations was in fact the perfect cover. Area 51 had not been used for ultra-classified operations for at least two decades, the press attention ensuring that it was simply too well known to be a secure location. Instead, the American military had moved its most sensitive operations to Dugway in the early 90s, a place perhaps even more remote and inaccessible than Groom Lake.

'Now what?' Greg asked as he started the cameras recording.

Kyle smiled as he observed the site through a pair of powerful binoculars. 'We wait.'

'Great,' Greg mumbled, 'endless hours on top of a cold mountain looking at nothing but stars and blackness.'

Kyle turned to one of the laptop computers, and he accessed a small program. The little application ran in the blink of an eye. Upon it, he could see a map of the continental United States, and upon that map were thousands of constantly flickering and moving red spots. Probability graphs and charts recorded information at a tremendous rate while algorithms that he had lovingly crafted hummed in digital symphony. Once again, just as the program consistently had for the entire week, a flashing gold star appeared on the map located directly over where they were standing.

'Oh, ye of little faith,' he said to Greg. 'We'll be waiting for precisely eight minutes, and then it'll be here.'

***

XII

Even as Kyle spoke, so he saw headlights appear on the distant base. It looked as though a small convoy of trucks had begun moving parallel to the runway. Although he could not see it in the darkness, Kyle knew that out there was an entire airbase and massive bombing ranges.

'Look,' he said triumphantly. 'They're on the move.'

Greg could see the convoy from where he stood, but he seemed unimpressed.

'It's just some trucks and stuff, what's the big deal?'

'The big deal,' Kyle replied, 'is not the fact that they're on the move, but *why*. It's half past two in the morning and they're out on manoeuvres? They only get out of bed at this time in the morning for a damned good reason, trust me.'

The convoy moved across the base, apparently driving down the main runway toward the south eastern corner of the airfield. Kyle could see that they were aiming for the general direction of where he and Greg were standing, but he knew that he had nothing to fear: as long as they stayed low and out of sight of infra-red sensors, they would remain concealed. His excitement was driven not by the trucks but by what he might see in the next couple of minutes.

'Any time now,' he said. 'Check the cameras are all running.'

'They're all running,' Greg said without glancing at any of them.

'Check them again,' Kyle snapped. 'I didn't come all the way out here for you to leave a lens cap on!'

Greg grumbled again but he strolled to the cameras one by one and made sure that they were operating normally.

'There, they're working fine. Can I go now?'

Kyle shook his head, his eyes fixed upon the skies above them. 'You go now, you'll miss a once in a lifetime event.'

'Sure,' Greg nodded and patted Kyle's back. 'You have a great night out here, and make sure you don't leave any of these cameras behind. They cost thousands and my ass is on the line if you…'

'There it is.'

Greg paused and looked up into the night sky. The vast blackness was sprinkled with dozens of pin-prick stars glistening in the heavens, but he could see nothing out of the ordinary. He chuckled.

'There's nothing there, Kyle.'

Kyle shook his head.

'Not up there,' he said, and pointed at one of the laptop screens. 'There.'

Greg looked at the screen and Kyle felt his friend tense up.

The laptop screen was displaying the view through one of the infra-red cameras that they had set up. The camera was overlooking the airbase, tilted upward slightly to see a bit more sky than ground. The airbase glowed with vivid reds and oranges against the cold blue and black of the surrounding deserts, and there, hovering above it, was an angular shape that was showing clearly on the IR camera despite being utterly invisible in the night sky.

'Jesus!' Greg uttered, his throat suddenly hoarse.

'Nope,' Kyle replied as he moved almost reverentially toward the laptop, trying to look both at it and the night sky before them. 'Not quite, anyway.'

Kyle had seen this before several times now and he knew precisely what to do. The craft, whatever the hell they were, generated large electro-magnetic fields, which appeared to be something to do with their propulsion. As far as he could tell, there was no engine as such at all aboard these craft, no exhaust emissions like a normal aircraft. These objects typically radiated energy at frequencies on the spectrum that were beyond human senses, only occasionally becoming visible in certain light and temperature conditions. Kyle was convinced that these things were whizzing about over the heads of humanity all of the time, and only occasionally did people get lucky enough to catch a glimpse of them. Kyle had made it his mission to remove luck from the equation, and had succeeded in spectacular style.

'How have you done this?' Greg asked in amazement, his eyes fixed to the object on the screen.

'Make sure we're running at the highest resolution and frame rates,' Kyle snapped. 'This one's about to light up.'

'It's what?' Greg uttered. 'How do you know th…'

Greg's sentence was abruptly cut off as from out of the darkness across the wilderness a brilliant, shimmering orange and yellow orb of incandescent light flared into life. Kyle cursed as he jerked his head away from the light, keen to preserve some level of night vision. The orb bathed the desert in light a few miles from where they stood on the hills.

'Resolution!' he snapped to Greg in a harsh whisper. 'Frame rates!'

Greg performed the necessary tasks, staring in wonderment across the night sky as the object shimmered. To Kyle it looked as though it were made from a liquid sunset, the colours as vivid as those seen every night across the deserts of Utah when distant storms kicked up dust and debris that tinted the evening sky with shimmering hues of colour. Kyle slipped on a pair of sunglasses, to help him see the object that he knew was veiled by the brilliant lights.

He did not know why they chose to conceal themselves so carefully and then promptly light up the desert for miles around. It was as though they liked trying to sneak up on people and then were disappointed that they hadn't been noticed. The only solution he had ever come up with was that they were doing something important, and had to de-cloak in the manner of a *Star Trek* Klingon warship in order do whatever mysterious functions they came here for. One thing that Kyle was certain of was that they did this most often when close to military and nuclear facilities, and that was one reason why he knew in advance where they would appear.

'What is it?' Greg whispered.

Despite the brilliant light the desert was utterly silent, the air still. Kyle shook his head as he looked at the bizarre shape concealed behind the light.

'I don't know, but it sure as hell isn't one of ours.'

Kyle could see the triangular form of the craft, which had one light on each corner that blazed white and another larger light beneath the centre that cast an orange light, the powerful flare that was illuminating the desert. Kyle could see that the craft was absolutely a solid object, and that its lower hull faintly reflected the glow of the lights as though made of metal. Everything about the object screamed that it was man-made, but only one thing assured Kyle that it was not: the triangular craft was the size of half a football field and was hovering in absolute silence.

'The air's charged,' Greg said, finally coming to his senses. 'You can feel it.'

As soon as he said it, Kyle realised that his friend was right. There was a faint electrical charge around them, teasing fine hairs on their necks.

'Stay focussed on the object, it might move at any time.'

Greg nodded, the motors in the tripods whirring softly as they tracked the object. Slowly, Kyle reached into his pocket and produced a theodolite and a laser range-finder. The two objects were essential in measuring angles and distances respectively and would allow him to assess the precise size of the craft. The more data that he could gather, the more he would be able to say to the public when the time came, and it was data after all that had got him this far.

Kyle used the theodolite and measured the angles, recording them in the device with the press of a button, and then he used the range-finder. He fired a single beam directly at the object and got an instant reading of just over eight kilometres.

'Wow,' Greg whispered as the data fed automatically into the cameras to sharpen their focus on the central object within the lights. 'It's massive!'

Kyle was about to reply when he saw a thin red beam of light extend slowly from within the craft toward the ground below. His skin tingled as he witnessed the incredible sight of a beam of light advancing at a controlled velocity, not zipping into existence like the light of a laser beam. The beam of light touched the ground and moved slowly back and forth as though searching for something. Almost at the same time, Kyle removed his sunglasses and saw thin red beams sweeping the sky around the object on the IR monitor, coming from the rapidly advancing column of vehicles.

'They're using night-vision goggles,' he identified the beams. 'The infra-red signals can be seen on our cameras.'

'They're coming this way.'

'Don't worry, they're not going to be interested in us.'

Suddenly, the object in the sky vanished as rapidly as it had appeared. The desert was plunged into a deep blackness as the convoy of lights came to a halt several kilometres out into the deserts.

'Unlucky boys,' Kyle grinned. 'Close, but not as close as me.'

Kyle was about to start packing up the cameras when he saw the red beams of the soldiers down in the desert suddenly snap around and point straight at them. Kyle froze in motion, staring at the laptop screen as Greg grabbed one of the cameras and held it up to him.

'I don't believe this! This is going to change the world! We need to get this out to as many people as we can!'

'Greg, get down,' Kyle snapped.

'What?'

Kyle opened his mouth to repeat his command when he heard what sounded like someone walking on an eggshell. Greg's head snapped to one side and he dropped vertically, his legs collapsing beneath him. Kyle glimpsed a faint splatter of dark blood spill onto the dusty ground at Greg's feet, and only then did he hear the report of a sniper's rifle.

***

XIII

Kyle had never really thought about what he would do if someone was shooting at him. As a teenager he'd had fantasies of tackling some deranged shooter at his high school, valiantly disarming him and winning the affection of the hot girls and the admiration and respect of the jocks.

Now, his guts convulsed inside him as he ducked down, his legs turning to jelly beneath him. Through gaps in the rocks he could see the approaching convoy of vehicles now tearing across the desert toward the hillside on which he crouched and he knew that they had been spotted. He stared wide-eyed at Greg, who was lying in silence with blood glistening in his hair where the sniper's bullet had taken off the side of his skull and scattered it across the hill top.

'Jesus,' he uttered, not in anger but in nauseating fear.

He could hear the car engines approaching and he knew that he had to act. Greg had been standing on the edge of the hillside and probably in plain view of the soldiers with their night-vision goggles. Even at two or three miles, his heat signature would have stood out vividly against the cold black rocks and night sky.

Kyle scrambled across to the cameras and took them down, yanking their hard-drive memories from them and stuffing them into his pockets. He turned and grabbed a flash-RAM drive from his pocket before using it to download the film and data they had captured from each laptop, careful to leave the computers in place. He could not help but look again at Greg, his lifeless face illuminated by the glow from the screens, one eye wide open and staring at the desert, the other missing entirely along with his skull and half of his cheek.

Kyle rolled alongside his friend, trying not to look at his ruined face or think about the horror of what had just occurred. Quickly, he rummaged in Greg's pockets and pulled out his cell phone and his wallet, stuffing them into his own pockets before he rolled away again. He could hear the sound of the approaching convoy now, growling engines echoing through the cold night air as he got to his feet and ran in a low crouch off the hillside toward the track that led back down to the main roads.

He knew that he could not hope to outrun the troops that would be deployed onto the hillside in search of him. They had just shot an unarmed civilian at a range of over a mile and he knew that they would not hesitate to kill him if they found him. The cover-up would be underway the moment they discovered Greg's body, and Kyle knew that he had only one chance to escape; make them think that there was only one person up on the hillside.

Kyle scrambled down the slope, his eyes adjusting to the darkness as he stumbled around boulders and rocks, following the trail back down to the desert floor. He could see the distant lights of Vernon to the east, seeming so close and yet so terribly far. He would be easy prey for that sniper once the troops crested the ridgeline, their night vision goggles marking him out easily against the cold desert darkness.

Kyle stumbled to the bottom of the hill, his breathing ragged as he staggered to the right and hunted around the mountainside until he found what he was looking for. Greg's battered old Ford pick-up was parked where they had left it at the base of the hills. Kyle, tears streaming down his face and his heart battering at the walls of his chest, staggered across to it and yanked open the driver's door. He climbed in and started the engine in one smooth motion, but he kept the lights off as he stamped down on the accelerator and drove away from the hills.

The troops would be supremely fit, but they would take time to crest the hill. If he could only make the main road before they did so, he could turn either north or south and appear to be just an ordinary vehicle making its way along the freeway. Kyle could only guess at how quickly those soldiers would reach their camera site: maybe four minutes from reaching the foot of the hills? The troops would be Special Forces or something most probably, able to ascend even steep terrain at a ridiculous speed. Three minutes?

He realised that he might be hit by a sniper even as he drove, and the thought of a high-velocity round ploughing through his back and out of his chest made him think of Greg's blood splattered remains again and he promptly vomited into the footwell. The truck careered left and right on the dusty trail but he managed to keep the vehicle from running off the road.

He saw the main road appear ahead of him, barely visible, and he bounced up off the track and onto the asphalt. Kyle yanked the wheel to the left and straightened out, then turned his headlights on and drove slowly north. He forced himself not to accelerate, and knew that the only way for him to survive now was to appear completely innocuous.

The tyres whispered on the asphalt and he wondered whether he would see the brilliant red speck of a sniper's scope flickering on his window. He forced himself not to look over his shoulder at the mountains, and as he drove he heard a terrific noise and flinched as over his head thundered a helicopter. The chopper was jet black and carried no navigation lights as it roared overhead and flew into the night, heading into the darkness toward the mountains.

Kyle kept on driving, focussing ahead on the twinkling lights of Vernon and hoping, praying, that he could make it there and skip town before the military realised that he had ever been on that hillside.

*

The troops made it onto the crest of the ridge within a few minutes of the sniper's shot being fired. They had little doubt that the individual they had seen on the hills to the east of the base had been a civilian that had somehow managed to sneak through the perimeter. What they could not believe was the lousy timing of their appearance.

Lieutenant Rico Savage surveyed the hilltop as he joined his men, who had cleared the area and confirmed one dead at the scene. Savage was a robustly built man who had served in the Green Berets before being posted to security at Dugway. Stern, wide-jawed and unforgiving, he was used to handling breaches like this but not used to seeing civilians shot dead right in front of him on U.S. soil.

'They're well inside the base boundary,' a trooper reported to him as he arrived. 'Lethal force was well justified, despite what's happened.'

Savage walked into the centre of a ring of cameras and surveyed them one after the other. Each was set up to watch over the deserts between here and the Dugway airfield, each recording a different wavelength of light. Laptops were arranged and connected to the cameras, which were mounted on powered tripods. In the centre of the arrangement was a young man, perhaps in his late twenties, lying face down in the dirt with half of his face blown off.

Savage sighed and closed his eyes briefly. In the darkness, his men could not see his expression and his leadership of them would not be questioned, nor his resolve to do what must be done. The mission with which he had been charged was to ensure that the security of the perimeter was not breached, especially when sensitive operations were being conducted across the Dugway proving ground. They had been half way to the site, after reports of movements on the hilltop, when that damned light had burst into life. If it had not appeared, there would have been an arrest, not a shooting. But with its arrival, his men had operated under their SOPs and had conducted themselves excellently. Stop the convoy. Observe the object. Do not attempt to intervene or intefere.

'One dead,' his soldiers confirmed. 'No sign of anyone else up here.'

As he spoke, a pair of helicopters thundered across the desert nearby, swinging around to come in closer to the hilltop. One of the troopers was in close contact with the pilot and called out to the lieutenant.

'No other individuals sighted in the vicinity,' he reported. 'One vehicle headed north at low speed on the freeway a couple of miles out, doesn't look like it's anything to do with this.'

Savage frowned as he looked around at the various pieces of equipment around them.

'That's a lot of gear for him to have hauled up here on his own,' he murmured out loud.

The soldiers glanced around them. There was no vehicle detected anywhere around the hills, and this guy must have got the stuff up here somehow. The darkness meant that it would not be possible to track anyone else who might have been up here, and as if on cue one of the troops completed a quick search of the dead man.

'Nothing,' he said, 'no identifying documents.'

Savage thought for a moment. He could see the laptop computer screens held images of the recently seen craft in the desert, and he could guess at what the individual had been doing up here, but what he couldn't understand was how they had been so well prepared for what had happened. It was almost as if they'd been ready for it.

'Confiscate everything, and get it all off this hillside,' he ordered. 'I want nothing left here to identify anything or anyone. Search teams to be deployed at first light. If there was anyone else up here, any tracks that give them away, I want them found!'

***

XIV

Indian Springs, Nevada

The heat was probably the worse thing about being back in the United States. It was different to the warm breezes of the Pacific Ocean, dry and harsh, sweltering. Ethan drove with the car window open and tried not to think about their tropical home as he guided their rented Chevy Tahoe along the 95, headed north west out of Las Vegas.

To his right, Lopez leaned back in her seat with her sunglasses shielding her eyes. She seemed remarkably calm despite being back in the states, perhaps because their mission this time would not involve gunmen and the imminent threat of death. Being paid merely to investigate and not get too involved seemed to suit her.

The desert stretched in every direction for endless miles, vanishing into a milky horizon of haze beneath the white flare of the Nevada sun. Indian Springs, Ethan had noted when he checked a local map, was just eighty kilometres south of Groom Lake, the home of the infamous Area 51 facility. Vegas was to the south east, and between each there was little more than scrub desert and lonely mountain ranges blue with distance. The terrain was spectacular but the same wherever one looked, and Ethan found his mind wandering over his past, the conflicts in which he'd fought and the investigations he'd conducted with Lopez at the DIA. They had seen some tremendous things in those years, things that even now he could not explain to his family, or even to himself some days.

It was only after some time that he realised he'd had one of those moments where he had been driving on automatic pilot, his mind far away from the present. He couldn't really remember the past few miles of their journey, as though they had passed in a daze. There was also a vague numbness in his belly and chest, a sort of pain that made him shift in the driver's seat to try to get comfortable. The pain passed and he looked to his right.

Lopez was dozing on the passenger seat, and he realised that he too felt uncharacteristically tired. He figured it was down to the desert heat, which was so dry and draining compared to the ocean breezes of the islands they had made their home. Lopez stirred and dragged herself from her torpor.

'Man, I must've checked out there for a few minutes.'

Ethan smiled.

'Nicola, you were out for half an hour at least,' he said as he glanced at the digital clock on the car's instrument panel.

Even he was surprised at how long they'd been driving. Damn, these long straight roads and the seemingly static scenery sure played havoc with the mind. It wasn't any wonder that so many people claimed to have had strange experiences while driving alone out here.

'So, what's the story?' Ethan asked as he drove, forcing his torpor from his mind.

Lopez had read the file that Mackenzie had sent them via secure e-mail when they'd landed at McCarran International in Vegas, while Ethan had sorted the Tahoe.

'Sophie Taggart, aged eight,' Lopez replied. 'She started playing up about going to bed. Her parents figured that she was acting out for some reason, maybe problems at school or something. But she became hysterical about sleeping on her own to the point of losing consciousness. Her folks tried everything but eventually it was getting her to talk about why she was so afraid of going to bed that got the truth out of her, or what she believed was happening.'

'That creatures were coming into her room?'

'Pretty much,' Lopez agreed. 'There's a lot of interview testimony from a psychologist whom the parents hired to try to calm Sophie down, and he went from being sceptical of the girl's story to fearful that people were trying to steal her from her parents. He called the police, they couldn't handle it and referred the case to the local military station right across the road from Indian Springs, Creech Air Force Base.'

That got Ethan's attention. He had heard of Creech during his time with the Marines, an airbase with a location so close to Area 51 that it was routinely associated with events at the mysterious test facility to the north. Creech actually acted as a diversion field for aircraft operating within the Nevada Test and Training Range and was home to a number of Special Operations and Reconnaissance Squadrons, whose activities were highly classified and had often, crucially, operated unmanned aerial vehicles known as Predator drones.

'What did they say about it?'

'Canned response,' Lopez replied. 'They said that they had no knowledge of any such events in the vicinity of that or any similar airbase anywhere in the inventory.'

Both Ethan and Nicola were used to hearing that from the military and government. Where there was any doubt whatsoever about an unusual event, a simple denial of knowledge, or an admission of ignorance, depending on how one looked at it, was the official response. When it came to UFOs, anything from misidentification of stellar objects, airplanes, satellites and even swamp gas was routinely used to explain the oft-sighted flying craft witnessed by people all over the world.

'Then how did the CIA get involved with them at all?' Ethan asked.

'The parents took matters into their own hands. They set up the cameras that took the images that Mackenzie showed us. The father then sent the images to the

FBI and demanded to know what the hell was being done about it. The FBI clamped down real fast when they saw the images, and pretty soon the CIA were involved. They covered everything up of course, confiscated the images and film, but they knew that wouldn't stop what was happening and were afraid that the parents would simply film more events and go public with it if something wasn't done. That's where Mackenzie got involved, and where we come in.'

Ethan shook his head. Their history with the DIA and the ARIES program was one thing, but in all that time neither Ethan nor Lopez had actually witnessed the appearance of an alien being or craft in full flight. They had seen countless incredible things in their investigations, evidence that mankind had never been alone in the universe, but most of that evidence was historical. Now, they were heading into uncharted territory.

Lopez's cell phone buzzed and she checked it.

'The psychologist is there,' she said, 'and the family are ready.'

'We'll be there in ten minutes,' Ethan confirmed.

Indian Springs was typical of most desert communities, compact and with a population of less than a thousand. Ranks of trailer parks dominated the east and south of the town, along with a small school and community store, gas station and postal service. Ethan reckoned that the town would not have existed at all were it not for the sprawling Creech airbase on the north side of the Veterans Memorial Highway. Ethan pulled off and found the address on the far eastern edge of the town, where low slung gated condos stood on the edge of the barren desert.

The Taggart family were there to greet them on the porch. Ethan liked them at once, despite knowing that much of the population of Indian Springs lived below the poverty line. The father, David, was an IT guy who worked in Vegas for the casinos, his wife Rebecca a stay at home mom to their two young children, Sophie and Mark. A young family, David had not yet risen in the ranks for them to be able to afford living closer to his workplace, but being out here allowed them to save money more easily for the future.

One glance at Sophie was enough for Ethan to know that she was traumatised. Her big, wide eyes flared with concern at every movement, and she often went into catatonic phases where she drifted off to stare into space as though rejecting the world around her. Rebecca and David filled them in as they sat on chairs in the garden beneath the shade of an acacia tree, the mountains dominating the view to the south.

'We don't feel safe in our own home,' Rebecca whispered, not wanting to alert the children to their conversation as they played nearby. 'We want this fixed. Why do they keep coming here?'

Ethan could see the anger and frustration in Rebecca, her fists clenched until her knuckles were white, her jaw tight. They had been dealing with this for some time and nobody was helping.

'The authorities just write it off publicly,' David uttered with contempt. 'But they're real quick to confiscate any evidence. One of their officers even suggested that we shouldn't record any more film of these things. I've half a mind to send footage to the national press, but the airbase guys hinted that would be a bad idea.'

'They'd seek to discredit the story,' Ethan confirmed. 'They won't want the mass media down here sniffing around the airbase and any classified operations.'

'Would you believe that it's the damned CIA that are being helpful?' Dave went on. 'The spooks are the only ones getting anything done.'

'We don't care about national security and classified operations,' Rebecca added. 'We just want this to stop, for Sophie to be able to sleep without being afraid.'

As soon as the parents had finished speaking, the psychologist guided them to one side and they spoke softly. A small, bespectacled man named Clifford, his voice sounded tiny against the vastness of the nearby desert.

'I'd seen a lot of these kinds of cases over the years, but I'd been able to ascribe most of them to night terrors, lucid dreams, that sort of thing.'

'Wait one,' Lopez said, 'lucid dreams? What are they?'

'Lucid dreams are what one experiences when one wakes up *within* a dream,' the psychologist explained. 'They are almost completely indistinguishable from normal reality.'

'Really?' Lopez said. 'Sounds cool.'

'It is, if you're ready for them. Many people experience them briefly without realising it, and call them "false awakenings". Essentially, people go through their normal routine of waking up and getting out of bed, getting dressed and so on, only to then wake up again and find themselves still in bed. It's caused by our brain becoming lucid of our surroundings but the body is still asleep and is the reason why our dreams are most vivid in the last hour or so of sleep – our increasing wakefulness makes them seem more immediate and real. Lucid dreaming is simply this process but under control of the person experiencing it.'

'But if you're asleep, how can the dream seem so real as to be indistinguishable from reality?'

Clifford gestured around them with his arms.

'We see the world around us through our eyes but it is our brain that interprets those signals and creates our perspective on reality. When we're asleep, we dream, and yet we can see the world of our dreams despite our eyes being closed. Lucidity within a dream transforms the dream into reality, and unless you know that you're dreaming, it can be completely the same as normal reality with the caveat that none of the rules of our universe apply. One can fly, become a whale or go into space, our imagination is the only limit. But the downside is of course that, unaware of what a lucid dream is, those who experience it can have a negative and often horrific experience. Children who undergo this are said to suffer from "night terrors", lucid dreams that become nightmares.'

Ethan glanced at Sophie Taggart, who was playing in a den with her brother but watching them with that cautious, damaged gaze.

'What convinced you that Sophie wasn't having night terrors?' Ethan asked, almost uncertain if he wanted to hear the answer.

'It was before we had the video of that creature in her room,' the doctor said. 'It was the way that she described the tumbleweed caught on the roof of the house that made me realise that she was witnessing something incredible.'

***

XV

'Tumbleweed?' Lopez echoed in confusion.

Clifford spoke softly, letting the weight of his words carry their gravitas.

'Sophie told me that small people would come into her room and take her up through the ceiling and into the sky. I didn't believe her at first and considered her experiences to be the lucid dreams or night terrors I suggested. But then she began describing the things that she could see as she was lifted away, and she mentioned tumbleweed caught in the roof between the tiles along with one of her toys. David here went up to check, and sure enough there it was, the tumbleweed and one of Sophie's toys. We figured that a bird of prey perhaps picked it up but later dropped it when it realised the toy wasn't food.'

Ethan glanced at Sophie as she sat on a swing and held a baby doll clutched in her arms, cooing to it softly.

'Anything else?' he asked. 'Is there any way that this can be resolved as an illusion, something other than actual abduction events?'

'No,' Clifford replied, 'and believe me, video evidence not withstanding I've looked at everything. What's most incredible about it is that this sort of thing has been going on for hundreds of years, for as long as people have been able to record the events, and we had no idea about any of it. Many of our most enduring legends and mythical beings appear to have been inspired by abduction events.'

'What kind of legends?' Lopez asked.

Clifford shrugged his shoulders as though he didn't know where to start.

'Angels, demons and gods,' he said. 'Beings that can enter any place and appear to speak directly into the human minds. In the Middle Ages people wrote about how they would awaken in their beds but were unable to move. Sleep paralysis is well known these days and happens to everyone occasionally – it's a kind of false awakening where you become lucid within a dream but can feel that your body is rigid, as it always is when you're asleep. The experience is often quite frightening and leads the dream onto a more sinister path and leads many sceptics to suggest this as the start of most alien abduction experiences. But those who have experienced both say that the two are very different. Chiefly, with sleep paralysis, little grey men don't come wandering into the room.'

'First hand testimony doesn't mean much without evidence though,' Ethan pointed out. 'They might believe that their experience is different or real when in fact it's just a lucid dream, right?'

'Yes,' the doctor agreed, 'but lucid dreams typically cease quickly as the person becomes more agitated or excited and wakes themselves up. Abduction events persist without any such interruption. In the Middle Ages, people spoke of awakening in their beds unable to move and with a demon sitting on their chest, and other creatures standing around the bed. Of course, they had no concept of alien life as we understand it, so they believed that the interlopers were demons rather than extra-terrestrials, and the similarities don't end there.'

Clifford gestured to the girl's toys scattered nearby, one of which was a figure of a wizard of some kind with a wand in his hand.

'Many accounts from ancient history concern non-human figures who carried with them rods, staffs or other hand–held objects that held great power. Legends abound of figures such as these entering the rooms of ordinary people, speaking directly into their minds, and waving these objects to take them away to other places, fantastical realms of light that they did not understand. Today we see these objects in works of fiction, such as the staff carried by Moses in the Bible or Gandalf in the *Lord of the Rings*, and the wands of wizards and witches such as *Harry Potter* and others.'

Ethan almost laughed. 'You think that *Harry Potter's* wand was inspired by extra terrestrial visitors?'

'History records such encounters,' the doctor replied, not taking offence at Ethan's mirth. 'They of course could not understand what they were seeing and so wrote it down in terms that they recognised, but unknown creatures or people holding wands and staffs and directing great energy is a common theme in many historical accounts and is backed up by the vast literature describing encounters with forest people, fairies and other phenomena written off by modern science as fanstasy.'

'Fairies?' Lopez asked.

'Almost any supposedly mythical creature of lore could in theory be an eye-witness account of an extra terrestrial being, although of course they could be anything else but, we simply cannot tell from the records themselves as by definition the witness did not understand what they were seeing. However, given the sheer number of sightings and experiences, it's perhaps fair to say that they were seeing *something*, and these accounts go right back into ancient history.'

David and Rachel moved to join them.

Ethan looked at David. 'Can we see the video you recorded of these things appearing in Sophie's room?'

David beckoned them to follow him. They walked into the cool of the house, and David produced a laptop computer.

'We've got a few seconds of footage. It's weird, the camera seems to malfunction whenever they're around it and we only get snippets of imagery before everything goes blank.'

Ethan watched as David selected the video and hit the play button. Ethan saw Sophie's room and the little girl asleep in her bed, her body clearly visible curled up beneath the sheets. For a moment nothing happened, the bedroom dark and the camera shooting in black and white with a rudimentary night-vision setting active. The footage was a little grainy but everything was clear to see in the room.

The image flickered slightly and then Ethan saw it appear in the doorway to Sophie's room.

'Jesus,' Lopez murmured.

Ethan knew that something like this could easily be faked, but he was equally certain that the family were in earnest and more concerned about their daughter's safety and well-being than making hoax videos.

The creature was about Sophie's size but it's features were unmistakeably those of the classic alien "grey" that had become synonymous with abduction events. Big, slanted black eyes stared silently at Sophie as she slept, and then it advanced into the room. It moved with awkward steps, as though automated in some way, and then the image flickered out and the screen went black.

'That's it,' David said. 'When the screen comes back, Sophie's still in her bed and it's like nothing happened.'

True enough, moments later the screen came back to life. Sophie was still in her bed asleep and appeared not to have moved. Ethan frowned as he looked at the image. Something wasn't right but he couldn't put his finger on it.

'How many times has this happened?' Lopez asked.

'As far as we know, Sophie has been taken six times this year,' Rebecca replied as she stood alongside them. 'It's affecting her in a lot of ways; her school work is deteriorating, she's shutting out her friends and family, she's not talking, she's…'

Rebecca choked on her own grief and turned away from them. David watched her go and then turned to Ethan.

'We just want this to end,' he said. 'I don't know how these things are getting into our house, how they're doing it without us knowing.'

'Is Sophie staying in your room now?' Ethan asked.

'She sleeps with us in the living room until we go to bed, and we bring her with us. We don't have any video, but she says it still happens even when we're in the room. I don't understand it: we don't hear a thing, it's as if nothing's happened, but in the morning when she wakes up she's crying.'

David clenched his fists, anger radiating from his every pore as he stood before Ethan. Ethan had known many people suffering as David now did, not from alien abductions but mothers and fathers whose children had vanished, victims of abductions for money in Mexico or slaughter in Africa and the Middle East or dropped ordnance in Palestine or the Ukraine. They all looked the same, their bodies wired for action but their faces begging for help, their rage impotent, their worlds ruled by frustration and helplessness.

Ethan could not be sure that Lopez would want to join him, but in that moment he knew that he wouldn't be heading back to the islands any time soon.

'We'll do something,' he promised David. 'I don't know what it is yet, but we'll figure something out.'

Ethan led Lopez out of the house, and when they reached their car he turned to her.

'Call Rhyss Garret. I don't know if we'll need him, but I don't want to walk into another investigation unprepared. Ask him to meet us in Las Vegas.'

***

XVI

Vernon, Utah

Kyle Trent huddled alongside a trash dumpster near a mall, the shadows of the night concealing him from the cameras he could see surveying the parking lot. The city lights glowed in the darkness but their light was hollow, like the lights within the mall or the soulless heart of Las Vegas, the bright lights blinding tourists to the uncaring greed of the giant casinos. They represented a world of which he was no longer a part, and now the desert night was turning cold again and he shivered.

He was still wearing his black camouflage gear, which was a bonus at night when he wanted to remain undetected but would make him stand out like a sore thumb once daylight arrived again. He had made it into Vernon without being detected, at least as far as he knew, but his first course of action, to return to his parents' home and gather what he could, had been derailed when he had seen the black vehicles parked outside.

Kyle did not know how the soldiers at Dugway had identified him so fast, but now he knew that he could not return home. They had killed Greg and now he felt sick with fear over what they would do to his parents. Would they kill them also? How could he stop them? What could he do?

Kyle had always been a fan of stories of lone warriors standing up to the "man", to the government, the solitary and uncompromising voice of mercenary truth in an uncaring world. Now, he was that man, but the world he inhabited was unpleasant and lonely. He was cold and hungry, had little money and nobody that he could turn to. The troops would by now know the names of the few friends that he did have, and they would probably put a watch on all of them in case he showed up there. Kyle was a fugitive from the most secretive armed forces in the world, but unlike most fugitives he could not expect due process if he was captured. His fate would be a shallow grave on some lonely desert plain miles from anyone.

Kyle didn't feel like the lone, mercenary warrior. He felt like crying.

He shoved his hands deeper into his pockets and his fingers brushed against the memory stick onto which he had downloaded the footage. That was all he had. Video of Greg's shooting. His only hope was to show the enemy, which was what they now were, that he was in possession of proof that his friend had been shot and killed by soldiers working for the United States Government, and that he had video of UFOs over Dugway Proving Ground to boot. That was, of course, if they didn't already know that he was in possession of such material.

Kyle cursed. There really was no way out of this. He couldn't bargain with them because he'd already taunted the government with his images and threats of disclosure to the public. There was nowhere left for him to go. His only hope was that going public now, before they could find him, would make his name quickly enough that to kill him would simply draw more attention to the government than they would have wanted.

Yeah, that was it. Full disclosure. That was the only way for him to get this out there, to protect him from the killers who had iced Greg. Proof that he was being hunted. Proof that he was a victim of a conspiracy that went all the way to the top; ruthless, savage military leaders intent on silencing the heroes, determined to keep a lid on the truth.

Kyle felt his resolve stiffen and he took a breath. All he had to do was find a media outlet that he could talk with and who would hear him out. He could admit to trespassing on a military installation, confess everything. Sure, the use of deadly force would be the military's standard fall back, but he could at least ensure that they wouldn't be able to come after him, and he could then reveal the UFO footage that would change the world.

Kyle nodded to himself and checked his meagre financial funds. He had enough to get him out of Vernon and away to Vegas. From there, he could start discreetly approaching journalists to see if any of them were interested in his story.

*

Rico Savage stood in the living room of the house and looked down at Mr and Mrs Trent.

They were in their sixties, he guessed, ordinary folk who were clearly nervous about the uniformed man towering over them. Savage stood with his hands behind his back and spoke in clipped, terse tones that betrayed no emotion.

'When did you last see Kyle?'

The man's father spoke, his voice trembling with what might have been fear and his eyes wide with uncertainty, the deer caught in the headlamps.

'Two nights ago. He said he was going to stay with a friend in Vernon.'

'Do you know the name of this friend of his?'

The man shook his head, but the mother nodded.

'Greg,' she said confidently. 'He said he was staying with Greg.'

Rico Savage considered this for a moment. The body they had found up on the hillside had been without any form of identification, not surprising considering the boys had been trespassing on federal land where troops were cleared to use lethal force. They wouldn't have wanted to be easily identified. Still, it was kind of unusual to find civilians that far inside the base perimeter and he knew that he simply had to find out both how they had done it, and how they had done it at the same time as the uniquely classified event that had occurred. Rico had served in several war zones during his career and had seen at first hand the suffering inflicted by governments willing to wage war on each other. He didn't believe in coincidences.

'Do you have a surname for this Greg?' he asked the mother.

'I'm sorry, no I don't,' she replied. 'Kyle met him at work in the convenience store, we never actually met him ourselves.'

'The convenience store?' Rico echoed, sensing a lead. 'Which one?'

'Old Joe's, in Vernon,' the mother replied, but then she seemed to tense up. 'What kind of trouble is Kyle in?'

Rico considered his response. It was clear to him that Kyle was operating alone and that his family knew little or nothing of what he had been up to. They had been shocked to know that he was at Dugway and not with his pal in Vernon playing video games as they had believed. Rico relaxed himself by force of will and took a seat opposite Kyle's parents, pressing his hands together as he spoke.

'Mrs Trent, your son is in tremendous danger and we need to find him as quickly as we possibly can. I need access to any phones and computer equipment that he possesses.'

'Danger?' Kyle's father echoed. 'What kind of danger?'

Rico chose his words with care. He knew that he needed the parents on his side if he was going to locate Kyle and the sensitive data he possessed.

'We found a body at the scene where we believe Kyle and his friend were camping,' he explained. 'Although I can't be sure, I suspect that it will be identified as your son's friend, Greg.'

The mother's concern collapsed into fear and grief as tears spilled from her eyes. Her husband held her shoulders as he looked at Rico.

'He's only twenty-one, he doesn't know what he's doing.'

'He knows enough,' Rico countered. 'Greg is dead from a gunshot wound to the head and your son has disappeared. I don't have to tell you how that looks both to us and to law enforcement. If they encounter your son before we do, they will believe him to be armed and may well open fire.'

The father struggled to keep his features from collapsing into the same grief that had consumed his wife.

'Kyle's a lot of things, but he's no killer. He's never had a violent streak.'

'It doesn't take a violent streak to mis-use a gun,' Rico countered. 'Often, it doesn't take anything more than a mistake.'

A group of troops behind him were walking out of the house carrying a home computer and two laptops, along with a pair of cell phones that the officer presumed must have also belonged to Kyle. He knew from experience that anyone walking around with more than one cell phone was usually up to no good.

'He doesn't even own a gun,' his mother bleated. 'How could he have killed someone?'

Rico knew that as Kyle was old enough and had no criminal record, he could walk into a store in the United States and buy an assault rifle that was more usually the preserve of the military, along with ammunition sufficient to take out a city block. Tragically, it was no secret that civilian access to military-grade firearms in the United States had resulted in some of the worst atrocities against ordinary people in the world. That said, Kyle had no history of ownership of weapons or any connection with gun clubs, terrorist networks or anything of the sort. Overnight psychopaths were not unknown but they were uncommon, and again Kyle displayed none of the traits known to such individuals.

'Greg may have owned the gun, or one of them may have bought it that night, we just don't know right now. All I can say is that we need to find Kyle and fast. If he were on the run and afraid, where would he go and what would he do, do you think?'

The parents looked at each other, and the officer saw them share the glance and with it certain knowledge.

'He would go to the media,' the father said. 'He's passionate about that kind of thing, freedom of speech, the truth movement, all of it. If he thinks he's in danger, he'll try to use the media to get the message out and protect himself.'

Rico Savage nodded once and stood to leave. This was going to be worse than he had thought.

'You will find him?' the mother begged. 'You'll find him and protect him?'

Rico nodded without smiling. 'We will find him.'

***

XVII

CIA Headquarters, Langley, Virginia

General Mackenzie sat at a long table in a room filled with half of the country's top brass facing a projection screen on one wall. There was enough military might within the room to launch a war, all branches of the armed forces represented as they were briefed by a CIA operative known only to them as Forty-Eight. The numerical moniker was merely for protection in the field; high–ranking officials were open targets for abduction by foreign powers and thus knowing the names of operational agents was forbidden in order to protect assets in the field.

Mackenzie was looking at the screen, where an image of Dugway Proving Ground in Utah dominated. The agent leading the briefing had been called in after a momentous event the previous evening out in Nevada, one that had gone horribly wrong in more ways than one.

'The breach was on the eastern border of the airbase perimeter, via high-level computer hacking, and it resulted in two individuals gaining access to the Dugway ground. Although the individuals were spotted by surveillance teams within the base and an armed team approached their location, before they could be reached and apprehended a gunshot was heard. When they reached the location they found a single, dead male in the vicinity who had been hit with a rifle shot to the head from medium to long range.'

Mackenzie began to feel a creeping sense of doom overshadow him as he listened. Civilians gaining access to locations as remote and well protected as Dugway was almost unheard of, meaning that whomever these interlopers were, they had devised some cunning means of avoiding the plethora of cameras and sensors that protected the perimeter. However, even then it would be extremely rare for patrols to carry out the threat of lethal force – such an action would itself draw unwanted attention to the site from the media. Threats of lethal force were more of a deterrent than a literal consequence of incursions onto military land. Mackenzie knew that in reality trespassers would be locked up, perhaps roughed up and certainly made to fear for their life before being released into the custody of local law enforcement, the military well aware that word of a trespasser's treatment would get out onto the street and help to prevent further transgressions.

'We have a team on site right now who are identifying the individuals at the scene and they're due to report in within the hour. This is a containment exercise, and as such we absolutely need to prevent any access by the media and ideally prevent them from learning anything about the incident. Should such media awareness become an eventuality, then it is our purpose to ensure that we play up the fact that the individuals were trespassing on an area known to be protected with the threat of lethal force, while playing down the fact that our troops were in any way hostile to the interlopers.'

Mackenzie frowned as he made notes, glancing up at the other brass around him and noting the same veiled confusion on their expressions.

'Do we know what their purpose at the Dugway grounds was?' Mackenzie asked the question that everyone else was thinking. 'And why are we coming down so tightly on this? Did they see something that they shouldn't have?'

The agent thought for a moment before he replied, hesitating just a little too long for Mackenzie to entirely believe the explanation.

'From their vantage point it is considered possible that they might have witnessed the transportation of a covert spy drone across the airbase.'

There was a long silence as the military chiefs digested this piece of information.

'It was nightime when the shooting occured,' Mackenzie noted. 'Did these witnesses possess any kind of photographic equipment or some kind of recording device?'

'There were several cameras retrieved from the site where the body was found,' the agent confirmed.

Mackenzie smiled inwardly. Say everything while saying nothing at all, or at least as little as possible. CIA standard operational procedure when there's something you'd rather not say.

'And did they *record* anything?' Mackenzie hazarded.

The spook looked a little uncomfortable. 'At this time, I don't have any information on that.'

Mackenzie didn't want to put Agent Forty-Eight under any unnecessary pressure, but he knew that there was something going on here that the spook wasn't imparting about events at Dugway. A civilian had died and there was an all-agency BOLO for an accomplice, yet there was something being held back.

'So, these two individuals break into the perimeter of the base, sneak cameras in with them, take some photos and then one of them gets killed. I get that we don't want undue interest in the site but how did one of these folks get shot? Did one of our guards take them down?'

'I'm not aware at this time of any one of our troops firing a shot at Dugway during this incident. The officer commanding the intercepting detachment reported that he heard a gunshot prior to the site being reached by his team.'

So he says, Mackenzie thought. There had been no mention of the calibre of bullet used in the shooting, no autopsy yet, no nothing. If the troops had fired in anger despite the lethal force allowed there would be recriminations, especially if the two individuals were found to be unarmed.

'How do we know that there were two individuals on the site? The report only details the one, the shooting victim.'

'There was a trail leading off the mountain,' the spook replied, on more comfortable ground now. 'The track was identified at first light and corresponded to a vehicle's tyre trails seen leaving the area on the main highway at the time of the incident. It appears possible that one of the individuals killed the other and then made off.'

Mackenzie nodded.

'And what of their equipment? Had they managed to take any images of the airbase or the supposed drone sighting?'

Again, the agent hesitated. 'There were several images on the cameras which were seized by the airbase authorities and remain classified.'

So, they *did* see something, Mackenzie guessed as an admiral piped up further down the table.

'So, this second person is a fugitive and they possess sensitive material that we're trying to track down, correct?'

'That's right,' the spook replied, clearly at pains to avoid discussing what the sensitive material actually was. 'It is a matter of national security that this material is recovered and secured before it can be disseminated to the public.'

Mackenzie glanced up as the image on the screen changed to one of a young man who looked suitably like a millennial – skinny, unkempt and sullen.

'Kyle Trent, twenty-one years of age, college dropout and apparently an accomplished computer hacker. It's likely that he managed to disable at least some of Dugway's perimeter sensors in order to infiltrate the base, so we're currently looking into his computer files to figure out what else he may have been up to. There's also the issue of legal repercussions for the use of…'

The spook's voice drifted away out of Mackenzie's awareness as he suddenly thought of the Unidentified Aerial Phenomena images he'd been sent at the intelligence desk. They had been taken in various light spectrum wavelengths, providing virtually perfect proof of a solid object in the camera lens. If those images had been taken by the same person, even the ones in Scotland, then it was possible that Kyle Trent was the person he'd been searching for.

'What kinds of cameras were they using?' Mackenzie asked.

Agent Forty-Eight regarded Mackenzie with interest for a moment. 'Why would you ask that?'

'The interlopers were some miles from the base,' Mackenzie replied as though it was obvious. 'They would have needed high-powered telephoto lenses, perhaps night vision. It takes money to get hold of these things, connections, the skills to use them. It might give us leads on where this Kyle Trent took off to.'

The agent nodded.

'There were four cameras, and lenses varied from macro to zoom, from optical to infra-red. These guys were up there to look into Dugway. Looks like they got more than they bargained for.'

The briefing ended, but Mackenzie did not reveal anything. As the officers dispersed to their duties, Mackenzie slipped out of the room and made his way quickly down the corridor outside. He waited until he was well out of earshot before he used his cell phone to make a *call*. Within moments, the section secretary answered the phone.

'Yes, general?'

'Cathy, the agency has a BOLO out on one Kyle Trent, twenty-one, out of Vernon, Utah. Can you run a check for me and find out if this guy was in Scotland any time in the past few weeks?'

'Will do, it should only take an hour or so.'

Mackenzie shut off the line. If Kyle was his guy, then he probably had no more than twenty-four hours to find him before either the CIA or local law enforcement.

'General?' Mackenzie turned and saw Agent Forty-Eight waiting for him. There was a gleam in the old agent's eyes as he glanced at the cell phone. 'You got anything for us that you want to share?'

'The case you described jogged my memory on an older, similar case,' Mackenzie replied, telling as much of the truth as possible without giving anything serious away. 'I called the sec' to see if she could dig anything up that might affect it. The case rested on imagery but we didn't have the software to identify the suspect in the shot, I figured we might have something by now.'

The spook nodded. He looked neither convinced nor suspicious, but either way they both understood the game here: neither was lying, but neither was entirely telling the truth either. It was a bit like the Cold War, all over again.

'You get anything on this Kyle Trent, you call me right away, okay?'

Mackenzie nodded like it was nothing, as though almost a dumb question to ask. The spook moved off and Mackenzie decided that he'd better get himself a burner phone and maybe another property, an apartment downtown or something. If whatever the hell was going on here turned nasty, he wanted somewhere for his wife and kids to go.

He waited until he was sure that he was alone, and then he dialled another number.

***

XVIII

'Kyle who?'

Lopez answered the call as Ethan drove south toward Las Vegas, the Tahoe's air conditioning keeping the car cool from the blistering desert heat scorching the landscape around them.

'Kyle Trent, twenty–one years old, currenly a fugitive from Special Operations out of Dugway, Nevada. He's one of a pair that infiltrated the base there last night.'

'They got into Dugway?' Ethan said in amazement. 'How the hell did they manage that?'

'At great cost,' Mackenzie replied. *'One of them's in the morgue, the other probably won't last past sundown once the Spec Ops guys get their teeth into him. They're saying that the other kid was shot by Trent but I'm not buying it, they're too heavily involved in the search and they all but admitted that Trent is carrying sensitive material. He and his accomplice were equipped with multiple cameras and apparently witnessed something over the base.'*

Lopez's eyes narrowed as she joined the dots. 'You think this could be our guy, the one behind the photographs?'

'Closest I've seen yet and he's right on your doorstep. Sit rep suggests that he'll make a play for the media in a major city and try to protect himself by threatening to disclose whatever he's got to the public. Chances are that won't happen. Special Ops are looking out for Trent and are on the road already, it's only a matter of time.'

Ethan kept one eye on the road as he replied.

'He could use the Internet,' he suggested. 'He doesn't have to raise his head above the parapet to get noticed. Hell, if he got into Dugway then public disclosure of images or video should be a piece of cake for him.'

'The spooks are running around like headless chickens looking for this guy, so whatever he's got could be explosive. I don't need to tell you what that means for him, regardless of how he tries to get himself out of this.'

'We're out of the game,' Lopez replied, but Ethan could tell that their encounter with little Sophie had softened her resolve. 'If you're thinking we're going to put our necks on the line for this guy's holiday snaps you can think again.'

'I'm not asking you for anything,' Mackenzie replied, *'I know the score, okay? But if you can find him and get him to law enforcement rather than radio stations, somewhere where Dugway's heavies can't tear him apart, then I can take over.'*

'Where was he last seen?' Ethan asked.

'Vernon,' Mackenzie replied. *'State troopers found his vehicle abandoned north of of the town near a Greyhound lot, so it looks like he's high–tailed it out of there. Maybe he's thinking of Los Angeles or crossing the border?'*

Ethan frowned. Heading north sounded like a bad plan, when Vegas was closer to the south and he could hide within the crowds. North of Vernon there was nothing much but open desert and isolated freeways, a difficult place to hide when the spooks were after you and armed with night vision and helicopters. Tracking down a Greyhound wouldn't take long.

'We'll check it out,' Ethan replied, ignoring Lopez as she rolled her eyes. 'No promises.'

'Roger that, call me if you need anything.'

The line went dead and Lopez shot Ethan a dirty look. 'Really?'

'He's just a kid on the run,' Ethan said, 'probably knee-deep in conspiracy theories and now he's being hunted. You know how that feels.'

'Yeah, I do,' Lopez agreed with a sweet smile, 'which is why I don't want to have to do it again. Last time the CIA targeted us we spent six cheery months living under cover, hiding in crappy motels and sleeping with guns under our pillows. Such fun. How we laughed.'

'We're not getting too involved with this,' Ethan promised. 'It's just a run in and grab.'

'Yeah,' Lopez uttered as she leaned back in her seat and closed her eyes, 'that's how it always starts. And then there's running and screaming and gunfire. I don't have to remind you that we're not armed, do I?'

'Who needs guns when we have your wit and charm?'

Lopez thumped Ethan's arm and he grinned to himself as he drove. It was tough to admit it to himself but after nearly a year spent sunning himself on an island paradise he'd started to feel a bit flabby and twice as useless. It wasn't easy to be involved in high level operations for several years and then suddenly just retire. Old habits died hard. He'd spent much of his time jogging around the island to stay fit, all the while scanning parked vehicles for bail jumpers or upstairs windows for gunmen. He was fairly sure he wasn't suffering from any form of PTSD or anything like that, because he slept well enough and only thought about throttling Lopez when she was *really* annoying him. He could only chalk it up to the fact that he liked what they did together, the thrill of being on the hunt, or even being the hunted.

Lopez was right though. They were exceedingly lucky to be still alive after all that they'd witnessed, and even Jarvis and Mitchell were out of the game forever now. Only Lopez and himself remained and here they were again, seeking out something that the United States government wanted but could not find.

Ethan turned toward Vegas. He was certain that Kyle Trent was shrewd enough to know that heading into the desert was a bad move. Hiding within the throng of Vegas was a much better prospect and also allowed him access to the Internet, which would be sparse out in the deserts. Trent would do what all fugitives did, and try to find somewhere they felt comfortable, secure, somewhere safe to hide.

'You think he's heading to the city,' Lopez observed without interest.

'Seems likely. You?'

'I concur,' she replied sleepily. 'Although I will act in concert, it shall be in protest.'

Ethan smiled but said nothing as he drove down into Vegas. It wasn't tough to spot the dense urban cluster of humanity amid the mountain ranges and endless open scrub. Nellis Air Force Base dominated the northern edge of the city, while the famous "Strip" held court at the centre. Both he and Lopez had been here on operations before, when Stanley Meyer's Fusion Cage, an ultra-high efficiency engine, had been sought aggressively by major oil corporations eager to see the technology buried before old Stanley could give it away to the world for free.

Ethan figured that Trent would seek refuge among strangers. With the Special Operations branch covertly seeking him out he could not hope to stay hidden with friends or accomplices. That meant some kind of refuge that was both alien and yet familiar. If Trent had managed to break through security at Dugway, that meant at least some kind of computer knowledge to hack systems or otherwise deceive them, and with the Internet the only real way of communicating with the outside world he would need access. Internet cafes were a thing of the past now, but with most public spaces offering wi-fi connections, Kyle would be able to move freely as long as he was within reach of said connections. Ethan couldn't hope to pick the kid up in a motel as there were so many in a famous city full of tourists, so instead he would have to try to locate him when on the move. That meant focussing on basics.

Everybody had to eat. They had to wash, to look after themselves, to go to the bathroom, shop for food and find somewhere to sleep. Kyle would have to do all of these things while also formulating a plan to keep him alive, which meant staying under the radar and not moving too much using public transport. Ethan knew that only one kind of place offered all of those things.

'There are dozens of them,' Lopez said when she awoke and he asked her to search for malls in the city. 'Most of them on the strip, more in north Vegas, a few out in Spring Valley. If we're right, this guy could be in any of them and if he's smart he'll have put on at least some kind of disguise.'

Ethan thought for a moment.

'What about outside Vegas, somewhere big enough for a mall but away from the strip?'

Lopez dragged her finger across the cell phone screen.

'One in Henderson to the south east of the city, another in Boulder City but it's pretty small. Hey, here's one – the Galleria at Sunset. It's in Midway, a few clicks out from the strip and it's massive. He could hide out there all day and not be found but be close enough to the city to get a room.'

'We'll start there,' Ethan said as he negotiated the traffic on the 515 heading south past the city. 'Call Mackenzie, see if he has anything on Trent's cell phones or e-mail accounts that we can track.'

Lopez got on the phone again as Ethan dropped down the off ramp of the Las Vegas Expressway and into Midway. By the time they were pulling into the parking lot, Lopez had a stream of information coming in on her cell phone.

'He's signed up to dozens of Internet forums, most of them concerning UFOs, paranormal research and government cover-ups of aliens and such like.'

Ethan wanted to say something dismissive about conspiracy theorists and their websites, but then he considered all of the things he and Lopez had witnessed over the last few years and he held his tongue.

'Special Ops will be watching all of those sites,' he said instead. 'He might try to log in with another user name or something.'

'Hundreds of members on all these forums,' Lopez replied. 'We're chasing rainbows if we think we can narrow him down.'

Ethan parked the car and shut off the engine.

'What about most recent users to join, say the last twenty-four hours, located in Nevada? Can Mackenzie patch us in to that?'

The general was on an open speaker line on Lopez's cell and he replied immediately.

'Stand by and I'll have it with you.'

'What's the story with special operations?' Ethan asked.

'They followed the Greyhound link but it turned into a dead end,' Mackenzie replied. *'Looks like you guessed right and Trent duped them with a false trail and then headed south. They won't be far behind you though and will probably be at Nellis by now.'*

Ethan nodded. A helicopter could make it from Dugway to Nellis in twenty minutes, putting the Special Operations teams only minutes behind them at most.

'Okay, here we go, three new users from the Nevada area in the past twenty-four hours,' Mackenzie announced. *'Patty123, Centaur and Watcher1997.'*

'Watcher1997,' Ethan said instantly, 'that's Kyle's birth year, right?'

'It fits,' Mackenzie agreed, *'tracing the IP last used.'*

Ethan and Lopez looked at each other. Ethan grinned and wiggled an eyebrow at her.

'You're an asshole, Warner,' she muttered.

'A very clever one,' Mackenzie said over the line. *'Last log-in was eight minutes ago at Galleria Mall, Nevada.'*

Ethan didn't even reply and was out of the car door like a shot.

***

XIX

The Black Hawk helicopters had touched down only minutes before at Nellis Air Force Base, and now Rico Savage was sitting in a black SUV that was flying down the Expressway toward Vegas. Through tinted windows he could see the city skyline and the harsh blue sky above, traffic glinting in the fierce sunlight.

'Target was last seen on CCTV near north Vegas,' one of his men reported.

He was accompanied by three soldiers who were now dressed in civilian clothes, their communicators and ear pieces carefully concealed along with their sidearms. One was scanning the screen of a laptop computer.

'Where was he heading?' Savage asked.

'South,' came the reply, 'but that doesn't mean much. The footage is four hours old and he'll have disappeared into the crowds by now. We're gonna need something more direct if we're gonna find this guy quietly.'

Savage glanced out of the windows. There was no way he could afford to cause any uproar within the densely populated streets of Vegas, much less on the tourist-infested Strip. Trent had proved himself adept at deception, taking the Greyhound ticket north but then heading south. Hardly high-level tactics but it had thrown the soldiers assigned to track him, who had gambled that a scared twenty-one-year old would have already crumbled psychologically by now and handed himself in to police.

'He'll have got himself a burner cell and contacted people by now,' Savage suggested. 'He's one of the fringe guys according to his report, someone who spends time on conspiracy websites and other crap. Start tracking all the forums and web pages he's visited and focus on his user names or anyone who's recently joined – it could be Trent trying to sneak in under the radar.'

His men worked as they drove south, another SUV following with a further four-man team inside. Together, they were assigned with bringing Trent in, with his data upon his person. The fact that Trent could already have hidden the data for safe-keeping did not bother Savage. They knew just how to get that information from people like Trent.

'Got something,' his companion replied as he held out the laptop to Savage.

Savage looked at the screen, which displayed a website called "Full Disclosure", a group dedicated to the release of supposedly secret UFO files hidden for decades by the CIA and other clandestine organisations. A new log-in named *Watcher1997* had accessed the site in the past few minutes, having joined in the small hours of the night and sent messages to several users. It took Savage only a moment to read the first few lines of the first message to know that they had found their man.

'Galleria Mall,' he said, 'prepare to deploy and bring him in, *quietly*.'

'Damn, this place is big.'

Lopez looked around at the plethora of shops, paying particular attention to one containing various high-heeled boots and women's clothes.

'He could be anywhere,' Ethan agreed as he scanned the various floors and elevators all around them.

'Don't suppose you think he's out for a new handbag do you?' Lopez hazarded with a wistful gaze. 'You don't know how long it's been since I went shopping in anything other than a palm-lined shack.'

'The only thing on your list right now is Kyle Trent,' Ethan insisted as they walked along. 'I'll take the upper levels. Stay within sight of the centre so if one of us picks him up we can signal each other.'

'Spoil sport,' Lopez grumbled as she headed off into the crowds milling around the lower level.

Ethan watched her go for a moment, then looked around. Kyle would keep moving most likely, if he was half as paranoid as Ethan suspected. He'd stay in the mall perhaps for a while, then move to another as long as he could do so without arousing suspicion or being easily recognised. Trent was young and relatively inconspicuous, and the trend for young males to wear hoodies wasn't going to help.

Ethan figured that the only thing that would help him would be boredom. Trent had empty days to fill and nothing to do but wander around the malls while he waited for replies to his messages and posts on the forums. Someone like him would probably be most at home in shops with computer games, skateboards, that kind of junk.

The mall was huge, with multiple floors and open areas filled with everything from palm trees to a skating rink. Crowds flocked this way and that, tourists milling with locals and delivery men going about their business. Ethan weaved through the crowds, scanning left and right, up and down. There was no way he could analyse the situation further to locate Kyle Trent – this was going to come down to luck, timing and perseverance.

Ethan took an elevator up to the third floor, giving him a panoramic view of one section of the galleria. There was a large computer games store at one end of the mall and he headed towards it. There were also a couple of computer and periphal stores here and there, the kind of thing that he imagined someone like Kyle Trent would feel comfortable hanging about in.

As he turned a corner he spotted a uniformed guard, one of several security personnel that kept an eye on the shoppers. He wandered over and got the guards' attention.

'Hi, I was wondering if you could help me. I'm looking for a twenty-one-year old named Kyle Trent, about five ten, mousy hair, your typical sullen youth. He's been missing from Vernon since last night.'

The guard, a portly Latino who looked bored, shrugged.

'Only about a thousand of those coming in and outta here every day,' he replied. 'You got anything a little more specific?'

Ethan held out his cell phone, an image of Kyle on the screen. The guard shook his head.

'Ain't seen him,' he said, 'but I'll keep watch.'

Ethan thanked the sullen guard and made his way into the computer game store. Filled with cases of games featuring everything from racing cars, monsters, space combat and flight simulators, Ethan watched a couple of kids with virtual reality headsets over their eyes. Both were squealing in delight as they controlled massive machines that were battering each other, their jaws agape as they swung their arms in mid-air to the sound of digital destruction.

Ethan frowned. Maybe this stuff was all a little too juvenile for someone capable of breaking into a high-security military base. He headed out of the store and along the upper level of the mall, then cast his gaze down as he walked. It was then that he saw them.

From ground level he might not have noticed, but from up here he saw the four-man team split as they entered the mall, like an aerobatic display team breaking over an airfield in perfect coordination. Everything about them screamed military; their bearing, keen eyes and alert expressions all traits of men on the hunt.

Ethan looked down and saw Lopez standing near a shop full of women's jackets, eyeing them up while scanning the mall around her. She caught sight of Ethan on her second sweep and he held up four fingers and pointed to her left. Lopez surveyed the crowd and a few moments later she spotted two of the new arrivals. She didn't signal Ethan back, but she turned and began moving down the mall in earnest, searching now for any sign of Trent and staying ahead of the four men.

*

'We've got something.'

Rico Savage glanced at the agent alongside him in the vehicle. They were parked outside the Galleria's immense arched entrance, the tinted windows of the SUV concealing them from prying eyes as the agent handed him a laptop computer.

'Fascial recognition software just got a hit on one of our targets inside the mall. He's on the move.'

'Trent?' Savage asked as he looked at the screen.

'No.'

Savage could see the image of a man with shaggy brown hair and broad shoulders walking through the mall. Although it was a static image, it still conveyed something of the man, his gaze purposeful and his eyes alert as though seeking prey amid the crowds.

'Ethan Warner.'

Savage knew the name. Warner had at one point or another been involved in a number of operations out of Langley alongside the DIA and other intelligence units. The guy had developed something of a reputation for himself and not always a good one – he seemed to be followed around by waves of destruction and a bad-tempered partner named Lopez. But Savage had believed them to be out of the business for some time, after the collapse of the cabal known as Majestic Twelve.

It was rumoured, and only in whispers, that Warner and Lopez had slipped away with a few million dollars once hoarded by the cabal, but nobody was entirely sure and their records were classified to all but the most powerful in the intelligence community, a fact that annoyed lots of serving officers as these two renegades had operated as civilian contractors.

'He can't be here by coincidence,' Savage said. 'He must be looking for Trent for some reason, although nobody else should know anything about what happened at Dugway. How the hell did he get here so quickly?'

The laptop made a soft buzzing sound and the agent flipped to another screen.

'They,' he said. 'Nicola Lopez just got pinged by another camera.'

That was it. Savage knew that they were here for Kyle Trent and he had to assume that the entire operation was now compromised. He reached for his door handle.

'Alert the men to their presence and tell them to apprehend on sight. We can't let those two gumshoes get to Trent first or we'll lose control of this whole thing before the sun sets.'

***

XX

Ethan hurried to the far side of the mall, heading away from the four-man team now sweeping the lower levels and keeping his head down just in case they were looking out for him. Ethan and Nicola had been out of the game for many months now but people had long memories in the intelligence game and Ethan couldn't be sure that despite the covert nature of the team's unit they didn't have official government support, which would mean local law enforcement, local cameras, everything and everyone looking for them. All it would take was a few calls by someone with sufficient rank and muscle.

He reached the far end of the upper level and scanned left and right for some sign of Kyle Trent. Lopez appeared among the throng below and looked up at him as she gave a brief shrug of her shoulders. Trent was here, but he wasn't in plain sight. Ethan wracked his brains as he spotted the four men advancing on their position. Kyle had to be here, but he must be hiding somewhere. The interiors of shops were not the best place to be, so Ethan tried to figure out where he would hide himself were he a teenager in deep trouble seeking to avoid law enforcement.

The answer came to him almost immediately.

Kyle would head for the most unobtrusive, calm environment he could with the maximum visibility, somewhere he could both hide and yet be in plain sight, making it hard for his enemy to take him down without creating a disturbance in front of many witnesses.

'The cafeterias.'

Ethan mouthed the words down to Lopez and she understood at once, heading for an elevator and only a few paces ahead of the leader of the team sweeping in behind her. As she moved, Ethan saw one of the team look at her and the expression of recognition on his face was unmistakeable. In an instant Ethan knew that they had been compromised and were now also going to be targets for the Special Operations team.

In silent accord, the four-man team suddenly changed direction and began following Lopez. Ethan saw her begin to ascend the elevator and he moved swiftly, staying out of sight of the team as he circled around to a spot near the top of the elevator.

Lopez appeared a few seconds later, riding the escalator to the top and gliding off it as though she didn't have a care in the world. She spotted Ethan instantly and he gestured to her left. Lopez turned left, walking along the upper floor and drawing the gazes of the agents following her away from Ethan lingering on their right.

Ethan stepped out just as the lead agent was about to step off the escalator. His three accomplices were right behind him, their eyes fixed on Lopez like a pack of wolves hunting a gazelle. Ethan took two paces, hopped onto his left foot and then struck out with his right.

The lead agent's eyes widened in shock and one hand went for his sidearm at the same time as the other tried to block Ethan's blow, but he was way too slow. Ethan's boot landed flat in the centre of his chest and propelled him backwards down the escalator and straight into the agents directly behind him.

The four men tumbled in a frenzy of limbs and shouts of anger as Ethan turned to Lopez.

'Time to leave!'

Gasps of shock from shoppers and tourists turned to shouts of alarm as they saw the tumbling suited men pulling guns from holsters concealed beneath their shirts. Ethan whirled and scanned the cafeteria, but he could see no sign of the youth among the diners.

'There!'

Lopez's cry alerted him and he turned to see a youth in a hoodie dash away from them and hurl himself out of sight down a flight of steps, heading for the galleria exit. Ethan bolted in pursuit, diners leaping out of his way as he hit the staircase at a run. Lopez beat him to it, flying down the steps almost at a full run in pursuit of the hoodie.

Ethan could not tell whether their target was Kyle Trent or not, but right now they had no option but to get the hell out of the galleria before they were arrested. The Special Operations guys would have law enforcement on the scene in no time and would generate some kind of trumped-up charge to get them off the chase as quickly as possible.

Ethan hit the ground floor and turned, Lopez's long black hair flying just in front of him as they sprinted after the kid in the hoodie. The grey hood flipped back as the kid ran and he looked over his shoulder at them. To Ethan's surprise it was Kyle Trent, and he was scared for his life as he dashed through the galleria, heading for the exits.

Ethan glanced over his shoulder and saw that the Special Ops agents had got to their feet and were now racing down the steps toward the ground floor, their weapons drawn and a wave of screams breaking before them as terrified shoppers dashed for cover.

'Kyle, we're not with the law!' Lopez yelled. 'We're here to help!'

Kyle Trent kept running. Ethan could tell that he was fleeing in a blind panic now, filled with a genuine fear for his life and that he wouldn't stop for anyone.

'We know what happened to Greg!' Lopez tried again.

Kyle Trent ran harder, and Ethan knew that he was doomed. There would be a second team covering the mall exits, waiting for Kyle to run into their arms as the first team flushed him out.

'Kyle, they'll be waiting for you at the exits!' Ethan yelled. 'Go up!'

Kyle glanced over his shoulder and Ethan could see the confusion and uncertainty on his face.

'We're not armed,' Lopez yelled and gestured behind her at the pursuing agents. 'They are! Go up!'

Kyle Trent reached another bank of escalators near the main entrance and he darted left, dashing up them as Lopez and Ethan followed. Ethan's thighs began to burn as they ran up the escalator, straining to keep up with Lopez.

Kyle Trent reached the upper floors and dashed out of sight, Lopez right behind him. Ethan struggled to the top and then hit the emergency stop button. The escalator ground to a halt behind him as the armed agents reached the bottom, buying him a little extra time as he laboured after Lopez.

Kyle dashed down the length of the upper floor and reached the end, where a couple of locked doors were the only exits available to them. Ethan saw him skitter to a halt, look left and right in desperation, and then throw his arms in the air as his features crumpled with terror as Lopez bore down upon him.

'Don't shoot! Please don't shoot! I didn't mean to do anything…'

Lopez tore past Kyle Trent, running full tilt at the weaker looking of the two doors, and she hurled herself into it. The door shuddered but held firm as she stepped aside, Kyle Trent staring at her perplexed as Ethan thundered past him and slammed into the door right after her.

The door's hinges were ripped from their mounts and the door collapsed inward with Ethan on top of it, clattering down onto cement steps that climbed up toward the roof. Pain bolted through Ethan's shoulder but he forced himself to ignore it as he scrambled to his feet and ran up the steps.

'This way!' Lopez yelled as she propelled the startled Kyle Trent in front of her. 'Unless you'd like to chat with the guys from Dugway!'

Suitably motivated, Kyle ran in pursuit of Ethan, who reached the top of the steps and slammed the handle of an emergency exit. The door crashed open and a wave of heat washed in as Ethan hurried out onto the roof and turned immediately east.

'Come on, move it!'

Ethan grabbed Kyle Trent by the collar and ran with him toward the edge of the galleria, dodging left and right past air conditioning vents. The edge of the mall and the parking lot beyond loomed up and Kyle shrieked in his ear.

'We won't make the jump, it's too high!'

Ethan ignored the kid, kept his grip firmly on his hoodie as he accelerated, Lopez grabbing Kyle on the other side. They reached the edge of the mall and a dizzying forty-foot drop as Kyle screamed in terror, and then Ethan pushed off the edge and leaped into the void.

Ethan's stomach rose up inside him as he plummeted down and landed hard onto the roof of a parked utility truck that he and Lopez had scoped out earlier.

Kyle Trent landed alongside him with Lopez and together they tumbled over and then scrambled to their feet.

Ethan didn't look back, running the length of the truck's cargo trailer and jumping down onto the roof of the cab, then down onto the hood. Kyle followed with Lopez right behind, and they leaped down onto the ground and ran for the rental Tahoe parked just yards away.

Ethan got in with Lopez and Trent, started the engine and looked up in time to see the four agents reach the edge of the mall and look down to see them pulling away. He gunned the engine and headed for the parking lot exit, hoping that he could make it before the inevitable second team could intercept them.

He glanced in the mirror and saw Kyle Trent staring vacantly ahead as though in shock, Lopez sitting breathlessly beside him.

'No more armed agents, you said,' she uttered. 'No more guns. Just run in and grab.'

Ethan nodded, as out of breath as she was.

'I was right about the run in and grab bit,' he pointed out. 'Call Garrett, we're going to need a ride out of here real fast.'

Lopez pulled out her cell phone as Ethan drove out of the lot and accelerated onto the freeway. They would only have minutes before the Special Ops team were able to regroup and pursue them again, and this time they would likely bring local law enforcement in to ensure that there was no escape. Ethan knew that he would have to lose the Tahoe real fast.

'Okay,' Lopez said as she put her cell away. 'Garrett's got us covered, just head west and find this location. He's on his way and has a route organised for us.'

Ethan nodded as Lopez punched an address into the car's GPS system and a route opened up on the screen. Ethan checked it out and was pleased to see their destination was only a few miles away. Even as he did so he saw a helicopter closing in on their position, a civilian model that glinted in the sunlight.

'Great, we get off the freeway at the next exit and lose the car,' he said. 'The rest is on foot, as quick as we can. You got that, Kyle?'

The kid stared at him vacantly in the reflection of the rear-view mirror.

'Man, I don't know what the hell just happened.'

'We just saved your ass,' Lopez replied, 'when I could have still been sunning mine on a tropical beach. You're welcome.'

'Sit tight,' Ethan said to Kyle. 'We're here to help, but right now we've got to lose the Dugway goons before we're arrested.'

Kyle nodded vacantly, seemingly taken utterly by surprise at how quickly his circumstances had changed. Ethan was no longer concerned with Kyle's welfare, however. He was more worried about the fact that the Special Ops team had clearly recognised Lopez and had actively altered their mission to close her down.

Whoever was pursuing Kyle Trent knew all about himself and Nicola Lopez.

***

XXI

Casa de Shenandoah

Ethan pulled the Tahoe over and parked it behind a series of lockups to make it harder to find for the Special Ops teams hunting for them. With Kyle and Lopez, he jogged the last couple of miles, aiming for the sound of helicopter blades. Ahead, in a dusty clearing, a silver helicopter had touched down and was sitting with its side door open amid spiralling clouds of dust and sand.

Ethan helped Kyle aboard as Lopez leaped inside, and then he jumped in and hauled the door shut. Within moments, the helicopter lifted off and climbed away to the west. Ethan saw Rhys Garrett look over his shoulder and give him a thumbs-up from where he sat alongside the pilot as Ethan donned a set of headphones.

'Welcome aboard, glad you could make it!' Garrett chortled.

'We've got friends pursuing,' Ethan informed him. 'We're gonna stick out like a sore thumb in this helicopter.'

'Don't worry,' Garrett replied, 'it's only a short hop and then we'll be taking off.'

Lopez frowned. 'I thought we were already flying?'

Ethan looked down out of the helicopter's window and suddenly he realised what Garrett had in mind. Below them was a sprawling forty-acre ranch that had its own museum, tennis courts, stables and an immense estate house. But, astonishingly, it also had its own airport terminal and private runway.

'You've got to be kidding me,' Lopez uttered.

'For when you just *have* to avoid the queues at the airport,' Garrett explained cheerily over the intercom from the front seat as the pilot began descending for a landing. They had probably flown less than a couple of miles.

'You own this place?' Lopez marvelled.

'No,' Garrett admitted, sounding a little disappointed. 'It belongs to a friend of mine. He picked it up for a bargain a few years back. I would have taken it on if I'd been in the country.'

'How much was a bargain?' Ethan asked.

'Fifty million dollars,' Garrett replied. 'It's almost a crime.'

'Fifty million,' Lopez echoed. 'If only I'd known.'

Garrett's private jet was waiting for them as the helicopter landed on a pad nearby, and Ethan could hear the jet's engines already turning as they ducked out of the helicopter and hurried toward it. The helicopter lifted off almost immediately and continued on to the north west.

'The feds should follow the helicopter and probably won't have noticed it land here,' Garrett said. 'He's heading out to California. Even if whoever's chasing you work it out, we should have a decent head start and be able to help you both get lost, in the nicest possible sense.'

Kyle Trent appeared to be in some kind of a daze, having been shot at for the first time in his life only days ago in an attempted assassination and now being hustled aboard a private jet on a ranch worth tens of millions of dollars.

Garrett shut the jet's door behind them and called to the pilot. Even before they were strapped in they were taxiing onto the runway and moments later the engines roared and the jet accelerated along the runway and then rotated, soaring up into the hard blue sky.

Ethan looked out of the windows and saw Las Vegas sprawl before him, a vast patchwork of streets and buildings that glinted in the harsh sunlight. The jet banked around to head east, climbing rapidly. Ethan's ears popped as he saw Vegas slip into the haze, the deserts stretching for miles in every direction as they climbed up through ten thousand feet.

'Okay,' Lopez said as she turned to Kyle Trent. 'You've got lots of talking to do and we're all ears.'

Trent stared at her, stunned into silence. Ethan could see that he was looking at Lopez as though she were a work of art, while at the same time trying to formulate a response that didn't sound ridiculous.

'Try starting with why they're trying to kill you,' he suggested.

Trent blinked. 'Who the hell *are* you people?'

'We're the ones who aren't trying to shoot you dead,' Lopez said. 'We're working for the government.'

'But those people who were chasing me work for the government!' Trent snapped, panicked.

'There's government, and there's government,' Ethan explained. 'Some departments work in such secrecy that they become a law unto themselves. We're the ones who work by the book, more or less. Look, we were sent here to find you and possibly protect you, if it came to that, and it has so we need to know everything that you know or this could end really badly for everyone.'

Trent eyed them all suspiciously.

'What, you're going to throw me out of the jet without a parachute if I don't talk?'

'No,' Lopez replied. 'We don't do that sort of thing, and nor does the part of the government we work for. However, you're in deep *kim chi* Kyle, and we think we know why.'

On cue, Ethan produced copies of the images that General Mackenzie had given him. The perfect photographs of UFOs taken by an anonymous source were handed to Kyle and he looked down at them.

'Been busy, Kyle?' Ethan asked.

Kyle stared down at the images. 'Oh shit.'

'I'll say,' Lopez replied. 'Kyle, if you don't help us to help you, you're looking at thirty to life in a security max prison for conspiracy, trespass on military property and probably treason for attempting to coerce the government of the United States into disclosure about top secret operations.'

Kyle didn't put up much of a fight as he stared down at the images.

'I thought I was doing the right thing,' he pleaded. 'The government knows more about UFOs than they're saying. Everyone knows it and yet so few do anything about it! The people have a right to know about this! The government doesn't own us, we own the government and until someone stands up for that they'll continue to walk all over us!'

'I agree,' Ethan admitted, 'but not all conspiracy theories are what they seem. Our evidence is that the government does know more about UFOs than they're admitting, but they keep quiet because they don't know what the hell these things really are. Their biggest concern is the panic they fear would be caused if they were to admit that these things are flying around in our skies with impunity.'

'People already know that they're doing that!' Kyle argued. 'We haven't collapsed overnight into dribbling cavemen, have we? People would rather know the truth and deal with it than have that truth hidden from them and be denied knowledge of the existence of life beyond this planet. Don't you think that people would rather deal with what's real than live in ignorance?'

Ethan found himself performing a rapid recalculation of his perception of Kyle Trent. Far from being a socially outcast computer hacker with a millennial chip on his shoulder, the kid was impassioned and determined and even now was fighting his corner. The thing was, not only was Ethan starting to like the kid, he was finding it tough to counter his argument.

Like most all folk, Ethan wanted to know what UFOs were. He wanted someone to speak out and explain what the hell they were doing whizzing around all the time. The public fascination with the subject was displayed for all to see in the popularity of endless documentaries about unidentified flying objects and supposed alien encounters, some stretching back into ancient history. Likewise, the march of civilisation and the Enlightenment had taught humanity that religions did not possess meaningful answers to any of life's mysteries and that science and discovery, even if painful at times, were largely responsible for mankind's emergence from brutality and suffering. People could take the hit, even if it made them feel vulnerable.

'People have been seeing these things for thousands of years,' Kyle added. 'They haven't harmed us yet.'

Ethan and Lopez exchanged a glance.

'That all depends on who we're talking about,' Lopez replied. 'Look, start from the beginning, okay? How the hell did you get photographs of UFOs like these? Are they fake?'

Kyle Trent gave a snort of a laugh and shook his head. 'No, they're not fake. They're as real as we are sitting here.'

'Then how did you take them?' Ethan pressed. 'If they got out they'd cause a media storm like nothing we've ever seen. How did you even know where they would appear?'

Kyle smiled, almost ruefully.

'That's the big irony in all of this,' he said. 'It was the government who showed me how to do it.'

***

XXII

'You're going to have to give us a little more than that,' Lopez said.

Kyle sighed and leaned back in his seat as the jet levelled off at thirty-five thousand feet, high above the sprawling Nevada deserts that were flecked with white cumulus clouds.

'I want to know who I'm talking to first,' he said, glancing at Garrett.

'I'm Ethan Warner,' Ethan said. 'I served in the Marines in Iraq and Afghanistan, became a journalist and then was hired to work for the Defence Intelligence Agency. This is my partner, Nicola Lopez, former Washington PD and we've been working together for several years now. Believe me, we've seen some stuff and nothing you're telling us sounds impossible.'

Trent glanced at Garrett. 'Who's the money man?'

'I'm an international property developer,' Garrett replied. 'I got involved with these guys when researching my father's murder. They helped me solve it and put the people responsible behind bars. I'd trust them with my life and I think that you should with yours, because right now there are some real unsavoury people who would like to see it come to an end.'

Kyle seemed to sense that Garrett was both telling the truth and genuinely concerned for his safety.

'Where are we going?' he asked, glancing out of the windows.

'Virginia,' Ethan replied. 'From there, anywhere that's safe.'

Kyle suddenly sat bolt upright in his seat. 'My parents, they're…'

'Safe,' Garrett replied. 'I tipped off a media team about the lights at Dugway last night and sent them canvassing the area, gave them your parents' address. The media don't know that you're missing yet but I made sure that I got word to your folks that you're safe with us. The media are hovering around Vernon right now so the military, or whoever these guys were, will find it hard to threaten them in any meaningful way.'

Kyle seemed to relax again.

'The pictures, Kyle,' Lopez said, 'how did you take them?'

Kyle picked one of the images up and smiled, as though fondly recalling the night that it was taken.

'Because of something called big data,' he replied. 'You ever heard of it?'

'Sure,' Ethan replied. 'The Internet, marketing strategies, gathering information on browsing so that adverts are targeted more efficiently, things like that right?'

'Right,' Kyle agreed, 'except that big data is capable of so much more and the government have been using it to catch criminals. The irony here is that I used the same process that they use, in order to catch a UFO.'

Lopez frowned. 'How does that work?'

Kyle got himself comfortable in the leather seats as he replied.

'There is a program which gathers data in large quantities, called PredPol, which is short for Predictive Policing. It's been in use for some years in Los Angeles. It's a data-crunching program that lists all known crimes in a given area, compiles all the details about those crimes, and then is able to generate an algorithmic predicition of where crime will happen based on that prior data.'

Lopez blinked.

'That's awesome, and it sounds like that movie, *Minority Report.*'

'It's much the same, except that PredPol is reality and it actually works,' Kyle said. 'Trials in the Foothill area of Los Angeles saw a twelve per cent drop in crime when the software was trialled there in 2011. PredPol was used not just to predict crime based on past data, but to also factor in things like the time of day, the weather, how close pay-day was and a bunch of other data that might affect how criminals operated. The police were able to show up before crimes were committed and criminals were thus deterred and prevented from carrying out burglaries and assaults or whatever. Police forces are using or trialling the program all over the world now. Burglaries were cut by over a quarter in Manchester in the UK by routing police vehicles through areas when PredPol predicted crimes would take place at certain times.'

Ethan realised that he was starting to get a sense of where Kyle was going with this.

'So, you wrote a similar code or program or something?' he hazarded.

Kyle grinned, and shrugged, almost coy. 'Well, *sort of.*'

'You stole the code, didn't you,' Lopez said, seeing straight through the kid.

'I didn't *steal* it,' Kyle retorted, 'exactly. I borrowed it. It's not my intention to make money from what I'm doing, only to expose what the government has been hiding.'

'So, you borrowed the code, presumably via hacking,' Ethan said. 'Then what?'

Kyle resumed his story.

'So, I then wrote my *own* code,' he said as he directed a harsh glance at Lopez, 'which was designed to trawl the internet using PredPol and search terms such as UFO, sighting of lights, UFO photograph, dates and times, words like pilot or police and so on, so that I could have a reasonable chance of obtaining data from well-trained observers who had recorded their experiences with big organisations like MUFON, the Mutual UFO Network.'

Ethan had heard of the organisation known as MUFON. Established in Illinois in 1969, the organisation had grown to become the most widely respected civilian research group into the UFO phenomena, with chapters in almost every American state. The group prided itself on its efforts to introduce the scientific method into its investigations, in an attempt to understand the phenomena better in the face of dismissal by the United States government. The only official US investigation into the UFO phenomena, Project Blue Book, had concluded that the phenomena was nothing unusual and most often the result of mistakenly misidentified aircraft, meteorological events or even swamp gas, and rejected the hypothesis of extra terrestrial visitors entirely.

'MUFON picked up the slack where Blue Book left off,' Ethan said.

'Pretty much,' Kyle agreed, 'and they had been compiling data since 1969, literally thousands and thousands of sightings, many of them by civilian and military pilots, trained observers who could tell the difference between something ordinary and something extraordinary. I made sure that my program could differentiate between brief sightings and extensive ones, and especially that it could detect sightings with visual and radar confirmation. Then I let it loose and waited to see what would come back.'

'What did it find?' Garrett asked, intrigued by Kyle's story.

'Man,' Kyle shook his head. 'You wouldn't believe it.'

'Try us,' Lopez insisted. 'You wouldn't believe half of what we've dug up in recent years.'

Kyle shrugged, and from his pocket he produced a small Flash RAM drive.

'I can do better than that,' he said. 'I can show you. This contains a copy of much of my work, and it has film on it of what happened at Dugway last night.'

***

XXIII

Las Vegas, Nevada

Vigor Vitesky hated the heat.

The sun blazed down from a cloudless sky as he stood with his men near the entrance to the Galleria Mall and watched the American agents running around like headless chickens as they sought to figure out where Kyle Trent was.

Vigor's greatest assets in this business, he felt, were his patience and persistence. The Americans were overly emotional about everything, whereas he preferred to watch from a distance and evaluate with a clear mind. That Kyle Trent was a slippery customer was clear from the fact that two four-man teams of American agents had let him slip through their fingers. Vigor doubted that Kyle Trent had managed to pull that off on his own, however, and judging by the four police cars gathered around a loading bay where a large truck was parked, and the agents on the roof of the building, Kyle had gone up and then down before making good his escape.

'He had help,' came a voice from Vigor's right.

Vigor turned to the youngest of his team. Although a fully trained field agent, Ivor was also an expert in computer hacking and had already accessed a local traffic camera network used by the city to monitor automobile accidents and traffic snarl ups.

Ivor showed him footage on a cell screen of a youth, a man and a woman leaping from the mall roof onto the truck and then down to the ground. Moments later, they pulled out of the parking lot in a silver vehicle just before the second American team could cut them off.

Vigor watched the two Americans helping the youth, who could only be Kyle Trent. It had taken Vigor some time to make the connection between the American youth and the events in Scotland. The police officer whom he had persuaded to assist had been able to inform him that a CIA officer had gotten in contact with the police just days after the event. Following that lead had led Vigor and his men to the United States, both to monitor the CIA officer in question and also to pursue Kyle Trent.

It had not been easy for Vigor and his team to identify the American as being the youth behind the photographs, but careful thinking and planning had cemented in Vigor's mind that the person they sought was indeed an American. The photographs supplied to the American agencies had contained landmarks in some images that his team were able to pin down to certain locations. The majority of those locations were in America, and oddly when marked on a map they traced a near perfect line across the 37th Parallel, right through the centre of the United States. Only the image taken in Scotland stood out.

Vigor's men had followed his orders and undertaken a painstaking search through flight manifests around the time of the Scotland event, seeking a way of matching one or more travellers to the movements of another in the United States. After three days of intensive work, they had uncovered a name: Kyle Trent. The American had stayed in what was called a "bed and breakfast" in Bonnybridge for two nights, having flown in from Las Vegas. He then flew back to Vegas the morning after the event.

Further detective work revealed Trent's presence on various conspiracy theorist forums, cementing in Vigor's mind that Trent was the mastermind behind the UFO photographs. He and his team had travelled from Scotland to Vegas and arrived only days previously, intent on tracking Trent down. It was during that time they had intercepted transmissions suggesting that Trent intended to strike again, this time at the ultra secretive Dugway Proving Ground. This time things had gone wrong and he was being hunted by units within the Special Operations Group, his own countrymen now his greatest foes.

'Do we know who the people helping him are?' Vigor asked.

'No,' Ivor admitted. 'The footage isn't clear enough to obtain an identification. They could be family friends perhaps, other conspiracy theory allies?'

Vigor shook his head.

'They're too courageous for that, and they must have scoped out the mall before finding Trent to be able to use the roof as an escape route. That requires planning and forethought. They weren't here by accident.'

'They would have had to have known that Kyle was a fugitive,' the agent pointed out. 'That would mean they're employed by a government agency of some kind or another.'

Vigor nodded. That the various intelligence agencies of the United States had failed to work together on numerous occasions in the past was common knowledge, a fact that Russia had often used to its advantage when infiltrating them. Now, it was quite possible that one agency was warring with another to keep Kyle Trent and his abilities to themselves and were probably unaware that Russia was also on the scene with the same aim in mind.

'We need to remain in the shadows for now, and so does Kyle Trent,' he said, airing his thoughts out loud. 'They must have gone somewhere and they must have done so very quickly. There is little point in following the vehicle: if they're smart they will have dumped it by now and moved on. They know their pursuers will be able to identify and track the vehicle easily.'

'Then how do we find them?' asked his companion.

Vigor thought for a moment.

'Trace the registration of the vehicle they were seen in. It will most likely have been hired for cash under assumed names, but it might lead us to find out who these saviours of young Kyle Trent are. We're following them now, not Kyle. They will have their own agenda and if we can track them down, we'll find Kyle. I want to know everything about them; where they've been since they arrived, their histories, everything. And we need to pay a visit to the Army officer who has been keeping tabs on the events since Scotland. I want to send him a message that he won't forget.'

The agents around him got to work as Vigor climbed back into the cool of the vehicle and shut the door. He checked his watch: barely after noon. He had people he could contact in almost all of the American states. Getting to the right people would not be a problem. He had already turned Kyle against his own countrymen. Now he needed to disrupt the chain of command and ensure that when the time came, his men would be able to grab Kyle Trent and his two new friends and dispose of anyone who got in their way.

*

Rico Savage stood beside a pool vehicle and listened to his agents.

'They made it out onto the roof, and from there off the side. Warner and the woman must have already scoped the place out for alternative exits – they were ready for us.'

Savage nodded. Within minutes, his carefully planned capture of Kyle Trent had gone to hell and now Trent, Warner and Lopez were all in the wind. Worse, Trent was now probably more fearful for his life than ever. Warner and Lopez had successfully spirited him away from agents working for Dugway, the kind of people that Trent would see as his natural enemy after what had happened to his friend.

'Scan every single traffic camera and find out what happened to them,' he ordered.

'We're already on it, and a BOLO for a silver Tahoe is already with local law enforcement. They won't get far if they stay on the roads.'

'They won't stay on the roads,' Rico countered. 'They'll lose the vehicle as soon as they can and seek another way out of the city. Warner and Lopez have to be working for someone else. Get in touch with the Director of Operations at Dugway and have him call the CIA, DIA, FBI, the Office of the Director of National Intellligence, every damned agency you can think of and find out whether these two are working for them and why.'

'Yes sir!'

His men scattered to perform their work. Rico Savage cursed silently to himself, and was about to head back into the mall when he noticed a pair of vehicles parked across the lot. Both were non-descript SUVs, both manned by men who seemed to be watching Rico's men from a distance.

The vehicles were too far away for Rico to see the plates, but they didn't look like government plates and there was nothing to suggest that the occupants of the vehicles were anything other than innocent civilians other than the tingle in Rico's gut that said there was something amiss.

He watched the occupants for a moment longer, staring at them directly, and both men in both vehicles averted their gazes, started their engines and drove away slowly through the parking lot.

Savage watched them go for a long time before he finally turned away and headed into the mall, pursued by the sense that he was not alone in his search for Kyle Trent.

***

XXIV

'You've got film of the Dugway event?' Ethan asked in amazement.

'I managed to download the footage that Greg and I shot before I ran away from the hills. Greg died up there helping me, and I was damned if I was going to let them kill him for nothing.'

Lopez glanced at Ethan with a raised eyebrow, apparently impressed by Trent's courage. The jet was slipping through the high altitude atmosphere without even the slightest hint of turbulence, Kyle Trent eating ravenously from the generously stocked mini-galley.

Ethan watched as Garrett produced a laptop computer and switched it on. Within moments, Kyle had the device on a fold-out table between them with the Flash RAM plugged in. His fingers fluttered across the keyboard with a sound like falling rain as he spoke around mouthfuls of meatballs and potato chips.

'The data compiled by my software showed trends in UFO sightings like you wouldn't believe,' he said. 'You could actually watch them appearing and fading away again, which falls right in with what we observe in the historical record, that UFO sightings come in waves, which researchers refer to as "flaps".'

He turned the laptop screen toward them, and Ethan saw a map of the world before him. Upon the map were flashing red spots, which he assumed represented individual UFO sightings. At once he could see them flickering into and out of existence, and he could see clear patterns emerging from the chaos. Like bands of weather marching across the skies, they swept from west to east.

'There are patterns,' Kyle said, almost in awe. 'UFO sightings are not random.'

The waves swept across the globe, rippling lines of red spots drifting like clouds across the United States, Russia, Europe, Malaysia and even Africa, but at once he could see differences.

'There are less sightings in Africa.'

'Ah, but *are* there?' Kyle replied. 'There are less people connected to the Internet in Africa, and hardly any connections to MUFON. That limits the data that comes out of remote regions, and also those with closed borders such as North Korea. But where people live with the benefit of freedom of speech and a free press, we get a lot of reports.'

'Maybe the waves are caused by people getting on the bandwagon after a genuine sighting, or a media report,' Lopez suggested, 'and suddenly everyone's seeing UFOs in their backyard.'

'A very astute observation,' Kyle said, smiling at her in open admiration now, 'but I wrote in a sub-code that eliminated hearsay reports in the wake of multiple or radar-confirmed sightings that were featured on the news. I basically looked at the natural frequency of copy-cat reports of misidentified aerial objects and filtered out anything that had no corroborating evidence. It isn't perfect, but it helps to reduce the chances of so-called mass hallucinations or copy-cat reports. Even then, the wave signals remained strong. Once I had the data in place, I then ran it through PredPol to see if the program could make predictions on where and when further waves would take place.'

Lopez, to Ethan's surprise, smiled back at Kyle. 'That's genius.'

Kyle stared back at her as though she'd just offered to take off her clothes for him. Then Ethan realised why. Trent was somewhat like Joseph Hellerman, the courageous IT expert whom they had worked with for several years, before he had died at the hands of Russian mercenaries in Indonesia in one of their last DIA sponsored expeditions. Lopez had been fond of Hellerman in a motherly sort of way, and his passing had hit her hard.

'Yes, it is,' Trent chortled in delight, mesmerised by Lopez but also by his own handiwork. 'But look at this data first, just check out where the sightings in the USA most often take place.

Ethan looked at the screen and was shocked by what he saw. The country was split almost perfectly in half, with relatively few sightings on the east coast rising to large numbers of sightings on the west coast.

'This was the result of collating almost forty thousand sightings,' Kyle explained. 'While there are undoubtedly many more that are never reported that could sway this result, it does seem likely that the vast majority of UFO sightings are occurring in the western United States.'

'Why should that be?' Garrett asked. 'Isn't the east coast more densely populated?'

'Yes, it is,' Kyle said, 'mainly due to the large and sparsely populated desert regions like Nevada and Utah in the west of the country. You'd think that with more people in the east of the country there would be more sightings and more reports as there are more eyes to do the looking, but there aren't and that sort of reinforces the fact that people seem to see more UFOs in the west.'

'Sort of?' Lopez asked.

'You can't take even data like this at face value,' Kyle said. 'It took me a bit of thinking, but I realised that one explanation for the extra sightings was the fact that the climate in the western United States is hotter than that in the east, and as a result there are generally more clear sky days in the west. It's much harder to see a UFO if there's ten thousand feet of cloud between you and the craft. Not only that, but per capita the most sightings came from California and Arizona, both of which are close to seismic fault lines, part of the Pacific Ring of Fire. Strange lights in the sky are often attributed to the release of energy in seismic events in these sorts of areas. The same thing happens in Scotland, where an ancient fault line runs through the country and produces the most UFO reports in the United Kingdom. So, to some extent those factors might explain the discrepancy.'

'But not entirely,' Ethan guessed.

'It's still too one sided. So I analised a little deeper and uncovered another trait in the sightings, one that was much more sinister. The data revealed that even in the east of the country, people were much more likely to see UFOs if they lived within sight of a nuclear powerplant or missile silo.'

Ethan raised his eyebrows. 'Seriously?'

'Definitely,' Trent confirmed. 'These things routinely appear over and close to military establishments and nuclear facilities. In fact, it's happened so many times that military personnel are forbidden to discuss it. Did you know that in March 1967, UFOs twice deactivated the nuclear ICBM missile silos at Malmstrom Air Force Base in Montana?'

When Garrett, Lopez and Ethan all shook their heads, Kyle tutted.

'Why is it that people just don't hear about these things? The entire base was in meltdown. A UFO appeared overhead in a clear sky and moments later every system malfunctioned. Malmstrom was part of Strategic Air Command and the silo was live, meaning that in the event of a Russian nuclear strike they would fire in retaliation. There probably wasn't a more secure, classified and sensitive site in the entire United States military arsenal at that time, and yet a single UFO wanders into the middle of it and shuts down every Minuteman Missile's launch and guidance systems for an entire day. It was *decades* before retiring officers and other staff went public with what happened, and their reports were verified by documents from other witnesses both inside and outside the base. A later sighting, this time of another UFO hovering over another part of the base, was reported in to the officer manning the Command Post, who replied that such incidents "were no longer investigated", a standard-issue response of denial. In short, nobody wanted anything to do with the sightings. Our own most sensitive military bases and defence systems, and the official response is "it ain't happenin', don't tell us about it".'

Ethan looked at the laptop. 'You said you ran this data through PredPol.'

'Yup,' Trent agreed. 'So, the only way I could figure out if this data was valid was to run it through PredPol and see what popped. Then, I could head out to whatever nuclear facility was most likely to have a sighting and wait it out. I only have a menial job and no bills other than food and drink, so I figured I could spend a few months running with this and see what I could uncover. It seemed like a good idea at the time.'

'It was a good idea,' Lopez assured him, 'right up to the point where you started sending pictures to the CIA. What did you do next?'

'I ran the data through PredPol, but I introduced another routine within it that I called the Hydra.'

'The what?' Garrett asked.

'The Hydra,' Kyle replied, 'named after the Greek sea monster that could regrow lost heads. It could only be killed by striking at its heart, and so I decided to see if I could use the common trait of nuclear facilities with UFO sightings that would allow me to get up close and personal with them. Basically, I wanted to use PredPol to analyse the data and predict when and where a UFO would appear within the restrictions of doing so within ten miles of sensitive military sites within the USA. To be honest I didn't think I'd get any hits as the data was going to be so confined, but I was wrong. I got hits all over the place from Texas to California.'

Ethan saw little red specks appearing across the American west.

'Each of these potential sightings is assigned a probability,' Kyle explained. The closer to the present that you run the data, the more accurate the prediction is likely to be. The best predictions are those made for within six hours, and those made at night. The further out you go into the future, the more fluid and less accurate the predictions get.'

Kyle switched to another screen, and there Ethan saw the image of a UFO hovering in the darkness, captured in strange hues of light that might have been ultra violet.

'This was what we recorded at Dugway, after the Hydra predicted a sighting with a high probability of occurrence.'

Ethan could see clearly the UFO, which was emanating a strange glow that seemed to obscure some of the details of the craft. Kyle set the screen to show imagery from several of the cameras at once, and on the Infra Red image they could all see that the object was solid and radiating heat. What they could not see was any evidence of propulsion at all.

'This is sensational,' Garrett murmured. 'This footage will set the world on fire if it ever gets out.'

'I agree,' Kyle said, 'that's why I sent the images to the government agencies, to show them that I was serious. But it turned out that the images were not the biggest discovery the Hydra helped me make.'

***

XXV

'Seriously?' Lopez asked. 'You've got something bigger up your sleeve?'

Kyle nodded. 'I'll get to that. Watch the video.'

Ethan leaned back in his seat as he watched the footage of the UFO hovering over the deserts of Dugway, and then he saw the trail of headlights rushing out towards it from the base in the distance. It was obvious that the base had scrambled troops out toward the UFO, the vehicle convoy heading straight toward it.

Then, quite suddenly, it blinked out and vanished. On the IR camera, Ethan saw a wispy ring of smoke drift away on the desert wind and cool until it faded from sight, the only sign that the object had ever been there at all.

'Man, did you see that?' Lopez gasped. 'It didn't even go straight up or anything, it just plain vanished.'

'I don't get it either,' Kyle agreed. 'How that's even possible I can't imagine. Well, I can imagine but I can't quite get my head around it. This thing was there in plain sight on our cameras, and then it was gone. I used a laser range-finder on it to get a distance, and from field-of-view calculations I'm confident that this thing was half as long as a football field. It must have weighed hundreds of tons and yet it just hung there for several minutes making not a sound.'

Ethan saw a face appear on the screen, pointing at the convoy of vehicles now parked out on the deserts beneath where the UFO had appeared. Moments later, the head jerked sideways and twisted away from the camera before it fell out of sight.

'Greg,' Kyle muttered, his face paling. 'I told him to get out of sight but he didn't listen, got all excited about the sighting and then pow, he's gone just like that. They blew half of his face off…'

Kyle trailed off and he looked as though he might feint or vomit at any moment. Lopez moved to sit alongside him, and Ethan realised that being on the run for a few days had kept Kyle alive and focussed. Now, the reality of what he had witnessed was starting to hit him and shock was setting in. He'd seen the look before, the vacant stare as the brain tried to come to terms with something so awful that the conscience did not want to confront it.

'This kid's in way over his head,' Garrett said quietly as he moved alongside Ethan. 'We don't know who's after him and they're not afraid of pulling the trigger.'

Ethan nodded, watching the laptop screen in silence. He reached out and used the keyboard to replay the shooting a couple of times. Greg's head appeared in front of the screen in the wake of the UFO's disappearance, and he pointed at the convoy. Moments later, a bullet shattered his skull and hurled him sideways, the boy's body falling out of sight.

'Who do you think they are?' Lopez asked as she returned to his side, Kyle now reclined in one of the jet's leather seats with his eyes closed and a blanket draped over him. 'Mackenzie must know something. Dugway's an Army field and it's probably got CIA spooks moving in and out all the time.'

'Maybe,' Ethan said cautiously. 'We don't know enough yet, but we have enough to take back to him and see what we can do next. If Kyle has something else he can show us, then we're in an even better position and we can use it to trade for his safety with the troops from Dugway.'

'Damn,' Garrett said, looking wistfully at Kyle. 'I wanted to know what else it was that he'd found out.'

'There's time,' Ethan replied. 'It's going to take us a while to get to Virginia and while we're in the air technically we're safe. It'll take them a fair while to figure out what happened to us. Right now, Kyle's our priority along with Sophie. Whatever the hell is going on out here it's probably connected in some way.'

Lopez looked across at Kyle.

'That kid's exhausted and he's going to be out of it for quite a while. We need to trade off what he has here for his life. That means talking to whoever these Dugway guys are at some point or another, whether we like it or not.'

'You've changed your tune,' Ethan observed with a smile.

'This is a matter of national security,' she retorted with a playful elbow in Ethan's ribs. 'It behoves us to protect the innocent, to stand up for the underdog, to boldy go where no woman has go…'

'I get it,' Ethan grinned. 'And we have evidence, just the kind of stuff they're afraid of reaching the public. Kyle was working alone, but we can do a much better job of getting this out there if we want to. That gives us leverage over them, whoever *them* is. I say we head back to the Barn and show Mackenzie what we have here.'

'Not much else we can do,' Lopez agreed.

'Are you sure?' Garrett asked.

They both looked at him. 'What do you mean?' Ethan asked.

Garrett shrugged but he was looking at the laptop screen with a gleam in his eye.

'Well, you've got this program that can predict where UFOs will appear, we have a private jet than can travel anywhere in the world and we're on the run from the authorities. I figure that a few camera shots and footage isn't enough to convince the public that there's been an assassination here. They'll think that it's been faked, it'll be rubbished by the media, you know how the government likes to spin news to protect itself.'

'You just said it would change the world,' Lopez pointed out.

'I know,' Garrett replied, 'but I wasn't talking about the footage, I was talking about the software Kyle's developed. It's the first thing that crossed my mind, that he's only using this technology in a limited way because he doesn't have the resources he needs. Why just use it to go find UFOs? Why not use it to *capture* one?'

*

Langley, Virginia

General Mackenzie managed to get home from the office in time to see his wife and kids, which was sometimes a rarity these days. Both of his daughters were in high school and were going through a phase where boys and fashion were far more important than giving their old man a hug before heading off to bed, and his wife was always so busy that he often got home at night to find the house quiet and his family asleep.

Carla met him at the door and he was able to get a few words in to Charlotte, the older of his two girls, in between texts on her cell phone from school friends. Rachel, the younger girl, was still just young enough to run up and hug him before she went to bed.

'Dinner's in the oven warming up,' Carla informed him, a little frostily. 'There's some wine in the fridge if you fancy it.'

'I do,' Mackenzie said as the hugged Rachel and then sent her off up the stairs to bed.

Carla moved off into the living room to watch television as Mackenzie headed into the kitchen. There was no point in arguing with her. She had married into a military life and accepted it, but when he'd been posted to Langley he figured she thought that he would be able to come home a little more often. That hadn't happened, and although she covered it as best she could he could tell that she was annoyed.

He saw the oven aglow with light and heat, a meal inside, and the fridge looked inviting as the thought of a small glass of wine entered his head. He was halfway across the kitchen when he saw them through the window.

You could always tell a government pool vehicle. It wasn't so much that they always used glossy black SUVs, although that often was the case. It was more that they always managed to look somehow *out of place*. There had been some rain recently, bringing with it fine dust and sand from the mid-west. It had settled on most of the cars in the street where Mackenzie lived, and yet this SUV, parked on the opposite side of the street to his home, was clean. It hadn't been polished to a mirror shine, but the wheels were also clean and it bore no adornments of any kind. Two men were sitting inside. Neither were looking his way but the dead give-away was that one of them was sipping from one of those cheap coffee cups, the type served over the counter in fast food joints across the country. Observation team, setting up for the night.

Mackenzie watched them through the window. They weren't moving, they weren't paying his home much attention but he knew somehow that they were watching him back, observing the simple rules: don't look directly at the target, don't stay in the same place for too long, don't make yourself stand out. It wasn't like he hadn't done the same kind of work himself in his career.

Mackenzie was high enough up in the chain at Langley to know that this kind of observation was only done on known targets. It was not routinely performed on serving officers within the CIA, so that ruled out Langley as the source of the agents inside the car, if agents they were at all. Mackenzie could not see the vehicle's plates as it had parked in close behind another vehicle, another ploy to help concealement. They could of course be a protection detail, but he would have been informed and besides, he had not asked for one.

The temptation was for him to phone the office and send two of his own people out to see who was watching him, but he knew instantly that doing so would lose him the advantage. They didn't know that he was aware of them yet, as he hadn't noticed the vehicle when he had arrived home. It was only by chance that he had glimpsed it through the small kitchen side-window that looked out over their neighbour's front lawn and up the street.

Mackenzie decided that he would deal with this the old-fashioned way.

He strode to the front door of his home and out into the warm dusk air. The light was fading fast now, the horizon to the west glowing with last light and a few stars twinkling in the heavens above as he walked down his front lawn and turned left, heading for the parked vehicle.

If he had needed any further confirmation that he was being watched, the vehicle started its engine and pulled out as its headlights lit up. Mackenzie quicked his pace. He wasn't about to let them drive off without finding out which agency they worked for. Mackenzie strode off the sidewalk into the path of the car and blocked the way.

The vehicle began to slow as Mackenzie advanced towards it, even as his wife appeared at the front door to their home and called out to him.

'Scott, what's going on?'

Mackenzie turned to call his response, but his voice was drowned out as the vehicle's engine suddenly screamed and it shot toward him.

Then he heard the gunfire.

In a terrible moment he realised that the men in the car were armed and out to kill. The gunman was pointing a machine gun out of the passenger window of the car, the muzzle flaring with flame as he fired not at Mackenzie, but at his home.

'Get down!'

Mackenzie's voice was a scream, frantic in his own ears as the car rushed toward him. He hurled himself up into the air, one boot slamming down onto the hood of the vehicle as he vaulted up and leaped over the car as it shot beneath him. Mackenzie flew through the air and rolled as he landed, managing to get one boot down as he slammed into the asphalt.

He crashed down awkwardly but came up onto his feet and ran toward his home, panic giving flight to his legs as he rushed to his wife's side without thought for any injuries he might himself have sustained. The front porch was peppered with bullet holes and the living room window was shattered as he leaped into the porch.

'No!'

Mackenzie hurled himself to his wife's side where she lay and stared down at her.

'I'm okay!' she said instantly. 'I got down before they shot at me! What the hell is going on?'

Mackenzie launched himself up the stairs inside even as his daughters rushed out from their rooms, screaming in panic and hurling themselves into his arms.

'It's okay,' he said, over and over again as he wrapped them up against his chest and held them tightly.

Behind him, Carla got to her feet and brushed herself down as she looked up at him, and for the first time General Scott Mackenzie realised that he had gotten himself into something that was way over his head.

***

XXVI

Kansas

Ethan could see out of the jet's windows the lights of America coming on as darkness consumed the sprawling fields of Kansas far below. Here at eighteen thousand feet or so he could still see the sun setting on the horizon behind them, beams of light shafting through towers of evening cloud glowing pink and gold in the sunset. Below, the land sprawled in shadow, and for some reason he felt a sense of despair or foreboding overwhelm him from nowhere.

The America below them seemed strange, a place they had not been for some time that had changed it seemed beyond all recognition, and the growing shadows seemed to reach out for the jet as it descended through wisps of blue-grey cloud toward the glittering lights of a city far in the distance.

'We'll be on the ground in ten minutes to refuel,' Garrett informed him as he walked back from the cockpit. 'From there we'll fly you to Langley, where you can debrief your commander. What will you do then?'

Ethan shook his head.

'I don't know,' he admitted.

The truth was that he was deeply concerned about what had happened at Dugway. The footage of Kyle's friend Greg being shot in cold blood was troubling him more than he might have anticipated, but there was also something else not quite right about the shooting that he couldn't put his finger on.

Then there was Garrett's suggestion.

'Have you thought about it any more?' Garrett persisted.

Ethan was struggling to get his head around what Garrett had in mind. Sure, Kyle Trent's mission to expose the reality of the UFO phenomena was startling and ground breaking enough, but now Garrett was proposing something even more extraordinary. Ethan didn't even know for sure if it was actually possible.

'How the hell would we catch one of these things even if we did find it?' he asked.

Garrett shrugged as he took a seat beside Ethan's.

'I'm not the expert here, but I'd bet my bottom dollar that we could recruit someone to help us, and Kyle over there must know a thing or two about UFOs, right? If we could find a way to just disable one long enough to tether it or something...'

'Great work genius,' Lopez murmured sleepily from a nearby seat. 'They can cross entire galaxies, outrun fighter jets and vanish in an instant, but a rope lasso'll hold 'em down no probs. Maybe we should head down to Texas and send in the cowboys.'

'I'm not saying it would be *easy*,' Garrett defended himself, 'but these things are rumoured to have crashed from time to time all over the world. If they can crash…'

'They can be controlled,' Ethan finished the sentence. 'The problem is we don't have any idea of how they're controlled, so we can't really figure out a way of hijacking them. About the only way we could do it would be to…'

Ethan looked at Garrett, who nodded quietly.

'Forget it,' Lopez cut in. 'I know what you two are thinking and it's not a good idea.'

'How do you know what we're thinking?' Garrett asked.

'Because you're men, so the first think you're thinking is that maybe you could shoot one down.'

'I'm hurt,' Ethan said.

'And offended,' Garrett added.

'Am I wrong?'

'No,' Garrett replied with a cheery smile, 'but the idea wasn't to damage it, just knock it off balance a bit so that we can get a closer look.'

'Knock it off balance a bit,' Lopez echoed with a smirk on her face. 'Seriously, that's your idea?'

'You got a better one?'

'Yeah, quit dreaming and let's get this kid on the ground and back with his family. That's our priority. You want to get all E.T. on these things, go do it on your own time.'

'I am on my own time and this is my jet,' Garrett reminded her.

'Minor technicality,' Lopez shrugged, 'when your humanity is at stake.'

'Nicola's right,' Ethan said.

'I am?'

Ethan knew that they couldn't even think about pursuing such a challenge without Kyle Trent's skills and some serious support, and right now the kid needed help, not more dangerous running around.

'We need Mackenzie behind us on this first,' he said to Garrett. 'We can fill him in on what we've found, but his mission priority was to bring Kyle in and get to the bottom of how he got those images of UFOs. We've done that.'

'Aren't you even a *little* bit curious?' Garrett pressed. 'Imagine, this could be the discovery of a lifetime, perhaps the greatest in all history: the discovery of other intelligent life in our universe, right here on our own planet. We could utterly annihilate every government cover-up of this phenomena in every country in the world in one fell swoop.'

'Yeah,' Ethan said, 'and if any of those countries got wind of what we were up to before we achieved it, we'd be on the end of a major *fell swoop* ourselves. You know how much they do to cover up these kinds of things, how much energy they put into dismissing anything that even hints that UFOs might be a real thing. They'd gun us down on sight, and Kyle's experience is proof that they're willing to shoot first and ask ques…'

Ethan's train of thought slammed to a halt as an image of Greg being shot flashed into his mind. That was it. That was what was wrong with the video they'd seen.

'Christ,' he uttered and hurried across to the laptop.

'What is it?' Lopez asked.

Ethan opened it and hurriedly accessed the footage of the shooting. He began playing the video again. He could see Greg move in front of the camera, then Greg was shot, and then moments later he heard the report of a rifle.

'There,' he said. 'That's the problem.'

'What is?' Lopez asked. 'He got hit by the troops. They're far out, enough that the bullet hits Greg before they heard the report.'

'Yes,' Ethan agreed, 'but Kyle said he measured the distance to the UFO as being a quarter of a mile, and that the distance made the UFO half the size of a football field. That means that the report would have reached them within a quarter second or so, if the troops on the plain had fired the fatal shot. But the report takes almost three quarters of a second.'

Lopez blinked.

'You clever little boy you,' she said. 'That means the shooter was three times as far away.'

The three of them looked at each other.

'The Americans didn't shoot Greg,' they said together in unison.

'Someone else did,' Ethan added. 'And right now, we don't know who.'

Ethan was about to say something else when his cell phone buzzed in his pocket. He pulled it out and saw Mackenzie's number on it.

'General, we've got news for you,' he said as he answered.

'It'll have to wait. Wherever you are, get the hell out of sight. I just survived an assassination attempt and they shot at my wife and children. Someone's coming for us, all of us. Get undercover as fast as you can!'

The line went dead immediately, and Ethan's blood ran cold in his veins as he looked up and saw the jet's cockpit ahead, the city ahead of them, a line of shimmering red, green and orange lights in the blackness. Lopez was looking at him with a concerned expression on her face. Ethan gave her a feeble smile.

'You know what you said about this being a no-gunfire deal?'

'You're kidding me.'

'Mackenzie's under fire, literally,' Ethan said.

'Is he okay?' Lopez asked wearily as she slumped back into a seat.

'Probably into protective custody,' Ethan guessed. 'They tried to hit his family too.'

Garrett had heard everything, but so had Kyle Trent, who was awake and watching now.

'They tried to kill a general?' he uttered, suddenly aware of the sheer level of danger they were in.

Ethan moved to the side of the jet and looked down at the darkened plains of Kansas. They could have been tracked out of Vegas. The squads hunting them would by now have checked passenger manifests and other aviation records in an attempt to track them down. Ethan and Lopez had flown one-way into McGarran because they didn't know how long it would take to track Kyle Trent down. Although they were now without a paper-trail, it wouldn't take their pursuers long to figure out how they got out of Nevada.

'We need a new game plan,' he said to Lopez. 'We can't take Kyle back to the Barn, there will be people waiting for him in Virginia who will shoot first and ask questions never.'

***

XXVII

Virginia

'What the hell is going on?'

Deputy Director of the CIA Edward McCain shook Mackenzie's hand the moment he arrived at the CIA safehouse. Mackenzie had managed to get his traumatised wife and children settled down but now he was standing with a stiff scotch in one hand and a sense of futility in the other.

'I don't know, but they're deadly serious. These guys shot to kill and it was only chance that they missed. What do we know about them?'

'Not a damned thing,' McCain admitted. 'We traced the car, but it's taken some time as these guys were smart enough not to set it alight. Local law enforcement followed traffic camera evidence to narrow the search and found the SUV abandoned in a sidestreet twenty miles out of town. No cameras out there, no witness and the vehicle was wiped down real well.'

'Professional work,' Mackenzie replied without hesitation. 'They were well armed and they knew how to shoot straight. It was only luck that they missed my wife and if I hadn't stepped out right in front of the driver's side…'

'The shooter couldn't easily hit you without taking out their own windscreen,' McCain nodded, understanding immediately. 'We did a ballistics check on the bullet casings, but they're custom made with no stamp and nothing on the hammer residue or pattern that our computers have managed to match. If they're as smart as they seem to be, they'll have used custom bullets in a black market weapon, which means no trail and nothing that can be relied upon in court.'

Mackenzie slumped into a big armchair and took a pull on the scotch. It burned his throat and belly, felt good despite the gnawing agony of being powerless to strike back. Mackenzie had fought in two major wars, had even taken on the Taliban in close combat. It had been a dangerous time but he had never questioned the fight, had never been confused about what he was doing and why. But now, he was trying to think of a way to fight an enemy that he didn't know and who was trying to kill not just him but his family too. McMcain was thinking the same thing.

'Jeez Scott, you're on the intelligence desk at Langley, not out in the field. Who the hell would possibly want you dead? Is there anyone you can think of, maybe former terrorists who are now on the loose or something?'

Mackenzie shook his head. There was nobody out of his military past who would likely hold a grudge against him, and while it was known for former soldiers to join motorcycle gangs and other criminal enterprises, this hit was not of their stamp. This was professional, and besides the men he had been able to see were young, not someone from his past who had come seeking revenge for an unknown or forgotten crime.

'No,' Mackenzie replied. He wanted to say something about the new evidence from Warner and Lopez he was working on, but the message about "trust nobody" had gotten through loud and clear now and was working to complicate things. Although he did not for a moment believe that McCain would be working against him, much less to have him killed, he did now understand that there were people out there who were willing to kill to get the information that he had.

Suddenly, he realised something. He had told nobody about his involvement with the project, and yet he had been targeted. McCain spotted the change in his expression.

'What, you remember something?'

Mackenzie bit his lip. He couldn't say anything for fear of knowledge about his activities slipping out, and yet remaining silent had still gotten him nearly killed. There was nowhere for him to turn, and yet he had to do something. An image of his wife and daughters flickered before him in the firelight and suddenly he knew what his priorities now were.

'This place isn't safe,' he said to McCain.

The DDCIA raised an eyebrow. 'I've got eight men out there surrounding the property and the Chiefs of Staff are already aware of what's happened. It's all over the news too, a drive-by shooting in your area.'

Mackenzie nodded. Public knowledge could sometimes work in the intelligence community's favour if a figure was at risk. By putting the news out there that someone, say the North Koreans, were looking to assassinate a refugee, then it would often cause the enemy to cancel the operation as if the target did indeed die, it was tacit admission of guilt on the part of the regime and an extra penny in the pocket of patriotism for the serving government.

'It might hold them off any further attempts on my life, but it won't stop them.'

McCain frowned. 'Is there something you're not telling me, Scott?'

Mackenzie had no way out of this other than to disappear, and he couldn't do that without putting his family at risk. The murder of those close to targets of government conspiracies were more common than most civilians thought. Russia had repeatedly poisoned and killed refugees in the United Kingdom and the United States as it sought to rebuild the state of fear that had been its legacy for decades. North Korean agents repeatedly murdered others who had fled the regime in South East Asia, and both China and Israel were likewise keen to hunt down those who would dare to take a stand against them.

'The new project you gave me has gone all Cold War.'

McCain sat down in a chair opposite. 'Talk to me. What happened?'

'Scotland,' Mackenzie replied. 'Ever since I got in contact with the Brits out there, someone or something has been on my case.'

'Did you talk to anybody else about the case?'

Macknezie rubbed his eyes and shook his head. 'You're gonna laugh, Ed.'

'You just got shot for whatever you're about to tell me,' McCain replied with a stony face. 'I'm not laughing, Scott.'

Mackenzie nodded again, took a breath.

'Somebody out there has figured out how to track UFOs down and catch 'em in the act, right? We've got photos of the real thing that'd make Steven Spielberg cry. I didn't have the ability or staff to handle this, but at the same time as you showed up I got a file from the DIA.'

'The DIA? What did they want?'

'It wasn't official either,' Mackenzie admitted. 'From some guy called Jarvis, a former agent. He directed me to two former agents who worked for him, Warner and Lopez. They've been doing the field work for me ever since.'

McCain stared at him for a long moment, and his reply was one that Mackenzie would never have predicted.

'Scott, you're in greater danger than you think. Somebody, somewhere, wants those photos kept quiet real bad, and they want whoever took them just as much. You're right, we need to get the hell out of here.'

Mackenzie raised his eyebrows, surprised. 'You're buying into this?'

'I'm already fully paid up,' McCain said as he stood and pulled a cell phone from his pocket. 'You're damned right that organisations out there are going to want images like that and will kill to get them. Hell, we work for one of them. Do you have anyone I can call, someone right outside of the system, someone who can get your family out of here and somewhere safe?'

'Can't the Director handle something?' Mackenzie asked as he stood up.

McCain shook his head.

'The CIA leaks like a sieve, Scott. We keep you in a safe house within an hour of the District, you'll be dead before the sun's up.'

Mackenzie was almost afraid to ask the question now burning a hole in his brain but he knew he had to.

'You think the CIA is behind this?'

McCain shot him a shocked look.

'Hell no,' he said with a scowl. 'It's much worse than that.'

***

XXVIII

Garrett's jet landed smoothly on the asphalt at a Johnson City Executive Airport airport and taxied in to a parking area to the west of the terminal. Ethan and Nicola prepared themselves as Garrett gestured to the terminal, which was lit brightly in the darkness that enveloped the rest of the airport.

'We've picked a spot that will shield you from the view of any cameras in there. I have a Mercedes booked to pick you up from outside the terminal and drive you to wherever you need to go.'

Ethan shook the billionaire's hand.

'We'll hook up with you as soon as we can,' he replied. 'But we may be dark for some time.'

'Get in touch,' Garrett urged him, 'I want in on this and I have the resources to make it happen.'

The jet rolled to a halt and the whine of the engines faded away. Garrett opened the main hatch and Ethan hurried out with Lopez and Kyle Trent close behind. They stepped out onto the asphalt service area, the wind cool and the lights of the airport shimmering in the darkness as Ethan headed out toward one of the large hangars between them and the terminal.

A car rolled up almost immediately, some sort of executive service. Ethan, Kyle and Lopez climbed into the car and were driven in silence to the other side of the airport terminal. Moments later, they were out of the car and walking into the airport as though they had just arrived to fly out of the state.

'We're gonna have to be quick if we're to get out of here before our friends from Vegas find us,' Lopez said as they walked through the terminal. 'You think that Garrett will be a safe bet?'

Ethan knew what she meant. Any link to Garrett would be a weakness now, and they couldn't afford to take the chance that anyone connected to their billionaire benefactor would squeal. Besides, their pursuers would soon link Garrett's jet to their escape and he didn't want to lose the advantage they had.

'We book ourselves out of here and go dark from now on,' he said. 'We can check in with Garrett once Kyle's safe, which will mean we'll also be of no use to either Special Operations or anyone else who might be hunting us.'

'And then what do I do?' Kyle asked. 'I'll be running again with nowhere to go.'

'You said that you had something else,' Lopez said, 'some other piece of evidence that pointed to where UFOs would appear.'

Kyle nodded, but glanced instinctively up at the cameras mounted in the terminal ceiling, the Big Brother network watching all with soulless black eyes.

'We need somewhere we can talk without being watched,' he said.

Ethan led the way to a cafeteria. Although there were people everywhere, at this time of night it was slightly less busy and there were isolated tables where they could sit and talk. Although there was the slight possibility that facial recognition cameras could be in operation, it was unlikely that they would be actively searching for any of them this far from Nevada. At least, not yet.

As he waited in line, Ethan felt a dull ache in his belly, as though something had struck him. He rubbed his stomach, pleased to find that it was still washboard flat, and the pain passed once again.

Ethan got coffees and fast food and joined Lopez and Kyle where they sat at the back of the cafeteria, able to watch the entrance. Ethan sat down and saw that Kyle already had his laptop open and was showing Lopez something.

'This is insane, Ethan,' she said as she stared at the screen.

'So are we for even being here,' he replied. 'What have you got, Kyle?'

Kyle turned the screen around to face Ethan as he spoke.

'I ran some other data through the Hydra, but I didn't have chance to integrate it into the program until after it had compiled. I was at Dugway when it completed, and I've only just been able to run it through. The results are astounding.'

Ethan could see on the screen of the laptop a map of the United States, much like the one that Kyle had shown him previously, where various states were marked with the frequency of UFO sightings. But this one was different.

'I included another set of parameters, in an attempt to narrow down the odds against encountering a UFO. There have been reports of cattle mutilations all over the world, but especially in the United States and especially in the last twenty or so years. I managed to categorise the accounts into high-level certainty groups where the chances of the mutilations being the result of predators or other natural events were virtually nil.'

Ethan knew something of the cattle mutilations that had haunted the mid-west for decades. Typically, healthy cattle were found dead in the morning by a rancher, and they were also found to be missing ears, tongues, genitalia, each being cut away with surgical precision. The animals often had their bowels scoured out and were almost always entirely drained of blood. This would all have been unusual enough, but not only where there no prints of predators, humans or otherwise around the remains, the victims themselves had left no trail to the point of their death; they were almost always found lying on their sides with their ribs broken, as though dropped from a great height.

'There are almost always UFO sightings around the same time that these cattle mutilations take place,' Kyle said, 'and ranchers know the difference between coyote and mountain lion kills and these mutilations. They report burning smells near the corpses, scents of hospitals or biochemicals and no sign of birds or other scavengers around the corpses which would normally not miss the chance to feast on a free meal. They happen often enough that I thought I'd put them in the data and see what happened, and this is what I got.'

Kyle pressed a button on the keypad, and Ethan took a deep breath as the graphic changed. Suddenly, all the sightings and events lined up perfectly to form a line that ran right across the very middle of the United States from west to east, and this time there was no variation in the number of sightings. The line was solid from east to west coast, and all of it within a narrow margin.

'The 37th parallel,' Kyle announced grandly. 'I couldn't believe it when I saw it, but it's there for all to see and this is hard data.'

Ethan couldn't begin to think why such events would take place almost exclusively across a single degree of latitude that ran across the country.

'Why the hell would there be so many sightings in one line like that?' he asked. 'What would alien visitors see as so important about it?'

Kyle wasn't finished yet.

'Tell him,' Lopez urged.

'Tell me what?' Ethan asked Kyle.

'I ran some other data that I already had through the system,' Kyle replied. 'Other factors that seemed to result in UFO sightings. The number of links to the 37th parallel is startling. Fully one fifth of all paranormal sightings occur on the parallel. What's more, some of the most famous UFO related locations and events are right on the same line of latitude.'

'Such as?' Ethan asked.

'Area 51,' Kyle replied, 'and that's just for starters. Dulce in New Mexico, long a location associated with UFO sightings and a place suspected to house secret government facilities in local mesas. The Taos hum, in New Mexico, heard only by some but the hum often adversely affects their health. The Miller and Sanchez mutilations, both famous for their veracity and both occurring in the last decade; the Wichita UFO sighting right here in Kansas, the Piedmont, Missouri UFO mass-sighting; the Cape Girardeau, Missouri UFO crash and retrieval, which is only know due to the deathbed confession of Baptist Minister William Huffman who was called to administer the last rites to beings not of this world; the Mantell UFO incident, when Kentucky National Guard fighter pilot Thomas Mantell was scrambled to intercept a UFO and died as a result. That's not to mention the large number of US military installations arrayed across the 37th parallel.'

Ethan leaned back in the cheap plastic seat and thought for a moment.

'It's pretty fair to say that almost every US installation across that line is also associated with the highest levels of security clearance. We're not going to get anywhere near any of them.'

'Not without help,' Kyle said.

'Do you know anybody who could get us in, or close to these places?' Lopez asked Kyle, clearly warming to him with each passing hour.

Kyle seemed uncertain.

'There may be one guy, but he's been off the radar for years. He supposedly lives out somewhere in Nevada and stays off the grid, right on the parallel believe it or not. He might know enough to get us in the right place at the right time.'

'Nevada, huh?' Ethan echoed. 'It's probably the last thing they'll expect us to do, hop right back into the state after getting away again.'

'We could drive it,' Lopez said, 'stay off the grid ourselves.'

Ethan nodded. 'It's probably twenty hours or more on the road but it's doable. All we need is a vehicle.'

'Yeah, and we can't hire one and take it out of state,' Lopez said.

'I wouldn't worry about it,' Ethan replied.

They finished their food, and rather than book flights headed back out of the terminal, Ethan led them to the parking lot and scanned the ranks of vehicles and spotted an old Ford Ranger, one that had survived since what looked like the 1980s. Ethan walked across to it as he slipped out of his pocket a small survival kit that he had brought with him. It contained a number of items that all Marines would have been familiar with, such as medical dressings, a miniature can opener, weapon cleaning fluid and such like. Ethan's also held a small number of lock picks, and within moments he was tinkering with the Ford's locks.

'Seriously?' Lopez asked. 'You're going to help us hide by stealing trucks?'

'It's only temporary,' Ethan explained. 'We'll take this one west, then dump it for another. There's no way that they'll be able to track us.'

The Ranger's driver's door clicked and Ethan opened it and climbed in. Lopez and Trent joined him, and within ninety seconds Ethan got the ignition turned and the engine rumbled into life. Despite the truck's battered exterior, the engine sounded in good condition as Ethan hit the lights and pulled out of the lot.

They saw nobody as they drove out of the airport, except the black Mercedes booked by Garrett waiting for them near the terminal building with its lights on. If there was anyone watching for them to exit the terminal building, their eyes would be on the Mercedes and not on a shabby looking Ford Ranger.

Ethan turned west toward the I70 as Lopez settled in.

'Okay, so now what?'

Ethan shrugged and looked in the rear-view mirror at Trent.

'I guess we do what Garrett suggested,' he replied. 'We go grab ourselves a UFO.'

Trent's eyes widened, both with trepidation and terror as he began to consider the implications of what Ethan was suggesting.

'I don't know how we'd do that,' Trent said. 'I wanted to film the things, not go hijack one. If the US government can't do anything about these things, how are we going to figure out how to catch one? Right now, we can't even safely catch a flight out of the state.'

'You're the genius, right?' Ethan said. 'The only way you're gonna get out of this is if you're too valuable to kill. You need something to trade, and while those images you have are dynamite they're not enough to save your life. The government could easily orchestrate a campaign to render them fakes, and there would be nothing that you could do about it. What you need is hard evidence, something so tangible and solid and unfakeable that nobody could possibly suggest it's anything other than the real deal.'

Trent scoffed in the back seat. 'Huh, no big deal then.'

'He's right, Ethan,' Lopez said. 'Have you thought about what you're proposing? Nobody in history has been able to figure out what these things are, much less capture one.'

'Until recently we didn't have clear images of one either,' Ethan countered. 'We have a way of finding them, and that puts us one step ahead of whoever is tracking us. It's all we have. There's nowhere else to go for Kyle here except into permanent hiding, perhaps as part of the FBI Witness Protection Programme along with his parents.'

Ethan glanced in the mirror and saw Kyle pale considerably as he considered a life where he would never see his home again, where his parents would have to live out the rest of their lives because of what he had done.

'This is all my fault,' he uttered miserably. 'I should have just gone public with the pictures.'

'That would have made sense,' Lopez agreed, 'and probably earned you a lot of money in the process, not a death warrant.'

Kyle Trent punched his own thigh in frustration. Ethan had to feel for the kid. He'd had the best intentions, forcing the government of his country to stop lying to the people for whom they worked. But he had underestimated the lack of control Washington had over certain branches of the military and intelligence community. Not everyone answered to the President of the United States, and Ethan knew that in some cases the president was kept in the dark about much of what went on within the so-called "Black Budget", the tens of billions of tax-payer's dollars spent on military-industrial projects shielded from congressional oversight.

'Kyle, you did what you did and now you're going to have to help us get you out of it. We don't have anyone else we can trust or rely on and I don't want Garrett to stick his neck out any further than he already has. We're on our own, and all we have is that little box of tricks of yours so why not run it and find out whether there's anything happening in Nevada in the next twenty-four hours?'

Kyle sat for a moment in catatonic silence. Lopez leaned back over her seat and flashed him her best smile.

'Why not show the world just what a genius you are, instead of hiding it?'

Kyle's lips curled in a shy smile, and Ethan wondered again why he didn't just let Lopez do all the talking. Trent pulled out his laptop and started it up.

'I'm going to have to connect to the Internet to update any data on recent sightings but I'm well protected, it shouldn't flag up to anyone looking as the IP address is heavily cloaked.'

'Make it fast,' Ethan replied. 'I don't care if you think you're well protected, the people searching for us will have a dozen Kyle Trents working to find you. Once you're done let me know.'

Kyle Trent's fingers rattled on the keyboard as he worked. Ethan could hear the laptop's fan humming to keep it cool as the software began to work.

'Okay,' Kyle said, 'lots of recent sightings over Nevada. The routine will need a few seconds to add the extra data and analyse it.'

Ethan kept driving, one eye on the mirror to both watch Kyle Trent but also to see if they were being tailed. They were heading north on the 70 towards Nevada, probably the last place that the CIA or special operations thought they would go to. With Mackenzie out of the picture for the time being they would have had no reason to go anywhere near the state and so their enemy would not think to…

Ethan frowned.

'What is it?' Lopez asked.

Ethan hadn't really made the connection until now, but the more he thought about it, the more he realised that the attack on Mackenzie made no sense.

'If they hadn't attacked the general we would have taken Kyle Trent right to him, just like we were ordered to.'

Lopez considered this for a moment. 'And they wouldn't have had to track us at all, they could have just sat back and wait for us to walk through their door.'

Ethan and Nicola shared a glance.

'The CIA weren't behind it,' Ethan said. 'They can't have been and besides, Mackenzie said that he was operating off the books, that he hadn't told anyone about the operation at the Barn and had come to us directly on the recommendation of…'

'Jarvis,' Lopez gasped. 'But he's…'

'Out of the game,' Ethan confirmed. 'But if someone else picked up on the images that Kyle sent to the CIA, someone who wasn't really on our side but who had access to that kind of material then they could have sent it out into the world and set *everyone* looking for Kyle.'

Lopez nodded slowly, thinking back to their work with the DIA.

'Mat Zemlya,' she said finally. 'You think that they're involved with all of this?'

Mat Zemlya was the name of a secretive Russian covert operations unit that resembled and had perhaps even been modelled on the Defense Intelligence Agency's ARIES unit. The name meant "Mother Earth", but there was nothing motherly about the unit's operations or their methods. Covert, violent and answering to nobody, their purpose was the infiltration of American intelligence assets and the acquiring of advanced technology for reverse engineering back in

Russia. In the past the unit and its various leaders had shown no concern for human life or international laws and boundaries, killing indiscriminately wherever they were encountered.

'The Russians are involved?' Kyle asked from the back seat.

'We don't know yet,' Ethan cautioned. 'But it's one possibility.'

There was a ping from Kyle's laptop, and he looked down. Ethan and Lopez waited.

'Well?'

'We've got a target,' Kyle said.

'Where is it?' Ethan asked.

Kyle told him, and Ethan bit his lip as he considered the location. 'Damn, this isn't going to be easy.'

***

XXIX

Colonel Rico Savage strode into the mobile command centre that his men had set up in a disused warehouse on the edge of Las Vegas, and with him came a deep aura of displeasure that descended upon his men like a black cloud.

'Sit rep,' he snapped as he reached a pair of desks where operatives manned hastily connected computers.

'We're searching for them,' came the response. 'No information as yet on where they went.'

Savage peered at the screens. Each portrayed multiple law enforcement and public service cameras that were operational at the time of the hunt through the Galleria mall. The operators were skilled observers and were trained to monitor each of the feeds simultaneously in order to identify their quarry, but they were assisted with facial recognition software that helped pick out targets of interest from the throng of shoppers and tourists passing by the cameras.

That, of course, didn't help if the targets happened to be walking away from, or parallel to, the same cameras, which was where the operatives came in. Despite advances in computer recognition technology that could identify people from as little as the shape of their ear, that capability did not translate well to the low-resolution cameras typically fitted within civilian areas. Savage preferred "eyes on the ground" over any technical gadgetry, but this time the old-fashioned way had failed. He turned to the commander of his field team.

'What happened?'

'We identified the target within the Galleria mall and were closing in when another team grabbed him.'

That got Savage's attention real quick. 'Identity?'

'American,' came the response, 'former DIA team known to our database.'

That was a surprise, and in some ways something of a relief. Had the grab team been Russian, as Savage had feared, they would have been facing far greater consequences.

The team leader turned and handed Savage a slim file which he opened to reveal two images and an intelligence brief.

'Ethan Warner,' Savage murmured as he read through the report. 'Former Marine, journo turned PI?'

Savage could admit to himself that he was stunned. His men were some of the best trained covert operatives in the United States inventory and yet a former soldier and gumshoe had given them the slip. While stranger things had happened, he wouldn't allow the team to get away with this without venting his spleen at their commander.

'You got given the slip by frickin' Columbo?'

The commander raised his chin.

'All due respect sir, this man knew what he was doing. He and his partner were already in the Galleria and they had help.'

Savage turned to the operatives at the computers as they supported their commander.

'They had a vehicle waiting outside and they were able to get out of the Galleria and blend in with local traffic. We located their vehicle within a half hour but they had already switched. By the time we caught their trail they'd boarded a helicopter that took off and headed north for McCarran. We're tracking the pilot down now.'

'How long?'

'Already on it, sir,' the commander reported. 'The team should have something concrete within the hour.'

'Good,' Savage replied, 'because I'm going to find it tough to explain how a former Marine who's been out of the service for over a decade outwitted a team of Navy SEALS and Army Rangers. Is that something you want on your CV?'

'No *sir!*'

Savage's cell phone buzzed in his pocket. He gave the commander a cold glare.

'As you were.'

The team dispersed to continue with their duties as Savage walked outside into the darkness and answered the secure line.

'Savage.'

'Where are we with the Trent kid?'

'He's got some friends,' Savage replied. 'Looks like former DIA, they've picked him up and run. How the hell would they have known anything about this, sir? We kept a lid on it from the get-go and it's only been a day.'

There was a long pause on the line.

'I take it that I don't have to impress upon you the importance of finding Trent.'

'Trent isn't the biggest issue now,' Savage replied, unintimidated. 'If the DIA or another agencies are sniffing around this then they're gonna take him under their wing and we'll lose the advantage we've had. Chances are they knew nothing about any of this until Trent and his pal snuck into Dugway and started playing David Bailey with the visitors.'

It wasn't often that Savage could even bring himself to refer to the objects that occasionally appeared over American installations, and even then he could only refer to them as *visitors*. This was more to do with his own dislike of them as it was to do with security over communications. Although not a religious man, Savage was not comfortable with the idea of alien species, or whatever they were, wandering around on American soil. What was more, he was aware of the way in which his superiors held these *things* in regard. They did not know what they were. They did not know why they came or where from. They were not able to be aggressive toward them, because humanity's weapons and technology were feeble in comparison. The end result of all of that, for any military man, was that they were afraid, and that bothered Savage immensely. The most powerful and dangerous men in America did not conceal the presence of UFO activity because of government projects or secrecy or national security. They concealed it because they could not tell the American people that they were scared and that they could not hope to defend the public against these things if they ever turned hostile.

'*A base that you and your team were charged to secure,*' came the response.

'Lines of battle change daily,' Savage countered. 'New skills allow determined folk to break through, however briefly. Trent's breach has been sealed and cannot again be used against us. The focus now is on locating and apprehending him.'

'*His apprehension is no longer enough,*' came the reply. '*I want him silenced, permanently, is that understood?*'

'Yes, sir.'

The line went dead and Savage slipped the cell phone back into his pocket and sighed. Most kids got busted for carrying beer or drugs, or maybe fighting on street corners. Kyle Trent had leap-frogged over all of that, infiltrated one of the most sensitive bases in the world and now had the full might of United States' covert operations units bearing down upon him. The chances of him surviving much longer, even with this Warner and Lopez pair protecting him, were pretty slim.

As if on cue the team called him back in, to where a cell was on speaker phone to an operative in the field.

'Go ahead,' Savage said as he joined his team.

'*We've got camera footage from a traffic camera that shows the helicopter in question descending below 500ft while over the city. That's normally against federal aviation laws so we checked it out and found that it flew to a ranch on the edge of Vegas that has its own airport.*'

'Its own what?'

'*You heard me right sir; runway, terminal, the whole thing. We've got a record of a private jet leaving within four minutes of the helicopter's arrival, scheduled for a stop–over in Virginia. Passenger manifest records only the pilot and one male aboard, but chances are that's where our boy and his new pals went.*'

Savage blinked in amazement. How the hell this had all been arranged at such short notice confounded him for now, but he put that to one side and focussed on the job at hand.

'Who owns the jet?'

'*It was chartered by one Rhys Garrett, a billionaire property magnate. He's the passenger.*'

Savage leaned in toward the phone.

'Find Garrett and find out what he knows. Everyone else, let's pack up and get moving. I want us all in Virginia before nightfall.'

The team dashed to perform their duties, as Savage's superior's words rolled around in his mind; *I want him silenced, permanently.* It was a shame, but Kyle Trent's life was about to come to an abrupt end, and if Warner and Lopez got in the way Savage knew that they too would suffer the same unfortunate fate.

***

XXX

The tide had well and truly turned.

Vigor Vitesky sat in the darkness in an unremarkable car, wearing unremarkable American clothes and reading an unremarkable American newspaper. It was notable about the insular nature of the American press that he had to turn to about page nine to get anything resembling world news: everything else was the world according to America. It was the same on the cable networks he and his men watched in their motel rooms, everything America. The rest of the world might as well not exist, which suited Vigor just fine.

The small articles concerning the other ninety per cent of the inhabited world detailed the recent electoral victory of Vladimir Putin with around seventy-five per cent of the vote. The journalist brought attention to the fact that Putin had no real challenger, the only one who had existed having been barred from running due to corruption charges, a favourite ploy of the Kremlin to prevent "undesirable" candidates from achieving office. Putin's victory had come just a few days after a Soviet traitor and his daughter had been poisoned in the United Kingdom, a likely revenge attack by communist loyalists who yearned for a return of the Politboro and the hardline leadership so embodied by Putin and his entourage.

Vigor set the piece down, which was full of Yankee rhetoric over the lack of democracy and honesty in Putin's Russia, smiling as he considered the rank corruption of most western leaders and the bias of their journalism, at least in America. Their press was owned by corporations, as were their leaders. In Russia, back in the glory days, the Kremlin had been owned by nobody, and anyone who crossed it would find themselves lost to history in the *Gulags* of Siberia.

Vigor's father had served with distinction and honour in the KGB, only to see his rank and prestige, not to mention his respect, lost in the chaos and disaster that was *Glasnost*. Now, decades later and long after his father had drunk himself to death, Vigor was on the warpath for a return to the glory of Soviet Russia. Sadly, that meant a break with Putin's Kremlin, as they were nothing like the Politboro of old.

Though he could barely admit it to himself, he knew that Putin and his corrupt leadership were nothing more than pawns in a larger game. After the collapse of the Soviet Union and the ruinous leadership of Yeltsin, the Russia of old had spiralled into corruption on a scale like nothing ever seen before. While the west crowed about its supposed victory over Communism, Russia was overrun with organised criminal gangs that wormed their way into power from the shadows, holding aloft their strong-man leader Putin as the public face of a very secretive leadership. Putin, the former KGB officer and loyalist, was little more now than the diplomatic face of a country run by thugs and criminals. Most of the successful entreprenuers who had risen to prominence after *Glasnost* had been arrested and jailed on trumped-up charges of corruption or treason and their vast fortunes in gas and oil seized by the state, which of course meant that the companies became the property of criminal gangs keen to advance their power agenda. Forget the street thugs of Moscow or New York – these folks were vastly more powerful and capable of handling billions of dollars worth of business and trade in both legitimate and of course illegal goods.

Vigor had watched his country crumble from within, a place now where Moscow's new veneer of wealth and prosperity masked a landscape of ruin and poverty; where Soviet-era fleets of warships and submarines rusted as hulks in docks across the country, leaking nuclear fuel into rivers and oceans; where half the country could barely feed itself; and where a small few possessed the vast majority of the wealth. For Vigor, Russia was not the answer for it had become every bit as corrupt as the west it so claimed to despise.

For Vigor, a new purity of being was required, and he would stop at nothing to achieve it.

'There they are.'

Vigor watched as the small knot of men they had been following made their way out of an abandoned warehouse building and toward a pair of black SUVs parked near the sidewalk. Although they wore civilian attire, Vigor could tell at a glance that they were military men. Their bearing, the short haircuts, the sunglasses, everything screamed government agent. The Americans, he scoffed silently to himself, so obsessed with their personal image that they inadvertently make themselves conspicuous on what was clearly supposed to be a covert operation.

Vigor sat in a cheaply rented Chevrolet that was probably as old as he was. His men were scattered in several vehicles around the area, only one on watch at any one time and routinely switching to avoid detection and identification. Vigor himself wore simple clothes that the average American wore, and appeared completely non-descript himself. His hair was short, greying at the temples and slightly receding. He was physically fit but not made of cut muscle like the Americans he was watching. He wore unfashionable but comfortable slacks like any middle-aged American might wear, and he veiled his appearance slightly behind a low-brimmed American hat, something like an old cowboy out of Texas might wear. In short, he could vanish into a crowd and never be found, which was why he had been hired. Well, that and the fact that he'd been living in America as part of a sleeper cell for the past twelve years.

'Stay on them, hang back. We'll switch in ten.'

Vigor's driver obeyed without question, and they pulled out a few cars back from the SUVs as they made off east. Vigor's car contained no equipment, but a small van deployed a mile to the west and festooned with both hacking and radio-tracking equipment relayed data to him in real-time via one of his men.

'They're in contact with Langely,' came the information across the airwaves, 'they're tracking the individual as we speak. They'll probably head to the airport. It looks as though the targets made it out by helicopter somehow, Kyle Trent and two other Americans.'

That made sense, although Vigor was surprised that their quarry had moved so quickly. Kyle Trent had made friends fast, although Vigor suspected that the relationship was one-sided. The Americans now with him had merely located Kyle Trent first. What was interesting was that they had not handed him in to officials or law enforcement, but now appeared to be on the run alongside him.

Trent had no criminal record but was someone who was both somewhat anti-capitalist and who had the potential to be hacking into the United States military system. Both were traits incredibly valuable to Russian operatives like Vigor, people with great skills who could be turned to work against their mother country if the price was right. Kyle was young, rebellious, and poor. Vigor could change that in an instant, if he could reach the youth before the Americans yanked him off the streets and hurled him into Florence Super-Max or similar.

'He's right,' Vigor's driver said as he listened to the information being fed to him from the hacking team, 'they're heading for McCarran. Their people are booking flights for Virginia.'

Kyle Trent had fled the state then. Vigor considered his options. He had his own footage of what had occurred at Dugway, and if released anonymously to the American public it could generate shockwaves – an American boy murdered on American soil by American troops. That in itself would serve to shake up a presidency already thoroughly corrupt, unpopular and suffering from multiple scandals as well as burgeoning military problems in Syria. It might also serve to force the Americans to cut off or otherwise subdue their pursuit of Kyle Trent, leaving the way more open for Vigor and his team to whisk the boy away to somewhere where he could become useful to them.

Now, it seemed as though Trent was heading for Virginia, the home of the CIA. But if the people who were with him were intending to hand him over to the authorities, then why would they not have simply handed him to the Americans that Vigor was watching at that very moment?

'Something's wrong,' he said. 'They would not need to go to Virginia, they could hand the boy in anywhere. The FBI has field offices in every state.'

'Maybe it's their inter-agency squabbling at play again?' Ivor said.

Vigor nodded but he wasn't certain. Trent was a wild card, a maverick, he wouldn't want to give himself up to the very people who had killed his friend. He would want to go public, to shout to the world that he was being hunted so that the entire world would watch him, protecting his life in the process. So why had he fled Nevada in the first place?

'Stay put,' he said finally. 'The government teams are running around like headless chickens. Leaving the state only would have made sense before we shot rounds at General Mackenzie, to prevent a handover. They'll consider him a target and won't approach now.'

'Then they may intend to go to the CIA Headquarters and hand him in there directly,' Ivor went on.

'The CIA could have collected him from Las Vegas, or anywhere for that matter,' Vigor countered. 'There would be no need for him to be delivered to their doorstep. Someone as valuable as Kyle Trent now is would have been picked up from anywhere. No, they have another agenda.' Vigor smiled to himself. 'Perhaps they intend to gather more data to solidify their claims. Tell me, Ivor, where would they go to do that?'

Ivor shrugged. 'They wouldn't go anywhere. If they wanted to capture more evidence of UFOs, they would stay right here in Nevada or maybe go to California. They'd stay in the west of the country…'

Vigor smiled and nodded. Ivor realised what he was thinking.

'If we're wrong, we'll never catch up with him again,' Ivor warned.

'If we're right, nor will the Americans,' Vigor replied. 'We stay here. Do we know who Kyle's mysterious benefactors are?'

'Ethan Warner and Nicola Lopez,' Ivor replied, handing Vigor a file. 'Former DIA agents, they've been responsible for scuppering several Russian operations in international soil over the years. Someone, somewhere must have sent them in early.'

Vigor read the brief files they possessed on the two Americans, and the more he read the angrier he became. As he finished he reflected for a moment on how just two individuals could have created so much havoc around the world between them, and not be in early graves.

'They've been in Nevada for at least two days,' Ivor reported. 'They've been visiting various locations, one of which was near Creech Air Force base.'

Vigor's eyes narrowed.

'Find out what they were up to out there,' he said. 'It may have a bearing on our search for them. And find out what you can about that helicopter, see if we can get a sense of how they got away. It might help us anticipate their next move.'

Ivor began working as Vigor settled in. They would stay in Nevada, picking up what they could of the American transmissions and piecing together enough information about Kyle Trent to grab him from under the noses of their enemy. Trent was on the run from Americans, not Russians, and he had something to offer that the Yanks would never dare present to a teenage runaway.

'I want Trent on our team,' he said finally. 'Mat Zemlya needs people like him. He is not to be harmed in any way whatsoever, is that understood?'

Vigors men nodded in unison.

Right now, the only thing that could save Russia from the wolves of corruption was absolute power and control via an untainted source. If Vigor was right, and Trent was able to predict when and where UFOs would appear, then that was precisely the kind of technology that could turn his mother country around almost overnight. Vigor was damned if he would allow that crucial advantage slip to either the Americans or the thugs behind the Kremlin.

***

XXXI

'There's no way in hell we're getting in there.'

Ethan sat in the car, which he had driven into a truck stop fifty miles north of Vegas and parked around back to avoid being spotted easily by anyone who might still be in the area. They had been driving for almost eighteen hours, with only a few hours' sleep, and his belly and chest ached. He couldn't tell if the recurring pain he was getting was due to the long hours of travelling or just his age, but he periodically rubbed the same spots as faint surges of pain lanced deep within him. Maybe he should see a doctor or something, but right now that wasn't an option. Although he felt certain that they had given Special Ops the slip, caution had saved his life on more than one occasion.

'I know it's a long shot but this is what the data is telling us,' Kyle insisted.

'Even if we did get sight of something,' Ethan replied, 'there's no way that we could get close enough to capture one of these things. The best we could get is more video evidence, and as we've already seen that can easily be dismissed as hoax material, even if it isn't. People won't believe what they see anymore, only the experts would be able to tell it apart from a hoax and the government has plenty of experts it can hire to denounce anything you take to the media.'

Kyle slumped back into the rear seat of the car as Lopez shot Ethan a scolding look.

'You could at least *try* to consider it.'

Ethan dragged a hand down his face.

'A few days ago, you didn't want any part of this. Now we're on the run from government sponsored troops, with a fugitive in the back seat, and you're considering wandering into one of the most famous and well protected military bases in the world?'

'We don't have to get in there, just see what's happening if the Hydra says that's where the action is.'

Ethan shook his head in disbelief. 'You're talking about the Tonopah Test Range Airport. That place is closed down and has been for years and has security around it as high as that around Area 51.'

'Which begs the question,' Kyle interrupted, 'if there's nothing going on out there and it's been shut down, why is the security so tight and why can't anyone get close to the place?'

Ethan thought for a moment as he sat in the car and looked out at the lonely mountains. The states of Nevada, Utah and others were some of the most desolately beautiful in the United States, and also some of the least populated. Scorching deserts, barren mountain ranges and vicious temperature changes between night and day rendered some of the wilderness virtual no-go areas for people. And yet, despite the low population density, these were considered some of the most likely places for people to see UFOs.

'What do we know about this guy you say can help us?'

'Benjamen Freeman,' Kyle said.

'Benjamen who?' Lopez asked.

'Old Ben Freeman was a NASA physicist who worked on Project Blue Book for the US government back in the sixties, before they shut it down. He investigated hundreds of incidents, many of which were reported by military pilots and other officials. When the final report of Project Blue Book was released Ben refused to sign it, citing a cover-up and he left NASA the same year.'

'So, what's this guy got that we haven't?' Lopez asked.

'Well, Ben headed out west from Florida and settled somewhere out here in the deserts. He made it his mission to research the UFO phenomenon. After he left NASA he worked as a part of private research projects that created exotic materials, and he owned the patents to several that went on to be used in many household objects. That alone made him some serious cash and gave him the freedom to pursue his fascination with UFOs on his own time. The guy has published literally hundreds of papers on UFOs but none of them reach the mainstream because the scientific journals always reject anything to do with what they refer to as paranormal or pseudo-science.'

Ethan turned to Kyle.

'If this guy went to where the UFOs were most likely to appear, then he ought to be here in Nevada, right, somewhere on the 37th parallel?'

Kyle nodded, pulling out his laptop computer once again and tapping some keys.

'He might not know about the 37th but he would have headed to somewhere like Rachel, Nevada, or pretty much anywhere on the Extra-Terrestrial Highway.'

'The what?' Lopez asked.

'Nevada State Route 375,' Kyle smiled in response. 'It's the state highway through south central Nevada that runs close to the Nellis Test Range and Area 51. It's been associated with strange phenomena and UFO sightings since long before the phenomenon hit public culture, and it's now a bit of a tourist attraction for UFO nuts from around the world.'

Ethan had vaguely heard of the town of Rachel, which was located north east of the Nellis Range and was a Mecca of sorts for UFO geeks and anyone with an interest in what the government was up to and might be trying to hide.

'He wouldn't be in Rachel,' he said. 'Too much in the media. Is there anywhere else he could be hiding out?'

Kyle squinted at his screen and nodded.

'There's an area to the north of the town, within easy reach, called Quinn Canyon Range. It's the location of a ghost town called Adaven. There's not much there according to this, and it was abandoned somewhere in the 1950s. Just a few old ranches and buildings remain, but if there was enough to support a town once…'

Ethan nodded as he reversed out of their parking space and turned for the state highway.

'Then it might be able to support one man now,' he finished Kyle's sentence for him. 'We'll avoid Rachel and give this Benjamen guy a shot. If he's still alive, he might even be able to fill us in on what the government is really afraid of.'

*

General Mackenzie was pretty sure that his family were safe, but he wasn't so sure about himself.

McCain had booked him a room in a motel just outside of Langley but far enough away that he wouldn't be an easy target for anyone trying to watch him. Mackenzie had insisted that there be no detail assigned to him, despite the DDCIA's pleas to the contrary. Mackenzie was convinced that whoever was targeting himself and his family, they were doing so from within the CIA or at the very least within the government and intelligence community.

The room was small, spartan and set within a box compound of cheap rooms. Trash littered the parking lot situated alongside the west flank of the motel. Mackenzie peered through the grubby linen hanging across the windows of his room and looked down to see one man passing a small package to another, cash coming back the other way in return. The exchange was over in a moment as they went their separate ways. Drugs, most likely. Into another room staggered a woman in her forties, or so she looked, her high heels wobbling unsteadily, her long black hair unkempt and a cigarette smouldering between her fingers. Her skirt reached only half way down her thighs, and she was followed by a shabby-looking man with receding hair and a flabby gut who closed the door behind them. Mackenzie glanced up across the road and saw a truck stop nearby, which explained all that he needed to know.

He moved away from the window, feeling like an imposter in this cold and seedy world. The girl on the reception desk had looked him up and down as though he had come from another planet when he had requested a room. He could tell that she didn't see many guys looking like him come here, and then she had shrugged and swapped keys for cash. Mackenzie had felt dirty, as though she figured he was here to hire one of the hookers or get high on something.

McCain's instructions were clear: don't go outside.

That frustrated Mackenzie greatly because he wasn't the kind of guy who found it easy to sit on his hands and do nothing, especially when it was his family that were being targeted. His wife and daughters were now in deep cover in a cabin north of DC, owned by a friend of a friend who had no direct connection to Mackenzie. Cash paid, no questions asked, just for a few days while Mackenzie was tied up with high-security work. Now, he felt the need to do something, *anything*, to find out who was targeting him.

Mackenzie sat down on a simple seat in one corner of the room and closed his eyes. He allowed himself to slip back in his mind to the first time that he'd encountered anything to do with this project, the one that had suddenly placed his life in jeapordy.

The file had come to his desk at the same time as McCain had approached him regarding the event in Scotland, and its secrecy level meant that nobody could be contacted regarding its contents. Although there was no direct way for Mackenzie to back-track the files and locate Jarvis or whomever had actually sent him the project, there might be clues within the paperwork that would reveal the most likely source. It clearly had not been from the White House or any other official body, so that ruled out normal channels of communication with the Pentagon. There was nothing in the way that the report had been worded that struck him as out of place or indicative of a certain post or command. That left only one thing, the name; Douglas Jarvis.

The former DIA agent and Marine officer had been part of ARIES, a secretive DIA sponsored team tasked with what amounted to paranormal investigations. That in turn had led him on to Ethan Warner and Nicola Lopez. They appeared to be patriots through and through and were even now risking their necks to protect Kyle Trent, so the threat was not coming from them. When he had suggested to McCain that the CIA might be behind the hit, McCain had been shocked and had said that it was "much worse than that" but had not then explained what he had meant.

Mackenzie rubbed his forehead between the fingers of his right hand. Warner and Lopez. Their records indicated that they were routinely attacked by elements of various foreign powers, most often the Russians. Mackenzie thought for a moment, about everything that he had seen, and then suddenly it hit him as hard as the sniper's bullet had hit the kid, Greg, out there in the lonely deserts.

He saw the sniper's shot hitting the kid's head, and suddenly he understood what McCain had meant.

'It's much worse than that.'

Mackenzie bolted up out of his seat, grabbed his jacket and rushed for the door. The Dugway troops hadn't opened fire on anyone. That meant there was another player in the game, and suddenly the attempted hit on himself and his family made sense. He knew that he had to get the word out before this whole thing blew up in their faces and Ethan and Nicola found themselves face to face with…

Mackenzie opened the apartment door in time to see four men rush in. There was no time to fight, no time even to react. They ploughed into him and he crashed down onto his back on the threadbare rug in his room, the four men plunging down on top of him. Gloved hands silenced any cry he might have made and he felt a sharp pain in his neck as something icy cold was injected into his body.

Mackenzie cried out, but no sound came forth as his limbs became numb and his vision faded to blackness.

***

XXXII

Quinn Canyon Range,

Adaven, Nevada

The map barely marked the route as Ethan drove down a dusty trail that led off the state highway and into the barren hills of Quinn Canyon Range, the sun just rising over the desert wilderness. They had passed a couple of ranch stations on the way a few miles back, but that was the last they had seen of civilisation as they drove across the blistering desert toward the canyon wash.

The trail followed the winding canyon as they entered into its depths, the sand-coloured hills either side of them peppered with thorn scrub and devoid of anything approaching human habitation. They drove for a mile, and then another, Ethan cautious of their remote location.

'We'll have to turn back soon,' he said. 'Without spare water, we're in real danger out here. If the car quits it'll be a self-rescue job because nobody knows where we are.'

Lopez nodded, more than aware of their vulnerability out here. Kyle Trent seemed oblivious, shaking his head as he read from his laptop.

'The amount of work this guy did is incredible,' he enthused. 'I mean, some of his theories are right out there but he backs them up with hard evidence and examples. If even half of what this guy thinks is right, we're looking at the whole UFO phenomenon the wrong way around.'

Ethan was about to ask what Kyle meant when he spotted something in the brush ahead. Angular, awkward looking, it was as out of place in nature as anything he'd seen and the sign that they were encountering man-made objects.

'There's something out here,' he said as he slowed the car.

Ethan rounded the corner and saw the hood of an abandoned vehicle, its bodywork rusted to an orange-brown. It looked like something he had seen on black and white television shows, a 1930s vintage vehicle that had been out here in the deserts for close to a century.

'We won't be getting that running again if this car quits,' Lopez observed, and then she sighed. 'Nobody's been out here for decades, we're wasting our time.'

Ethan shook his head. 'No, we're not.'

'There's nobody here!' Lopez said as she pointed at the canyon around them.

'No,' Ethan agreed, 'but there was.'

He pointed over the hood of the car, and for a moment Lopez didn't get it. But then she realised what he was looking at.

'I'll be damned.'

The winds of the open desert constantly shifted, hiding trails and patterns in the sands, but here in the canyon Ethan could see the trail left by a vehicle, and that trail could not have been more than a day or two old to still be here.

'Someone's here,' he said. 'Let's just hope it's this Ben Freeman and he's...'

A gunshot shattered the silence outside and Ethan slammed on the brakes as a puff of dust burst on the trail a couple of yards ahead of the car. Ethan jammed the car in reverse and was about to hightail it backwards down the track when Kyle Trent leaped out of the vehicle and waved his hands in the air.

'Don't shoot!'

Ethan was about to yell at Kyle to get back into the car when he heard another gunshot and a spurt of dust whipped up near where Kyle stood. The sound of the shot echoed down the canyon, that of a double-barrelled shotgun. Ethan could not see the shooter but he knew for sure that no trained military soldier would use a shotgun in terrain like this, the weapon far too inaccurate to confirm a kill unless you were within fifty yards or so.

'They've fired warning shots only,' Lopez observed.

'On target,' Ethan nodded as he slipped the car into neutral.

Kyle Trent was standing in front of the car with his hands still in the air as he called out.

'Ben? Ben Freeman, is that you?'

His voice echoed down the canyon as Ethan turned off the engine. There was no point in running now, and neither he nor Lopez were armed. They waited in silence for what felt like an age, nothing but the hot desert wind moaning through the valley around them, and then a voice called back.

'Who's askin'?'

Ethan glanced in the direction of the voice. He could see nothing but scrub and rock on the hillsides, the canyon playing tricks and carrying sound this way and that.

'Kyle Trent! I'm a… a computer hacker. I managed to make a program that predicts where UFOs will appear. I need your help with something.'

Smart kid, Ethan thought. Kyle had left out anything about the government shooting his friend and pursuing them across the country. Despite his earlier misgivings, he was starting to like Trent. He got out of the car and moved to stand alongside Trent.

'Who's the bodyguard?' the voice yelled from everywhere and nowhere at once.

'Ethan,' Kyle replied, 'he's helping me with his partner.

As if on cue, Lopez got out of the car. She moved to stand on the other side of Kyle. Ethan wasn't sure if it was the wind or not, but as Lopez appeared he could have sworn he heard the man say "hot damn" and cough. Lopez certainly looked the part as her long black hair snaked like a banner on the breeze and the low sunlight illuminated her face.

'Who's the broad?'

Ethan smiled as he wondered how hard Lopez would hit the mystery man for that.

'Nicola Lopez,' she shouted back, 'and you call me that again, I'll take that shotgun and shove it up your ar…'

'I'm a comin',' the man yelled, and stepped out almost right in front of them as though he had appeared in a puff of smoke.

To Ethan's surprise, the side of the hills and gulleys just ahead and to their left was in fact a simple canvass hide, painted the exact same colour as the hill behind it and carefully disguised with scrub bushes. The narrow approach road meant that their perspective on the hide was limited to a narrow angle, and so they could not see that it was not a part of the natural hillside until the man stepped out from behind it into view and broke the illusion.

The man was in his sixties, Ethan reckoned, with a grizzly grey beard and half-moon spectacles. He held the shotgun at port arms, neither threatening them nor accepting them as friends either. Kyle took the initiative.

'We've got some footage here that I think you'd like to see, but some of the data we've gathered is too complex for us to understand. We need your help to figure it out.'

Again, Kyle played the old man like a fiddle, teasing him in with precisely what they figured he'd like to hear. Ben Freeman peered at them suspiciously.

'Government send you?' he half-asked, half-stated, then pointed at Ethan. 'You look like you've been in the military.'

'Marines, twenty years ago,' Ethan admitted, sensing an opportunity. 'We're not working for anyone, but we are interested in what you'd have to say about what we've got here. I've never seen images like it.'

'That so?' Ben chirped. 'That'd be just the thing to get me all excited and drop m'guard, don't you agree?'

Ethan smiled ruefully. The old man wasn't going to be swayed so easily, but it was Lopez who replied.

'Yeah, you got us. We're working for the CIA. We're a covert hunter team sent here to erase you from existence. We were offered a platoon of troops, an attack helicopter and explosives but nah, we just wandered out into the desert in a Lincoln, unarmed and with a geeky teenager in tow, 'cause we figured that would buckle you at the knees.'

The old man cackled a laugh that sounded like crows feasting on a carcass. The laugh instantly degenerated into a membrane-tearing cough that made Ethan's eyes water just to hear it. Ben Freeman doubled over and Ethan hurried to his side as the shotgun fell from his grip. He caught the weapon, and Ben looked up at him with eyes both streaming with mirth and also filled with sudden fear and uncertainty.

Ethan turned the shotgun around, set the safety catch to on, and then held it out for the old man.

'We're not here to harm you, and we really do need your help.'

Ben Freeman got his lungs under control as Lopez and Kyle joined them. The relief in the old man's eyes was plain to see as he realised that they were kindred spirits and not the government assassins he so plainly feared had found him.

'You'd better come this way,' he said, his voice rough.

***

XXXIII

Ethan could see that all that remained of Adaven was a few weathered shacks and what looking like abandoned mining equipment that lay scattered and rusting amid the thorn scrub. He followed Ben to what looked like just another abandoned homestead nestled against the hills, but as they got closer it became clear that the homestead was in fact in perfect working order, the battered walls merely a shell tacked on to give it a weathered appearance.

The canyon walls rose up either side of them to great heights, effectively concealing the homestead even from air traffic passing overhead.

Ben led the way inside. The living room before Ethan was little more than an immense library with some scattered chairs and a sofa. The whole place was scented with the odours of old paper, leather and books. Shelves lined every wall, filled with reference books on physics, astronomy, electromagnetism, chemistry and biology. Kyle wandered into this plethora of material, both wide eyed and confused.

'Do you have a computer?' he asked Ben.

'Pah!' the old man scoffed. 'I do have one but it isn't connected to the Internet, damnable thing.'

'You don't have an internet connection?' Kyle asked, stunned.

Ethan was mildly surprised but the old man looked at Kyle as though he were an imbecile. 'For every bit of valuable information on the Internet, there is a thousand times more garbage! The Internet is a trash can for the bile of humanity's wretched bowels, the repository of all the inane gossip and drivel that was once confined to conversations and could be denounced face to face. Instead, we have a digital crucible where anyone can say anything, where falsehoods and outright lies have become the currency of mankind.'

'Not on Facebook then?' Lopez murmured.

Ben didn't dignify her flippancy with a reply as he spread his arms to encompass the room around them. 'Once, the printed word was the currency of knowledge, and if one wrote drivel you could be assured that others would present them with that drivel and demand evidence, to prove that what they had written was real. Books required bibliographies, so others could also check the reference and validate or reject the author's claims. This, my friends, is knowledge.'

Lopez scanned the shelves. 'I'd have a tough time squeezing that lot into my back pocket, where my phone lives. I like to travel light. Kyle, show the professor here what you've got.'

'I don't want to see it,' Ben snapped.

'What?' Ethan uttered. 'You've got to see the pictures, they're electrifying.'

'They're worthless,' Ben insisted. 'I could sit and watch *Independence Day* and be told that it looked amazing, but I'd still know that it was produced with digital animation. It's just pictures.'

Kyle's wonder morphed into anger. 'My friend died to get these pictures here.'

Old Ben froze in motion and peered at them. Kyle's careful screening of the truth was shattered in an instant.

'What have you brought to my home?' the old man growled.

Ethan stepped in, not wanting to lose Ben's assistance.

'The photographs and video Kyle took were shot at a place called Dugway Proving Ground. Someone opened fire when they detected his presence, and one of his friends was shot and killed. They're hunting for Kyle right now, because of what he's come here to show you. That's about how real *they* consider it to be.'

Ben Freeman thought for a moment, and then he sat down on an old sofa and sighed wearily.

'I've managed to stay happily hidden out here for more than twenty years, and you bring the military to my doorstep?'

'You're not hidden,' Lopez replied. 'You need supplies, medicine, food. You're known to be in Rachel from time to time. It didn't take Sherlock Holmes to find you Ben, we managed it in a couple hours. The military likely knew you were here all along.'

'Yes,' Ben agreed, 'and they left me alone here. Now what's going to happen?'

'Look at what we've brought here,' Ethan urged him. 'Help us in any way that you can, and then we'll leave and dummy trail the military right past Rachel and right past you. They won't know we were ever here.'

'It's still just pictures,' Ben resisted.

'It's not,' Kyle replied. 'It's the data they're after.'

'What data?'

Kyle perched on the edge of a chair and started talking. Ethan and Lopez waited in silence as Kyle laid it all out for the old man; the data gathering and the PredPol predictive policing program that he had hacked and appropriated for himself; the development of the Hydra and the data crunching that he had peformed; and the big data from MUFON and other sources that had allowed him to begin predicting when and where UFOs might appear. Ben Freeman listened in silence as Kyle went on.

'The Hydra predicted a UFO appearance in Scotland, United Kingdom, and another in Utah at the Dugway facility a few days later. It was that information that allowed me to be present at the scene and film UFOs. We got images in optical, ultra-violet and infra-red light, like nothing anyone's ever seen. The government troops want the images but it's really the data they're after.'

Kyle did not mention the fact that he had been provoking the government into declassifying its UFO files, demanding full disclosure "or else" he'd go public with the images. Ben Freeman peered at Kyle for a long time before he finally spoke.

'You can predict when UFOs will appear?'

'Yes sir,' Kyle nodded, 'with about seventy-five to eighty per cent accuracy.'

Ben did not move for a long moment. When he did, it seemed to Ethan that he was doing so with guarded interest. He got up and walked to a shelf, unerringly selecting a folder tucked between ranks of books. He dusted it off and walked back to his seat, flopping down into it as he opened the folder.

'In almost forty years of investigations, I have found precisely five cases of what can definitely be termed alien spacecraft being encountered by human beings on this planet.'

Ethan moved closer to the old man without realising it, his eyes fixed on the folder in his lap.

'Seriously?' Lopez replied. 'Just five?'

'Oh, that doesn't mean there aren't more of them out there,' Ben said. 'It just means that with the data we have, five is the number of cases that are without doubt extra terrestrial in origin. They are the cases which I have studied the most, and they are the ones that have revealed the most intriguing and solid information I have on what these things are and what they're doing here.'

Kyle moved closer to Ben too, his laptop open.

'We need to share our information,' he said. 'If we can figure out what's been going on all these years, we might have the key to advancing humanity, not to mention getting a bunch of bad-ass dudes off my back.'

Ben Freeman briefly removed his spectacles and sighed as he replied.

'I'm afraid that won't be possible.'

'Why not?' Lopez challenged, as eager as Ethan to hear what was in the file. 'People have a right to know about these things. There's a seven-year old girl who's battling depression and seizures because of encounters with these things and you won't tell us what the hell's going on?'

Ben Freeman shook his head, despite his obvious sorry at hearing of the young girls' plight.

'I don't have a problem with telling you everything that I know,' he replied. 'The problem is that the government will never speak of it, will never fully disclose what it knows. It's not because they don't want to. It's not even because they fear other countries gaining access to exotic materials or technologies, because these things have shown up in countries other than the United States and you don't see Russians flying out of the Solar System aboard the USS Enterprise starship, do you now?'

Ethan frowned.

'Then why won't they release the information and tell the people what they know?'

'For the same reason that I haven't gone public with what I know,' Ben Freeman replied quietly. 'It's because, if I'm right, the reason we see UFOs in our skies is too disturbing for most people to adequately understand and cope with.'

***

XXXIV

'We need to know,' Kyle insisted. 'We don't have anyone else to turn to and nowhere else to run. It doesn't matter how disturbing it is, because having your friend's face shot off right in front of you kind of trumps everything else.'

Lopez moved closer to the old man.

'That little girl I mentioned? If her seizures keep getting worse, sooner or later she'll suffer a cerebral haemorrhage that will end her life. If you don't do it for Kyle or for us, let us know what you know so that we can maybe use it to help Sophie.'

Ben Freeman looked up at Lopez.

'You do realise that's blatant emotional blackmail of the highest order?'

'I do,' Lopez replied. 'It's a woman thing.'

Ben sighed mightily once more and opened the folder. Kyle almost tripped over himself as he moved closer and listened intently as Ben spoke.

'The five encounters that I spoke of as are follows and are supported by a plethora of physical or other evidence that over the years I have been able to verify as being legitimate; the Laredo, Texas encounter in 1948, when a disc-shaped craft of approximately ninety feet in diameter crashed in Mexico just south of the Texas border. The US Government actually requested permission from Mexico to allow a military team to cross the border and collect what they claimed was a crashed test vehicle. Mexico allowed the team in and the debris was retrieved and spirited away by the Americans before anyone could get a good look at it.'

Ben turned the page.

'The Dalnegorsk incident, in southeastern Russia in 1986. A spherical object of some sixty feet diameter crashed into a hill near the town of Dalnegorsk. Debris and residue collected from the crash site was studied by Soviet scientists in various institutes, their research carefully followed by the CIA. The scientists discovered that iron within the samples had different atomic arrangements to the iron we know, and that not only would the objects appear to defy gravity from time to time but they would also spontaneously vanish from sight, doing so once in front of four witnesses.'

Ethan noticed that the file contained only basic details, a summary of each of the cases in question.

'Kecksburg, Virginia, 1965. A bell-shaped UFO streaked through the night sky over much of the United States before crashing near Kecksburg. Tracked on radar, the object was examined by several local people who gave detailed descriptions of a bell-shaped object with strange writing around the perimeter that resembled Egyptian hieroglyphics. Within an hour of the crash, military teams with no insignia sealed off the area and the object was later carried away on a flat-bed truck under armed escort. Witnesses were intimidated by the military into remaining silent about the event, to which the government has never admitted sending any of its troops. The town to this day has a model of the UFO, based on witness descriptions, suspended near the main street.'

'Die Glocke,' Lopez said to Ethan, who nodded as Ben went on, remembering the scant descriptions in old Nazi documents of "The Bell", a strange device apparently recovered by Germans from a UFO crash in 1937.

'The Cash-Landrum incident, December 1980, Dayton, Texas. Two women and a seven-year old boy driving late at night witnessed a diamond-shaped UFO descend over the road they were driving along. It forced them to stop and came close enough for them to identify that it was made of metal and had flames or energy of some kind being emitted from beneath it. Heat from the object made the car exterior too hot to touch. As they were watching, CH-47 Chinook helicopters visible in the light from the object arrived in the area and the UFO moved off. All three of the witnesses suffered burns and radiation poisoning, with Betty Cash losing hair and skin as well as developing large blisters. She was hospitalised for almost a month after the incident. Investigators later discovered that the patch of road where the encounter had taken place had been resurfaced within days of the event, but that the local authorities knew nothing of the resurfacing work being done.'

Ethan felt the hairs on the backs of his arms tingling as he considered each of the cases and the supporting evidence that Ben was citing. These were not random, hearsay encounters with lights in the sky or cases of mistaken identity – these were encounters with objects not understood by mankind that had left lasting and tangible impressions on the witnesses.

'Japan Airlines Flight 1628 incident, November 1986, over Alaska. A JAL Boeing 747 cargo aircraft witnessed a UFO the size of two aircraft carriers, as well as several smaller objects, which followed their airplane for almost an hour. The UFOs were detected on ground radar shadowing the 747. After the incident, an investigator from the Federal Aviation Authority sent to examine the case was asked to present his material and evidence to a board consisting of CIA officers and Vice Admiral Donald D. Engen. At the end of the presentation, the CIA confiscated all of the evidence and warned everyone involved not to talk about the incident. The JAL pilot was grounded for years as punishment for talking about the UFO to the press, a clear message to all career pilots both military and civilian – don't talk publicly about UFOs or your job is on the line.'

Ben Freeman turned to the last page in his file.

'The USS Nimitz incident, off the coast of San Diego, California. Commanders David Fravor and Jim Slaight flying an F-18 Super Hornet from the carrier Nimitz were vectored onto an unknown radar contact flying nearby. When they intercepted, it was described as about forty feet long and shaped like a Tic Tac. The object would manoeuvre apparently at random, zoom climbing to eighty thousand feet and then descending to just fifty feet above the ocean. It completely and utterly out-performed the jet fighter, which was unable to get any closer to the object. Not only was it tracked on both the Hornet's radar and that of their wingman's, it was also tracked by the Nimitz herself. Video footage of the event shot through the Hornet's Heads Up Display was released recently and clearly shows the object being tracked, while recordings of the pilot's voices shows their astonishment at how the object is manoeuvring. You can watch it today on YouTube, so well known is the footage.'

Ethan knew then, in that one instant of time, that he was convinced of the reality of the UFO phenomenon. He'd seen the footage of the F-18 UFO intercept on the television, but the light-hearted way in which it was discussed by the anchors meant that he had forgotten about it almost as quickly as he'd seen it. This was a case where a military pilot had intercepted a UFO in broad daylight, at visual range, detected it on radar and even *filmed* the damned thing, and yet nobody seemed to know anything about it.

'This is why your pictures won't affect a thing,' Ben Freeman said to Kyle, as though reading Ethan's mind. 'We already have video of UFOs actually in the public domain, shot by military pilots during routine training flights. This already exists and anyone with an Internet connection can watch it at any time on YouTube. That's how far we've come.'

Ethan could see that Kyle Trent was looking somewhat defeated.

'We didn't come all this way to be told that what we have is useless,' he said. 'The government wouldn't be chasing us so hard if there was no value to what we have.'

'Indeed,' Ben seemed to agree, 'and what you have is indeed valuable. What I am certain the government does not, and never has possessed, is a working UFO. They only have crashed ones or debris from crashes, nothing they've been able to use properly. Even the Roswell event was merely the debris of a crashed flying object.'

Lopez rolled her eyes. 'Seriously, *that* one?'

Ben Freeman looked up at her over his spectacles. 'That, young lady, is what the Internet does, along with the media and the compliance of the government. It has been the government's mission for years to render any serious UFO incident the subject of ridicule, to the extent that many witnesses won't come forward for fear of that public ridicule. It's how they silence ordinary people, whereas with military and commercial pilots it's intimidation and the threat of losing their jobs that maintains the veil of silence and secrecy about UFOs. I won't bore you with unnecessary details about Roswell as it's obviously one of the best known UFO cases in the world, but what I will tell you is what happened on the day and what the people involved in it were able to say on their deathbeds and no sooner.'

Lopez retreated in silence as Ben went on.

'The crashed disc everyone knows about, reported to the authorities at Roswell by a rancher who discovered the debris field after a severe thunderstorm the previous night. The United States Army Air Force reported with some delight in the national press that they had discovered a crashed flying saucer. However, a day later it retracted the report and said that it was a crashed surveillance balloon from something called Project Mogul. The debate about the event has raged ever since, but what is most important is the testimony of those involved, such as Jesse Marcel. In the wake of the military retracting the article on a crashed disc, Marcel privately maintained that the disc was real and that the army had no idea what to do with it. He also never claimed to have found any alien bodies, or that there was a massive security shut down of the base around the event, or any of the other conspiracies that have been spouted as fact around the Roswell event.' Ben Freeman took a breath as he looked up at Ethan. 'The Roswell event occurred, and something unusual *was* recovered from the New Mexico desert. But beyond that we know very little.

'And Roswell doesn't make your list because…?' Lopez asked.

'Because it highlights so much about the flaws and the uncertainty surrounding UFO reports. We know something happened then, just as we know now that UFOs are seen commonly all around the world. It's not a secret – they're up there and they're real. What we don't know is what the hell they are and what they're doing here, but the military have made some progress and it can be sensed, if not seen, in their desire to downplay anything that constitutes a serious and well-observed sighting. They're afraid of what these things really are and what they're doing here.'

'And what *are* they doing here?' Lopex pressed the old man, losing patience.

Ben Freeman removed his spectacles and considered his words carefully.

'In line with all official investigations into these kinds of sightings, I consider it indisputable that we are being visited by solid, flying craft that were not built by human hands. Where they come from is not certain, but a number of common factors suggest that their purpose is similar. Whether they be diamond shaped, flame emitting, radioactive craft, white Tic Tacs as big as a boat or aircraft carrier sized mother vessels, there appears to be one common theme: they know we're here and they react to our presence. That does not necessarily signify intelligence, but it does suggest some level of control or awareness. In conclusion, there are only three real possibilities that make any sense against the canvass of UFO experiences. The first is that these things are extra terrestrial drones, somewhat automated, which react at basic levels to the human presence or that of biological life in general, which would explain their often-erratic behaviour that seems both intelligent and yet unpredictable at the same time.'

'And the second?' Kyle asked.

Ben Freeman replaced his spectacles.

'That these things are not alien craft at all and are in fact controlled by us. They're not aliens crossing the galaxy to find humans, they originate from here and are travelling not through space but through time.'

***

XXXV

'Travelling through time?' Lopez repeated.

Kyle Trent shook his head.

'Nah, I'm not buying that. They *must* be alien craft.'

'Why *must* they be alien craft?' Ben Freeman challenged. 'You're commiting the same logical error that hardline religious believers do: starting from a point of belief and then seeking only evidence that supports your position, while not considering any which does not. They don't have to be anything at all, but when you think about it it does explain quite a lot.'

'Such as?' Ethan asked.

'The lack of time travellers for one thing,' Freeman replied cheerfully. 'People who say time travel is impossible often cite the fact that future people haven't shown up here. But in UFOs we have a phenomenon which accounts for that. There is a celebrated case from 1960 when an Anglican Australian Missionary, William Gill, working in Papua New Guinea made the best-attested, longest and clearest sighting of a UFO in history. It hovered over the forests for more than twenty-five minutes in front of at least a dozen witnesses, all of whom signed independent confirmation documents describing what they saw.'

'I know about this one,' Kyle Trent said. 'Gill and the parishoners saw a large, silver, metallic disc with several lights and visible landing gear. What made the case so amazing isn't just the combined testimony, or the fact that Gill had no prior interest or connection with the phenomena. It's that they all reported seeing human figures aboard the craft who seemed to be working on something, and when Gill waved at them, the figures waved back.'

Lopez almost coughed. 'They waved back?'

'Right back at them,' Freeman replied, 'much to their surprise. After that, these beings then seemed to lose interest in their audience and got back to whatever they were doing. A lowering cloud base and deteriorating weather eventually concealed the UFO, and a while later the witnesses described hearing a tremendous crack of thunder about the same time that the UFO's lights disappeared. That was when the encounter ended. Gill, at the time, had believed the object to be some kind of advanced craft built by the Americans or similar, but we now know that not to be the case. What's so interesting about this is the fact that the figures aboard the craft were humanoid.'

Freeman gestured to a skeleton of a human male standing in one corner of the room, half hidden behind precariously piled stacks of books.

'The chances of our human form being replicated in an intelligent species from somewhere else in the cosmos, while not impossible, is highly unlikely. While eyes, limbs, ears and mouths are common throughout the animal kingdom here on earth, only primates have evolved a bipedal locomotion, grasping hands and so on.

In many ways our upright stance is an evolutionary weakness, exposing our soft abdomen and reproductive organs to attack from other creatures, so there must have been a valuable evolutionary advantage to walking upright. But beyond that, there is no reason to expect that aliens look anything like us.'

'What was the third possibility?' Lopez asked Freeman.

'Ah, the third is the most controversial. It states that we may not have been the first species of human to achieve high technology, and accounts for some of the legends in ancient civilisations of highly advanced peoples and of gods warring in the skies. The supposed legend of Atlantis is one example. This hypothesis states that the advanced people left Earth to travel into the stars and have changed greatly since, perhaps through genetic engineering to withstand long periods of high velocity space travel. They are now returning, aliens the scant remnants of some other, advanced species of Homo Sapiens.'

Ethan frowned. 'That doesn't make much sense. There would be more evidence of their high technology civiliations here on earth.'

'There are dozens of ancient cities, buried under hundreds of feet of water,' Kyle railed, 'and they had to have been built tens of thousands of years ago! Archaeologists just ignore them and pretend they're not there!'

'Sure they do,' Lopez agreed, 'but those cities are still built from stone, not steel. They're not real examples of advanced civilisations, just evidence that people could build big things a long time before accepted dates. It's not like we're finding ancient history's version of Cape Canaveral down there, is it.'

Kyle seemed suitably chastened as Freeman nodded in agreement with Lopez.

'Mega structures of great age only indicate early human technological understanding and achievement, not the arrival of alien spaceships to held us with some stone masonry. I leave such ideas to the fantasists. The hypothesis that UFOs might be visitors from a future isn't just an idea, it's the only idea which explains both the humanoid nature of alleged alien beings and their advanced technology.'

'Assuming that the UFO William Gill saw was, in fact, a time traveller from the future,' Ethan said, 'then what the hell were they doing here? Sight seeing? And why would they be abducting people and tinkering with them in medical procedures over and over again. These things have been reported for centuries, millennia even: if they're so smart, wouldn't they already have learned everything they needed to know?'

Freeman nodded, propping his chin beneath the point of his hands as he folded them together.

'So you would think,' he agreed. 'Investigators have come up with two possible solutions to that conundrum. The first is that UFOs are indeed from other civilisations, and that we are being subjected to waves of UFOs that come from all corners of the cosmos, each encountering us for the first time completely independently of each other. The second, more disturbing hypothesis, is that

UFOs are built by our future selves and traverse time itself, but they only visit us the once. The rest is down to the unnatural nature of time itself.'

'I don't get it,' Lopez admitted.

'Time is an illusion,' Freeman explained. 'If you were to walk outside and look at the sun right now, you're not seeing it as it is. You're seeing it as it was eight minutes ago, because that's how long it takes the sun's light to cross the space between itself and the earth. Likewise, we see the planets such as Saturn and Jupiter as they were a few hours ago for the same reason – they're just further away. But when you look at the stars, you're seeing them where they were and as they were thousands, if not millions, of years ago. The whole universe is an illusion of what we call the present, but in fact we can only see the present within our own frame of reference. Even distant hills appear as they were a tiny fraction of a second ago. Just by looking at me, you're looking into the past. It's just by such a small amount that we don't notice it.'

'That doesn't explain how they're able to do it,' Ethan pointed out.

'No,' Freeman again agreed, 'but there are several key points about UFOs that are noted again and again. They have no visible means of propulsion, they emit no exhaust, they manoeuvre often erratically and they seem only partially able or willing to respond to the human presence. Those factors, along with their apparent ability to vanish into thin air leaving only a smoking ring behind them, are consistent with an object that is present in much the same way as a hologram can said to be present. It is not a physical object but a transmission, something that reaches us from afar and can vanish just as easily.'

Ethan leaned back on the sofa. Freeman's concepts were flying way over his head, but he could see something of what the old man was getting at. If time travel were possible, perhaps it was not something that was done physically but merely through observation. Perhaps the humans of the future were able somehow to *observe* the past and be seen doing so.

'That doesn't explain the physical abductions,' Ethan pointed out.

Freeman inclined his head.

'No, but are these abductions what we think they are? Apparently about five per cent of the population of the United States believes they have been abducted by aliens. That's around fifteen million people. For that to be true, abductions would have to be taking place in vast numbers every single day and I don't believe for a moment that our skies are filled with UFOs racing this way and that with terrified human passengers locked aboard.'

'Sophie's suffering is real enough,' Lopez remined him.

'Because it might be real,' Freeman nodded, 'just not in the way we think that it is. I worked on a number of cases of supposed hauntings before I really got into the UFO thing, and one factor that always kept cropping up was that people were reporting seeing historical figures, people from the past, but never from the future. I started to think about time, and how we only ever see things from the past. Why not from the future? Why should hauntings of any kind only present historical persons or events? And these things are not just witnessed by individuals, but often large groups. Sceptics of course consider these events to be mass-hallucinations, but that to me is too easy an explanation.'

'So, you think that some abduction events have only happened once?' Lopez asked.

'I think that it is possible, however bizarre that it may seem, that our minds have the capacity to occasionally witness past events. Time is not linear. Ask any physicist and they will tell you that time can bend and warp and even turn back on itself. It is entirely a part of the fabric of our universe and is malliable. Time and space are different aspects of the same thing, and so it stands to reason that sometimes time can be displaced by powerful events; the merging of black holes, supernovae, all manner of powerful cosmic events produce ripples in space and thus time that have been measured by scientists here on earth. If a person happens to be in the right place at the right time, or their brain perhaps is susceptible in some way to such events, then they may witness things that others cannot see.'

Ethan frowned thoughfully.

'A recent case occurred in Scotland in the United Kingdom, where a UFO sighting that Kyle here witnessed coincided with the arrest of a man who, according to CIA reports, appeared to be from the Middle Ages.'

Now, Freeman leaned forward, his expression in earnest. 'A medieval man? Where is he now?'

'That's the thing,' Lopez said, 'the UFO returned, and this guy vanished from a locked jail cell. He hasn't been seen since and the UK Army and police are up in arms about it, as their suspect vanished after stabbing a local youth.'

Freeman stared at them in amazement, then leaned back in his seat and stroked his beard.

'Interesting,' he murmured.

'Interesting?' Kyle uttered. 'You're talking about the event of the decade, perhaps the century, and all you can call it is *interesting*?'

Freeman appeared to have barely heard Kyle.

'Intersting in the sense that if they're truly abducting people, regardless of how often, it appears that UFOs can make mistakes.'

***

XXXVI

'Mistakes?'

Freeman nodded, glancing at images in frames on his walls of some of the most famous UFO photographs ever taken.

'Why else would they drop a medieval man in modern day Scotland?' he asked. 'Unless they got the time wrong?'

To Ethan, it seemed like the perfect explanation and a complete abandonment of common sense at the same time.

'So, they're sufficiently intelligent and advanced to have the technology to abduct someone from the past, but they're dumb enough to forget to set their watches correctly?'

'You're talking about the technology required to traverse spacetime,' Freeman pointed out. 'Maybe they haven't quite perfected it yet? Maybe they do later and they're visiting us without us knowing anything about it, so all we're seeing is the screw-ups that came before? It's not like our own technology works perfectly first time: ask Microsoft. What I'm trying to say is that although UFOs have been reported for thousands of years in our history, maybe they haven't been able to do it for very long from where they come from. Their ability to visit the past might be somewhat limited, or dangerous even. They might not be able to maintain their presence very long or interact well with us.'

'That sounds as far fetched as governments saying that multiple sightings of huge, metallic, flying objects are in fact emissions of swamp gas or the planet Venus shining a bit brighter than usual,' Kyle scoffed.

'It's speculation,' Freeman acknowledged, 'but let's face it, these things may from time to time operate in a fashion that suggests intelligent control, but they also often act erratically and even dangerously, as though they're only half aware that we're here at all.'

Ethan sat for a moment in silence, and then he looked at Lopez as a realisation hit him.

'The video of Sophie's abduction event,' he gasped. 'I know what was wrong with it now. There was missing time in the video.'

'The video clock recorded without a hitch,' Kyle countered. 'We saw it, there was no time error.'

'Not the clock on the video,' Ethan said.

Lopez got her cell phone out and accessed their copy of the video. She forwarded it to the moment where the creature appeared and then vanished from sight.

'There,' Ethan said. 'Sophie's clock on her wall. I didn't spot it at the time, but it moves by an hour in a split second.'

'Damn,' Lopez said. 'You're right, it does. But how can that be possible?'

'Sophie's parents said that she could be taken from their own room and they still wouldn't notice it,' Kyle speculated. 'But if the abduction happens within a distortion of time itself, then there wouldn't be anything for them to notice.'

'None of this is gonna help us find whatever's behind these abductions,' Ethan said. 'We need to refine the technique and we need some guidance. We can travel anywhere, within reason, so what would you suggest is the best way to try to do something about catching one of these things?'

Ben Freeman got out of his seat and took a deep breath as he moved to past a row of images of a supposed spacecraft captured in California in 1952, images that Ethan knew were impeccable in that it had been tested many times using the latest in photographic technology and found to be genuine. Rex Heflin, an Orange County Highway Inspector, snapped four images of a metallic, saucer shaped craft that flew over a lonely stretch of highway in front of his truck. The last of the images was of a ring of smoke hanging in the sky where the object simply disappeared, leaving the smoke ring behind.

'They have a weakness,' Freeman said as he looked at the images. 'They can sometimes be seen, they sometimes crash, and they have been recovered. One of the things that ties in many crash reports is extreme weather, specifically storm cells and lightning.'

Freeman grabbed another document and held it open for them.

'One of the little-known facts about the Roswell event is that there were particularly savage storms ravaging the area on the night of the crash. What seems to be a common theme among UFO sightings is that the objects appear to have no means of propulsion and no means of staying aloft, at least as far as the technology we're familiar with suggests. That means that these objects, and we know that they're objects of solid materials because they frequently return radar reflections, must traverse our skies and perhaps interstellar space using some other means. Given that we cannot see them producing any form of thrust of their own, it is reasonable to assume that they may be utilising some force that we're either unaware of or have not considered as a potential form of energy.'

Lopez frowned.

'I don't know how that would be possible. We've had scientists studying our planet for decades, they would have found something like that by now.'

'Would they?' Freeman challenged her. 'The existence of radiation is as old as the universe itself but it was only at the turn of the last century that mankind, or more specifically a woman, discovered it. We didn't know anything about black holes other than theoretical physics until they were finally detected in the 1960s. The presence of an energy field that is used by advanced technologies is really only new in the sense that they might be using something we already know about in a way that we haven't even thought of. My guess, and it is a *guess*, is that they use electromagnetic propulsion by effectively riding waves generated by the planet itself, a bit like a surfer riding a roller into the beach.'

'What evidence do you have for that?' Kyle asked with some interest, as though he too agreed with the concept.

'Multiple witness reports that describe the same phenomena when UFOs are sighted,' Freeman explained. 'The first is that vehicle engines and other electrical equipment tends to malfunction in the presence of UFOs. This has been recounted in literally hundreds of cases but the most spectacular are those witnessed by military teams at US ballistic missile silos in Montana who were present when the entire launch facility was shut down in the presence of a UFO. Others, well documented by police and other trained personnel, confirm that car engines don't like UFOs. Although the combustion cycle itself is unlikely to be affected, the ignition systems and electrical systems would be disrupted quite easily by powerful electromagnetic fields.'

'The second is that UFOs seem to be adversely affected by bad weather, lighting in particular, as evidenced by the Roswell event and other crashes. Most occur when storm cells are active in the area. Several people who have worked on this and developed patents for flying discs have discovered the same limitations.'

'People have patents for flying discs?' Lopez asked in amazement.

'There are lots of them,' Kyle explained, apparently knowing as much if not more about the subject than Freeman himself. 'Nikola Tesla famously worked on it in search of a means of propulsion that was free, clean and powerful. He ran a high-voltage, high-frequency alternating current between two metal plates. He found that the space between the plates became a solid-state area, one in which a mechanical push could be exerted. The implication was that an engine for propulsion could, in theory, be produced anywhere in space. The result was a drive principal called the Magnetohydrodynamic Effect, or MHD.'

'It sounds like science fiction,' Freeman went on, 'but it's all perfectly within the bounds of currently understood physics. The solid-state condition within the plates caused by the high-frequency electromagnetic pulsing is hugely more efficient than a jet engine, and the thrust increases with the fourth power of the frequency, so if you double the frequency the thrust is sixteen times greater. This, if course, all works best in the vacuum of space where a small amount of input power could create dramatic accelerations, but it would work well within a planet's atmosphere and gravitational field as long as energy was being produced within the craft to power the electromagnetic frequencies, which leads neatly on to UFOs' habit of appearing over military and nuclear installations.'

'Tesla developed his Dynamic Theory of Gravity around this principal in 1897, and it still stands today,' Kyle said. 'In 2005, Boris Volfson was granted a US Patent based on this very technology. While the patent did not, sadly, detail a mechanism for a spaceship, it *was* granted. This is real science at work and work it does. The earth's electromagnetic field is immense – suitably trapped and amplified within a small device, enough energy could be produced to power a large craft because the force is 2.2 to the power of 1039 greater than that of gravity. It's far too big a number to visualise, but if the amount of energy required to lift a vehicle one hundredth of an inch off the ground were applied as an electromagnetic lifting force, then that same vehicle would be propelled literally trillions of miles off the ground and into space.'

Ethan nodded.

'Okay, so maybe they can fly in the way we see them and maybe, somehow, they can travel through time itself. So, you think that we should factor the weather into the equations too and see if something shows up?'

'The weather,' Freeman nodded, 'electromagnetic waves, the earth's magnetic field, literally anything that an advanced race might be able to use as a power source that we might not know about or have rejected in the past as un-workable. We have to think like a species that has achieved the things that we have so far failed to understand. They would have worked out how to generate energy on large scales without affecting their environment, at least in terms of pollution. To them such things would presumably be child's play, like making fire from twigs. It's a cliché, but to catch the alien you've really got to start thinking like an alien.'

'Be the alien,' Kyle enthused, already using his laptop to collect more data to run through the Hydra. 'I can have this data analysed within the hour. There's more than enough out there to use, it's all public domain stuff. And if we run it alongside the 37th parallel, we should get a pretty good prediction.'

'Plenty of summer storms along the 37th too,' Freeman pointed out, apparently already aware of the phenomenon. 'You could get a hit at any time of the year, but right now would be one of the best times.'

Ethan nodded, just as his cell phone rang in his pocket. He pulled it out and saw a number he didn't recognise on it. Cautiously, he decided to answer it.

'Hello?' he asked as he answered the call.

'Ethan Warner?'

'Who is this?' Ethan asked.

'My name is McCain, I'm the Deputy Director, CIA. Mackenzie asked me to call you. Do you have a camera on that phone?'

Ethan glanced at Lopez in surprise, and as she was sitting right alongside him she had heard the caller's identity. Ethan hit the camera button as he replied, and was shocked to see Deputy Director McCain looking back at him as the cell connected.

'Where's Mackenzie?'

'In a safe house,' McCain replied. *'Right now, you need to keep moving. There are other forces at play here and we don't know for sure who to trust. Is Kyle Trent with you?'*

'No,' Ethan lied. 'We figured it too big a risk to stay together.'

'Smart move,' McCain said. *'We know that the folks at Dugway didn't kill Greg.'*

'So do we,' Lopez replied. 'We think that the Russians might be involved.'

'*Mat Zemlya,*' McCain confirmed. *'We're trying to track them down now. You need to get Kyle into custody as soon as possible, before the Russians can locate him.'*

Ethan glanced at Lopez, who was out of McCain's sight, and she shook her head slightly.

'Kyle's off the grid and he's staying that way for now,' Ethan replied. 'The safest place for him is one where nobody knows where he is, even us.'

'There may not be time for that,' McCain replied. 'You need to bring him in now.'

'Why?'

'The family of the girl you visited, Sophie? They've just contacted local law enforcement. Their daughter went missing last night.'

Ethan felt his blood run cold in his veins. 'Did they have the video evidence this time, enough to go public with this?'

'They got video evidence all right,' McCain said, *'but it's not the ETs that grabbed her Ethan. Four armed men, masks, everything. They took her right out of her bed, and we think that they may be the same players who tried to kill General Mackenzie. This is about more than just Kyle Trent now. We need you to come in as soon as you can. Where are you?'*

Ethan sat for a moment in silence, staring into the distance as he thought of Sophie's parents, and of his promise to them that they would do everything that they could to protect the child. He shut off the line to McCain.

'Geez,' Lopez uttered, 'now what do we do? How the hell would anyone know about Sophie's connection to any of this unless they're in on it somehow? You trust this McCain?'

'You're talking about the Deputy Director of the CIA,' Kyle whispered. 'Surely we have to do what he says?'

Ethan turned to Kyle.

'We're going to need that next location real fast.'

***

XXXVII

The hood over General Mackenzie's eyes had been in place for almost an hour before it was finally removed. He blinked in the light, struggling to figure out where he was.

He had been bundled into a vehicle and driven away from the motel. His training as a soldier had kicked in instantly as soon as he had recovered consciousness, and far from fighting back against his abductors he had struck a deliberately defeated posture, shoulders slumped, head hanging low beneath the hood. Long experience had taught soldiers to remain passive in the face of being taken prisoner of war, and to make any attempt to forge a relationship with ones' captors. Mackenzie had not spoken yet, but by not hindering his captors' work he was indirectly causing them to be more considerate toward him. There was no rough shoving, no shouting or abuse.

He had been driven for half an hour, and when he had been instructed to get out of the vehicle the voice had been that of an American. He had heard the sounds of jet engines and had known without a doubt that he was at an airport. It would not have been an airbase, as he was a Colonel and that would have been a very safe location for him. Judging by the number of departures and arrivals, he figured he was at McCarran.

He was led up steps into the cabin of an aircraft, the height of which suggested a small regional airliner. He was sat in a seat and could sense the men surrounding him. The airplane had taxied out and taken off briskly, turning to the left during the climbout. Mackenzie's best guess was that they were heading north west, but he wasn't sure.

Then, the hood was removed.

He was in the centre of the cabin, and the view over the right wing revealed open deserts and mountain ranges basking in the heat. They were climbing through about ten thousand feet but strangely the airplane levelled off at about that height and entered its cruise, suggesting a very short flight indeed.

The men guarding him were wearing smart suits, earpieces, sunglasses, every inch an American team. Mackenzie could not fathom why they had whisked him out of the motel, unless perhaps he was in some kind of danger and they didn't want him to be recognised.

He turned to the nearest of the men.

'Where are we going?'

The man looked at him, not a trace of emotion on his face, and ignored him.

Mackenzie, a high-ranking officer in the military, was not used to being ignored. He knew that he should remain quiet, and he knew equally that he had not really done anything wrong. His subterfuge at the agency was more than offset by the need for security and the unusual nature of the case being studied. Mackenzie knew that if he was in trouble at the Barn he would have been hauled before the DCIA, not dragged onto a plane and flown out of Vegas.

'I'm a Colonel,' he said, trying again. 'There's no point in messing about, I'm not an idiot. We're flying north west out of Vegas. What's the story here and why the cloak and dagger routine?'

The agents all looked at him, and this time the one who looked the oldest among them spoke.

'You rank has no power here. You'll find out soon enough. Sit back and enjoy the flight.'

The agents, apparently deciding that he presented no threat, moved off down the plane and left him to look out of the window. Mackenzie did so for no more than about ten minutes when the airplane began to slow and descend. There was nothing to see but desert outside, distant mountain ranges and wide salt flats basking beneath the endless heat of the sun. It was then that he realised where they were going to land.

The deserts below gave way to the blinding salt flats of Groom Lake. Mackenzie, running their flight trajectory through his mind on a mental map of Nevada, knew for sure that they were descending into Homey Airport, better known to civilians as Area 51. Mackenzie had never visited the site before, but he knew that a small fleet of airlines served the airfield from Las Vegas, flying workers at the base in and out on a daily basis. They were identified only by a thin red line down the otherwise white fuselage and the "Janet" callsign, which became something else when the aircraft was handed to Nellis Air Base controllers, and something else again when it switched to the unknown frequency used by Groom Lake.

The airplane lowered its flaps and undercarriage and Mackenzie watched as the immensely long runway hove into view, dark ashphalt against the brilliant white flare of the salt flats. The airliner, a Boeing 737, touched down and came briskly to a halt under reverse-thrust braking before it turned off the runway and taxied to a parking spot. Mackenzie was directed to get out of his seat by his guards, but there was no hood this time. He also realised that he was the only passenger on the plane. The exit was opened to a waft of hot desert air, steps were wheeled into place, and just like that Mackenzie walked down into Area 51.

A white pick-up was waiting for him, crewed by two soldiers in camouflage fatigues and sunglasses. Mackenzie was directed to the vehicle and accompanied on board. The truck drove them across the airbase, where Mackenzie could see various hangars and buildings, all with their doors closed. He could see no signs of life on the base, and he knew that security directives would mean that his presence on the base would require a brief lock-down until he was safely ensconsed into whichever building he was being taken to.

From what little he knew for sure about operations at Area 51, every person who worked there was privy to information only concerning their own individual projects. Data was compartmentalised so that no individual knew everything, or even a sizeable portion, of what went on at the base. It was said that even the base commander himself was kept in the dark about many of the projects on-going at Area 51, for his own personal security: it would otherwise be too easy for a foreign power to abduct and interrogate him for information about the base.

Mackenzie was driven to a non-descript prefab building on the north west corner of the base that to him looked like little more than a storage shed. The vehicle stopped and the guards silently got out. Mackenzie followed and was led into the building by one of the men while the other three stood guard.

The inside of the shed was unremarkable in that it was completely empty but for an elevator shaft. The guard opened the grated metal doors and gestured for the colonel to get in. Mackenzie obeyed in silence and then the doors where shut behind him. The guard pressed a button and Mackenzie descended within a shaft that sank down through the floor.

It crossed his mind that perhaps those who encountered the secretive forces controlling investigations into the UFO phenomena within the government were sent down here into a seething lake of fire or something, never to be seen again. Right now, all he could see were hewn rock faces passing before him and the occasional glow from light bulbs connected by electrical wiring. The elevator rattled downward for what he guessed was a couple of hundred feet, and then it slowed before a steel door.

The door hissed open, and DDCIA McCain stood awaiting him.

'I knew it,' Mackenzie said as McCain yanked open the gate.

'Sorry about the heavy hands,' McCain replied, extending his own with an earnest look. 'That's just the way this stuff has to happen.'

Mackenzie shook the proffered hand. 'You'd better fill me in on what the hell's going on. I take it the Men in Black aren't waiting for me down here.'

McCain shook his head.

'I wish they did work for me, they'd probably be quite useful,' he replied mysteriously. 'Come this way, we need to talk about this.'

Mackenzie followed McCain down a corridor, off of which were various doors marked with what seemed like entirely innocuous names. McCain noticed his look of surprise.

'This is part of the research facility that works on lasers and directed energy weapons. Any regular physicist would be right at home. It's only the security level that keeps everything secret.'

'No alien spaceships, no invisibility cloaks?' Mackenzie asked.

'Sadly, no,' McCain replied. 'Although we are working on dynamic polymers which are used on airplanes and allow them to take on the appearance of their background. Quite remarkable when you see it in action, you can barely see the airplane at all.'

Mackenzie frowned. 'Not much good if you can hear its engines.'

McCain smiled. 'This is why I got you the FID job, I knew you'd be a great asset here.'

'Wait one, *you* got me onto that damned desk?'

'It's a long story,' McCain said as he gestured to an open door that led into an office. 'I'll tell you about it.'

***

XXXVIII

The office was small, containing only a single table and two chairs. On the far side was another door. McCain closed the door through which Mackenzie had walked, and then gestured to the table.

Mackenzie saw that in the center of the table was a clear plastic box, and within it were pieces of what looked like metal.

'What are they?' he asked.

McCain walked across to the box and spoke softly, as though even here in the most well-guarded and secretive place on earth there might still be those who were listening in.

'These are the remains of what was found at Roswell, New Mexico, in 1947.'

Mackenzie's breath caught in his throat. Like most everyone on the planet, he had heard about Roswell all of his life: the stories, the legends, the supposed cover-ups and conspiracies, the lies, the false histories. He had both believed and rejected all of it, convinced that whatever had happened was so far in the past now that the truth could never be recovered.

'Seriously?' was all that he could say.

'Yes,' McCain insisted. 'This is the real deal.'

'Why is there so little of it?'

McCain sat down, folding his arms as he looked at the fragments.

'People seem to forget that this thing didn't touch down gently at a local airport and welcome us aboard. The damned thing crashed, at high velocity, during a raging thunderstorm. By the time our people got there in '47, having finally realised that a flying disc had actually crashed, all that was left was fragments. All the stories you've heard, of workers here supposedly reverse-engineering UFOs and flying them about all over the place, all of it's crap.' He sighed. 'But then, so is the cover story of the debris being a surveillance balloon belonging to Project Mogul: they didn't tend to launch those balloons in heavy weather because they were so fragile, not that anyone in the media seems to have realised that.'

Mackenzie approached the box and sat down opposite McCain, his eyes fixed on the pieces of metal fragments before him. That they were metal was clear, the silvery, twisted chunks glinting in the light.

'What happened to the rest of the fragments? There must be more.'

'Destroyed over the years during tests,' McCain said. 'An entire department sprung up here to study the materials, and materials was all we had by the way. There was nothing found in the way of proper engineering, nothing that we could dismantle and re-build to understand. All that we had was the remnants of a shell, disc-shaped in form, with almost nothing that resembled an interior or cockpit that could be understood by engineers, then or now. All that they could do was try to figure out what this thing was made of, and attempt to speculate from that basis what these things are.'

Mackenzie nodded, peering closely at the metal. 'What did they learn?'

McCain smiled.

'Technically, I shouldn't tell you yet as you haven't been cleared, but I think that's a formality now. The metals contain recognisable elements such as iron, but the atomic arrangement is different to earth-based iron. That is, it was created or manipulated in processes different from those we're used to and understand. That difference gives the metal remarkable properties.'

'In what way?'

'Well, for a start it does not respond to normal forces in the way that we would expect. The metal is both ultra light and yet stronger than any steel, to the extent that large sheets of this stuff weigh little more than sugar paper but would protect you from a rifle bullet. The bonds are extremely strong. It does not reflect radar signals very easily. The scientists who worked on this in the 1970s managed to figure out that, in conjunction with a disc or boomerang-shaped form, radar energy would flow around the object and continue on its way, rather like water flowing around a pebble, thus preventing a clear radar signature on all but the most sensitive of devices.'

Mackenzie nodded, as though he'd known all along.

'Is that the only reason they're disc shaped?'

'No,' McCain replied. 'That seems to be to do with their propulsion.'

'I thought that no energy source was found?'

'It wasn't,' McCain confirmed. 'What has since been discovered is that the oval form of the original craft would have acted as a resonance chamber for electromagnetic energy. The best guess of our brightest minds is that the craft harnesses natural forces such as gravity or electromagnetism and essentially rides the waves through the sky.'

Mackenzie could not really add anything to that.

'What about occupants?'

'None,' McCain replied, 'and that's not the CIA uttering an official explanation for public consumption. There were never any bodies or indeed *any* biological remains discovered in or near the craft when it was recovered.'

A word slipped out of Mackenzie's mouth of its own accord. 'Drone.'

McCain slapped the table with an open palm in apparent delight.

'Exactly! It took the boffins here thirty years to come up with that conclusion. This thing was a drone, an automated craft. It got caught out in a freak storm and *bam*, it's in our hands. The United States Army Air Force admitted it had caught a flying disc and went public with the information because it genuinely assumed that the craft was Russian, and the capture would be a major public relations coup that would say to *Ivan*, "*Hey, we know what you're up to and we've got one of your new toys, so be careful whose backyard you're playing in.*" It was only when they got it under study at Wright Patterson Air Force Base that they realised this was nothing to do with Russia or any nation on earth, so they hurriedly issued a cover story about the crashed balloon and went quiet thereafter. Everything you've heard since is mere speculation and conspiracy theories.'

Mackenzie smiled.

'No smoke without fire. They were right then, that this was from another planet.'

McCain nodded.

'Yeah, they were right. But that's not the big deal, believe it or not.'

'You're kidding? Evidence of visitation from another species *isn't* the big deal?'

'Come on, Scott, you're a man of the world as much as we all are,' McCain replied. 'People the world over may not know the truth but they all think the same. It's spoken about in pubs and in family gatherings every day somewhere on the planet; the universe is too damned big for us to be here on our own. There must be other life out there. If you factor in the known facts that every chemical we're made from was forged in ancient stars, and that intelligent life could have first arisen several billion years ago, it becomes a no-brainer. It's not just that there should be life out there, or that there should be intelligent life out there: the universe should be bursting with life, and it's only the huge distances between star systems that prevents us from easily contacting, or being contacted by, other civilisations.'

Mackenzie knew that his boss was right. There had to be other life out there, and if there were, then it was probable that they would have the same curiosity about the universe around them as mankind did. If they were more advanced, they would spread out into that cosmos in search of new life, new planets and new experiences just as man had done on earth.

'They'd send out drones,' Mackenzie said out loud. 'Lots of drones, robots, AI, all searching the cosmos.'

McCain grinned.

'Of course they would, just as we send robots and satellites to other planets and moons in our own solar system. Send the machines in first to check things out and return data, and then send people in for a better look.'

Mackenzie realised that he was following a natural thought experiment and let it continue out loud.

'The drones find points of interest, send the data back to home base, and they come out to have a look for themselves.'

'And find us,' McCain said. 'They want to have a look at us.'

Mackenzie frowned. 'But it would take too long for the messages to cross light years back and forth to other star systems, that's the whole problem. If a planet is forty light years away, and we send them a message, it would take eighty years to get a reply, right?'

'Right,' McCain said. 'If you're thinking like us.'

'Like us?'

McCain leaned forward on the table. 'Scott, what you're about to learn is something that is kept between only a few people on earth. I'm not exaggerating. Believe me when I say that the secrecy is so high not because we want to control it, but because we don't know what the hell to do about it ourselves. I asked for you to be brought into this because of your patriotism and your reliability. Right now, you're in danger, your life and that of your family has been threatened and you've been abducted by your own countrymen, yet you're sitting here with me and fully engaged in what I'm telling you. No board of control is ever going to turn you away now but I need to know that I can count on you, because what's through that door will change your life forever once you've seen it.'

Mackenzie glanced at the other door, the one that had been closed the entire time. Somehow, he knew not to ask what was behind it. There was, he figured, no point. The point was that he could only see it if he agreed to whatever terms McCain was about to place before him.

'You can't speak of it, ever,' McCain said, 'although once you've seen it you won't want to.'

Mackenzie felt a little uncomfortable at McCain's choice of words.

'It's that bad?'

'It's not bad,' McCain said. 'It's just that you won't be ready for it, no matter what you think you know.'

The hairs on Mackenzie's arms rose up and pulled at his skin, shivers running along his limbs as though insects were scuttling across them.

'I gotta go through that door, before you say anything more, haven't I?'

'Pretty much,' McCain replied. 'It's how it started for me. It's how it starts for everyone involved in this program.'

Mackenzie thought for a moment. 'How many have left the program since it started?'

'None,' McCain replied. 'And before you ask; no, none were assassinated for threatening to talk. It doesn't work like that. All held their silence because they wanted to. I do. You'll understand too, if you decide to go through that door.'

'My family?' Mackenzie asked.

'Safe, but you won't be able to share this with them. Scott, we need to know where Kyle Trent is, before the Russians can get to him. You should know Scott, that the girl mentioned in your investigation, Sophie Taggart, has been abducted by armed men we believe to be the same bad actors who went after you.'

Mackenzie winced in frustration.

'I can't tell you,' he insisted. 'Ethan and Nicola are with Kyle Trent but they've gone dark. The number I gave you was all I had, have you tried calling it?'

'Yes,' McCain replied. 'I don't think they're playing ball.'

'They don't know you well enough to trust you yet,' Mackenzie replied. 'But if you called them you can track them, right?'

'There are teams on the way to their location right now,' McCain assured him. 'Don't worry about them. Right now, your only concern is what's behind that door.'

'Sophie Taggart is a concern,' Mackenzie insisted.

'Then do what you can to help her,' McCain urged him. 'You'll be better equipped once you go through that door.'

Mackenzie nodded. The door beckoned him in silence. Slowly, he stood up and turned to face it. He glanced back at McCain, who gave him a small nod of encouragement. Mackenzie took a deep breath and reminded himself that he'd fought in several theatres of war in his time and seen too many things he'd rather not dwell on. He could handle one more.

Mackenzie opened the door and walked through, and as he saw what McCain and others before him had seen he knew that nothing would ever be the same again.

***

XXIX

Rico Savage peered out of the open door of the Black Hawk, his rifle cradled in his lap and his men waiting with him as the sleek helicopter raced along barely thirty feet above the desert floor. The rotors thundered somewhere just above his head and the hot wind buffeted him as he leaned out and saw the canyons ahead.

The military from the Nellis Range often trained here, flying through these very canyons on a regular basis. There was nothing unusual for the local residents to see, just more mysterious aircraft and helicopters thundering this way and that beneath the scorching desert sun.

He checked over his shoulder and saw that his men were ready and were watching him with stern, silent expressions. They knew what had to be done. He knew they would follow him through the gates of Hades if he ordered them to, and though they were not expecting heavy resistance they were treating this mission with the same dedication as they would when storming a terrorist cell's hideaway in Afghanistan.

The Black Hawk's engine note changed as the pilots adjusted the controls. The helicopter was all black and unmarked, no squadron patches adorning its fuselage or airframe numbers to identify it. Photographs taken of the helicopters typically showed little detail, and never enough for civilians to identify where the helicopters originated. Mostly operated at night, this broad-daylight mission was unusual but necessary.

'Sixty seconds!'

The helicopter remained low, skimming the brush at over one hundred knots, the Black Hawk's shadow racing them across the desert. Rico saw the canyon loom before them, and even as he spotted the ramshackle buildings tucked within it the helicopter suddenly leaned over and pulled up. The huge rotors thumped the air as it slowed and turned, blue sky and sunlight flashing through the interior as it broadsided the entrance to the canyon. Clouds of swirling dust and sand coiled into the air in great spinning whorls and the noise of the engines reverberated like drums through Rico's chest as the Black Hawk came to a hover fifty yards from the canyon wash and some six feet off the ground.

Rico leaped out and landed in the desert, his men spilling out after him as they sprinted for the entrance to the canyon: far enough away to prevent anyone attacking them in a crossfire, close enough that nobody could flee. As he ran, Rico ducked as a second Black Hawk thundered overhead, tasked with blocking the canyon off further up by deploying more of Rico's men onto the heights either side.

Rico ran to the entrance of the canyon, digging into cover on one side as his team fanned out into position. The helicopters thundered away into holding positions three miles out and the silence returned to the desert. Confident that nobody could escape, Rico waved his men forward and they began advancing up the wash.

McCain had called him only an hour ago with a cell phone trace on Ethan Warner. The coordinates were located within a long-abandoned ghost town out in the Nevada deserts associated with a man named Freeman, who had apparently been a thorn in the Defense Department's side over the years.

Rico had read a detailed file about Benjamen Freeman on the way here. A radical, anarchistic former scientist with a passion for writing complex papers on the UFO phenomenon, he was regarded as a hero by the fringe lunatics and almost a traitor by the military. In his released works he had revealed complex formulas used by NASA projects that, while not classified, were certainly sensitive. It was grounds enough for arrest and given the old man's advanced years and penchant for criticising the US military there seemed possibility enough that he would booby-trap his secluded home or otherwise seek to impede or harm Rico's men.

Rico advanced past the rusted hulk of a century-old car and saw ahead a shambolic homestead that looked abandoned, but he suspected was perfectly serviceable. There were no people between him and the homestead, the canyon eerily quiet. He waved his men into an arc formation, their weapons trained on the homestead as he called out.

'Ben Freeman, come out with your hands up and your back turned to us!'

A hot wind moaned up the canyon, carrying dust that caught in Rico's eyes. He brushed them clear with one gloved hand and called out again.

'Ben Freeman, this is your last chance. Failure to comply may result in the use of deadly force. Come out with your hands up an…'

The front door to the homestead opened and an old man walked slowly out with his hands on his head and his back turned toward them. Rico peered at him, but he could see no evidence of anything strapped beneath his shirt or in his hands. Still, better safe than sorry.

'Hands held high, fingers splayed!' he yelled.

Ben Freeman complied, standing with his hands in the air and his back still turned to them.

'Turn around!'

Freeman turned to face them, and it was clear that he was unarmed. Rico broke cover and moved forward, his pistol aimed squarely between Freeman's eyes.

'Is there anything on your person that could harm myself or my men?' Rico demanded.

'No,' Freeman replied, his voice soft on the warm air, 'only my mind.'

Rico ignored his flippancy as he moved behind Freeman and yanked his hands down, cuffing them behind his back. Satisfied, he jabbed the pistol into Freeman's back.

'Is there anything in the homestead that is intended to hurt or impede my men?'

Freeman frowned.

'The iron's a bit warm,' he shrugged.

Rico jabbed the pistol harder. 'You want this to go easy or hard?'

Freeman glanced over his shoulder. 'You're the ones who barged in here. You could have just knocked.'

Rico glanced at his second in command and jerked his head toward Freeman's home, and instantly his men swarmed upon the homestead, rushing inside with yelled orders to *get down and stay down*! Rico waited as his men cleared the room with military efficiency, and then he heard one of their voices on the comms channel.

'They're not here, all rooms cleared.'

Rico spun Freeman around, kept the pistol jabbed into him.

'This is going to be a very short conversation. Where is Kyle Trent?'

'Gone,' Freeman replied. 'You missed them by barely an hour.'

'Where did they go?'

'I told them not to tell me. I knew you would come here eventually, so I didn't want to know.'

'What did you tell them?'

Freeman smiled almost pityingly at Rico, as though somehow the soldier was just some pawn in a big game that he didn't understand.

'Everything I know.'

Rico saw his lieutenant hurry from the homestead, a scanner in his hand.

'They're not here,' he reported. 'Nothing on infra-red either but they *were* here, recently. I've got hot spots in several seats inside, and there's evidence of recent tyre tracks all over the wash.'

Rico nodded. He too had noticed them, some going in, others going out. The freshest tracks, the ones that rode over all others, seemed to be of a vehicle leaving the area.

'What was the vehicle, and where was it headed?' he demanded of Freeman.

'A Lincoln, silver, and I told you I didn't want to know where they were heading.'

'You have an idea,' Rico snapped, knowing enough about the wily old man to know that if he helped Trent then he would be able to surmise their next move.

'I told them what I knew, just like I'm telling you,' Freeman replied. 'They came in here just like you did, all heavy handed and panicked. I didn't know if they wanted to talk to me or shoot me. I just wanted them gone.'

Rico's eyes narrowed. Freeman could be telling the truth, and the Warner guy was known for leaving a trail of destruction and sometimes bodies behind him. But there was no evidence of any true ruthlessness towards other people, only a dogged determination to get the job done that Rico could sympathise with.

'Who was *them*?' he demanded, deciding to catch Freeman out a little on his slip up.

'Some guy called Warner, and a woman, Mexican probably. They seemed to be protecting Kyle, who looked like the whole world was after him.'

'Keep talking,' Rico snapped.

'They wanted to know everything I'd surmised about UFOs. The kid had some gizmo that gathered big data and crunched it. They wanted to input what I knew about the phenomenon in order to improve their chances of seeing one, I think.'

Rico's mind started turning quickly. Trent was almost certainly the kid behind the images that the CIA had gone ballistic about, and that explained why he had showed up at Dugway when he had. The two figures had been on the hilltops inside the base, their kit all set up *before* the lights had appeared over the base. Either they had been the luckiest UFO spotters on planet earth or they'd known that something was going to happen at Dugway that night. Given that they'd broken in at great risk to their own lives the latter seemed the most likely, however impossible it may have seemed.

Now Trent was on the run and likely his best course of action was to gather more evidence, go public with it and cover himself using the mass media. If he got killed, somehow, then the public would believe that some kind of shadow government was at work behind the scenes and it would draw even more attention to Dugway and other classified sites around the country.

'He's going for another sighting,' Rico said out loud.

The lieutenant said nothing, waiting patiently for orders.

Rico believed the old man when he said that he had deliberately not asked where Trent was going. If he supplied data to the kid then he could have input it into whatever data crunching program he had and got the result after they had left. About all that Rico had on his side was the fact that they were travelling in a silver Lincoln, and that part could easily be fabricated.

He turned away from Freeman and moved to crouch alongside the recent tyre tracks. They looked like normal tyres, not those of a truck or SUV. A smaller vehicle, lighter. A Lincoln would be a good fit, and there were countless Lincolns across any state in many colours. Tracking the vehicle down would be almost impossible, given the limited time and resources available.

He stood and turned to his lieutenant.

'Get every traffic camera feed that you can into play. We're looking for a Lincoln, of any colour, heading away from this area on the interstate. Maybe we can identify them and start tracking.'

The lieutenant dashed away to carry out the order as Rico returned to Freeman.

'You don't know what you're doing,' he said. 'Kyle Trent is in immense danger.'

'Yes,' Freeman nodded. 'From all of you.'

Rico's eyes narrowed. 'What makes you say that?'

'Must make you real proud,' Freeman almost spat, 'chasing an unarmed kid in the defence of secrets the government has no right to keep from its people.'

Rico's fists balled at his sides, but somehow he managed to keep his voice level.

'Trent and a friend knowingly trespassed onto a government facility where lethal force can be used in defence of national security.'

'And you shot one of them,' Freeman agreed.

Rico shook his head.

'Trent's friend was killed by a sniper,' he replied. 'But I can assure you that none of my men fired a single shot that night. We're not looking to kill anyone. We want Kyle Trent's technology, we want him on our side and we want to know who the hell killed Greg Parfitt. Just tell us what we need to know, or your friends are going to wind up dead by tomorrow morning.'

The old man peered at him suspiciously.

'You're just saying that to cover your own arses. I don't tell you what you want to hear you're going to shoot me too, right?'

Rico kept his temper in check.

'Nobody's going to shoot anyone. Kyle Trent and Greg were in plain sight on the hills, couldn't have got away from us if they'd tried. We'd have arrested them, charged them, the whole nine yards, but not one of my men would have opened fire without my express order unless they felt directly threatened. That's how it works! The only reason Kyle Trent got away was because we thought *we* were under fire when we heard the shot! By the time we reached the hilltop, his friend was dead and Kyle was gone. I can't tell you who fired upon them but I have a good idea and I think I know why, and right now your friends are carrying it around with them. We need to know where they are.'

***

XL

Ethan drove, with Lopez alongside him and Kyle Trent in the back seat.

They had ditched the Lincoln in favour of a small truck, the likes of which could be found in the possession of farmers all across the state and which would therefore blend in better with their surroundings.

The sun was sinking toward the horizon as they drove along the empty highway before them, the asphalt a long straight line that vanished into the heat haze ahead where mountains sprawled like slumbering demons over the lengthening shadows.

'Man, this place is insane.'

Kyle was for once not looking at his laptop computer, which was humming alongside him as it crunched the extra data that Ben Freeman had fed it. They had seen the Black Hawk helicopters in the far distance not long after they had left, and Ethan had guessed that they had been bound for Freeman's homestead. If they had ever needed confirmation that the government were now following them with intent, that had been it. Ethan only hoped that they would not see Freeman's face on the news that night, under arrest or worse killed at the hands of covert government troops.

Kyle was instead looking out of the windows at the immense deserts and mountains surrounding them. Ethan didn't have a picture in his mind of the perfect UFO spot, maybe thickly wooded roads in rural Oregon, but this desolately beautiful landscape with miles of empty roads seemed as likely as any.

'This is where it all goes down,' Kyle added. 'Tonopah Test Range. It's an airfield and support base about seventy miles north west of Groom Lake and just about the best kept military secret in the United States arsenal. Weapons and security experts talk about the place with fascination, because it's considered ultra-deep black and yet sits in plain sight.'

'What's so special about the place?' Lopez asked.

'Well, this is where they ran the MiG projects in the 1960s until the 1990s. Covert CIA operations were conducted under the codename Project Have Donut to capture and bring back to the US Soviet MiGs for testing against our own aircraft. When they did so, they were brought to Tonopah.'

'They had MiGs here?' Ethan asked in surprise.

'Lots of them, variously stolen by CIA contracted pilots or captured via Soviet defections,' Kyle confirmed. 'The airplanes were tested, and the result was the formation of the Fighter Weapons School in the Navy, better known as TopGun, and a similar school in the Air Force. You'd have thought that such prizes would have been hidden away at Area 51, but no, they were tested at Tonopah. This was where the super-secret F-117A Stealth Fighters were tested and stored before they became public knowledge. Most experts refer to Tonopah as Area 52 and suggest that because of the public interest in Area 51 from the 1980s onward, most truly covert operations were moved to Tonopah instead to avoid observation.'

'How come nobody's caught on then?' Lopez asked.

'Mainly because the government doesn't hide Tonapah in any way. It's kept as unremarkable as possible, although it sits well inside the Nellis Test Range and in many ways is harder to observe than Area 51. Commercial airliners over-fly the base on scheduled routes, there is no denial of its existence by the government, and there are no swathes of UFO sightings to suggest that anything untoward is going on.'

'Maybe nothing's going on,' Lopez suggested with a smile.

'The clue is in the activity,' Kyle countered. 'The base is supposed to be under caretaker status, with only occasional flights using the base for either normal training operations or emergency landings. But there is an entire drone squadron based at Tonopah, the airfield is kept operational, and security is as tight there as at Area 51 but without the overt fuss. This place is where the Hydra suggested we would best go even before the new information we now have, and I'm willing to bet it still will be when Ben's information is factored in.'

Ethan glanced up into the late afternoon sky. Billowing towers of cumulonimbus were soaring into the heavens, then anvil shaped storm cells driven by the huge amounts of heat rising up from the deserts below. They towered as high as sixty thousand feet into the atmosphere, and the sheer amount of energy within them would be unleashed upon the state as the terrific electrical storms it endured.

'We could be in luck,' he said. 'Those storms will let loose within a few hours, all we have to do is be in the right place at the right time.'

Kyle's laptop pinged, and the kid looked down at it and tapped a few keys.

'Okay, location remains the same, Tonopah, sometime just before midnight tonight.'

Lopez shook her head in wonder.

'Seriously? You mean that there will be an *actual* UFO, in that spot, at that time, tonight?'

'It's been right on the last four times I've run the program, and now it's even better with Ben's knowledge added into the mix. I hacked the state's aviation weather report, or METAR, into the data feed, so it's factoring that in too.'

'Don't suppose that program can predict state lotteries, can it?' she asked.

'You think I'd be sitting here with you two if it could?'

'So,' Lopez said, 'we get the UFO in front of us. Then what? If you're going public with this then we need something solid and we don't have your fancy cameras with us.'

Kyle gave her a sheepish look.

'We may need to buy some equipment.'

'Right,' Ethan murmured. 'We'll just drop in the next mall we see and grab everything you need.'

The car hummed along the deserted highway, in the middle of the desert, for a few moments.

'You got any better ideas, genius?' Kyle sulked at him.

Ethan grinned as he drove. 'As it happens, yeah, I do.'

Lopez looked at him questioningly but he said nothing, keeping his eyes on the road as they covered mile after mile. After an hour or so, and with the sun sinking further toward the distant mountains, they arrived in the town of Tonopah itself. Situated thirty miles north east of the base, Tonopah was one of those towns that clung to existence on the fringes of the inhospitable deserts. Ethan knew of it largely due to his and Lopez's exploits of a few years' earlier when they had been involved in a major shoot out at the Crescent Dunes Solar Project a few miles to the north. Unincorporated and with a population of less than three thousand, Tonopah was about as remote as it got in the state of Nevada.

Ethan drove past the town fire house, the wall of which was emblazoned with images of Stealth fighters, denoting the fact that the locals were well aware of the close proximity of the secretive airbase. There were no major stores, only hotels and convience stores plus a couple gas stations at each end of the town, but Ethan knew what he needed and even here he knew that he could find it. He pulled up outside one of the stores and hurried inside, taking a few moments to find what he needed before paying and walking back to the car. He got in, Lopez and Trent both looking at him expectantly.

Ethan placed several packages into Lopez's lap and she frowned at him. 'A satellite phone and a bunch of cells?'

'Not just any satellite phone,' Ethan said. 'This one has the ability to connect to more than one satellite at a time, making it much harder for anyone to jam a signal. Farmers and landworkers often carry them out here in case of accidents or injuries out on the ranches.'

Kyle Trent understood immediately.

'You want me to broadcast the UFO live,' he said in delight. 'Record using the cell phone cameras and then broadcast via the satellite phone.'

Ethan started the engine.

'We're all being hunted now, and I've spent too much time with one government or another on my back. Let's just get this over with. We show the world what you know and what you've done. Even if the broadcast was wiped from every server in the country, it would still be saved by UFO enthusiasts and organisations like MUFON and will probably make the national news if it's good enough. You'll be a television celebrity and it'll be tough for the government to arrange an accident for you if you use the broadcast to highlight Greg's death and their awareness of it. Brace yourself kid, you're going live with this one.'

*

Vigor Vieski sat inside an air-conditioned SUV and waited patiently for the call.

He felt as though he was sitting inside a surreal bubble of all-American contamination. Outside the tinted windows he could see American automobiles, American hotels, American people and wall murals of American wild west scenes. America seemed to overwhelm him with its capitalist, gung-ho exuberance like a song stuck in his mind that wouldn't go away.

Vigor knew that success, here, in this case would be essential in ensuring his return home. So far, he knew that the American boy, Kyle, was running from his own people, precisely as Vigor had intended. *Demonise your target's friends, angelicise their enemies: bring the target to you of their own volition.*

Kyle had travelled west, out into the deserts. Initially Vigor had been somewhat surprised, expecting the youth to hide within the throng of Las Vegas. Out here, there was nowhere to run and nowhere to hide. But he had underestimated the boy's determination, the American do-or-die attitude when their backs were against the wall, and he had underestimated the government's willingness to engage personnel to support the youth.

Warner and Lopez.

Vigor knew enough about them now to be certain that they would scupper his plans given half a chance. He had put people onto General Mackenzie but he had vanished, probably into a CIA safe house along with his family. Communications had been brief, but Mackenzie had made several calls to one number that had turned out to belong to none other than the Deputy Director of the CIA. Tracking that cell had revealed calls to a location in the deserts of Nevada, and Vigor's hunch had played out. With the American team having to rush back from Virginia, Vigor and his men had been able to stake out the roads leading out of the area where the calls had been received.

They had picked up Kyle Trent's tail shortly thereafter, an hour before the Americans raided a lonely home far out in the deserts.

The situation was delicate. Many of his predecessors had underestimated the two Americans to their great cost. Several high-ranking Russian officers had gone to their graves at the hands of Warner and Lopez over the years. Vigor did not intend to be the next.

One of his men, who was sitting in the front seat, got a message from the lead car and turned in his seat to look at Vigor.

'They're close,' he said. 'The've stopped in the town of Tonopah, twelve miles from here.'

'Good,' Vigor replied. 'It was almost common sense that they would come to a spot somewhere out here. Follow them, at a distance. Wherever Kyle is going, we must allow him to reach his destination before we strike. Let him do our work for us, and then we shall wipe the slate clean and take what we need.'

The agent nodded as the engine started and they drove out of the parking lot. Vigor settled into his seat and allowed himself a small smile. He was about to do the United States a great favour. If Kyle Trent would not join him, then he would die like his friend at Dugway. With Kyle Trent dead, the American troops would no longer fear their secrets being exposed, and Vigor and his team could slip from the country with the Hydra in their hands, and as a bonus finally kill Warner and Lopez to avenge the many Russian lives lost at their hands.

***

XLI

Groom Lake, Nevada

Rico Savage drove an unmarked sedan through the wilderness and tried to stop himself from grinding his teeth in frustration. Benjamen Freeman had been unable to supply him with the information he needed to locate Kyle Trent, other than to say that he was heading north-west out of Vegas. That could mean anywhere in the Nellis Test Range. Rico was not surprised that they were coming out here, the area one of the legendary hot spots for supposed UFO activity.

He saw the entrance to the huge airbase ahead, having taken the standard route off the 375 onto a dirt track called Groom Road that led across the tractless desert wastes toward distant ranges of hills. The sun was low in the sky, the horizon a sheet of molten metal pouring across the hills. In the growing darkness behind the car he could see ranks of huge thunderheads marching across the heavens, their tips bathed in the orange glow of the setting sun. Those storms were heading west and would catch up within an hour or two.

'We don't have long,' he said to his companion, one of his men who had liased with the base commander at Groom Lake.

The truck accelerated, dust plumes coiling from its wheels as it led a convoy of four vehicles down Groom Road. They drove the ten kilometres across the desert and reached the hills, cruising past vivid warning signs lining the infamous entry to the most secretive airbase on the planet.

Rico's second in command had called ahead and security clearances had been obtained. Even with his rank, driving into Area 51 without clearance would have resulted in several gunshots and flowers being sent to his wife, such was the classified nature of the facility. As he drove, so a pair of four by four trucks with silver body work appeared, having waited for them on a dusty slip road, and pulled out. One drove in front of Rico's convoy, the other slipped in behind it.

The trucks led them over the ridge of hills, following the winding contours of Groom Road until it descended on the far side. The deep shadows gave way to the brilliant sunset once more, the blinding light helping to conceal from view the vast salt flat of Groom Lake. But there, on the far side, deep in shadow now but visible as twinkling lights and a vast runway, was Area 51.

The airbase dominated the far side of the salt flats and the runway was almost ridiculous in its length, running alongside the entire airbase and then north west across more of the salt flats. All of the hangars were low slung, the buildings around the base all on the western side of the runway and equally innocuous. Rico had heard, from time to time, from people who had worked on the base, and only in whispered conversations, that there was far more below the surface than there was visible above it. Area 51 was now well and truly in the public knowledge as a place of great secrecy, but what really lay beneath the surface was anyone's guess.

The pick ups led them along the road that circled the northern side of the base, sweeping left back in toward the main buildings. As they turned, Rico saw flashing red and white lights hovering in the sky to his left. Despite himself his heart leaped into his throat and for a moment he thought that they were about to bear witness to either a super-secret test programme or an extra-terrestrial visitor. Moments later he identified the Janet flight aircraft on finals to land at the base, bringing in workers from Las Vegas. Like the buses that ran up and down Groom Road to bring workers in from Alamo, there was a constant shuttle service by road and air to supply the base.

Rico checked his watch. They had taken an hour to get here, a helicopter flight not possible due to the intense air traffic restrictions around the airbase. The short notice clearance had allowed for vehicular access only. As the vehicles pulled up in a parking lot at the northern end of the base, Rico saw a pair of Apache attack helicopters parked nearby, and an F-16 Fighting Falcon which appeared to be armed and ready for immediate flight should the need occur. That meant pilots on alert status twenty-four-seven, ready to scramble against any intruder.

Rico got out as soon as the vehicle stopped and hurried across to the drivers of the escort vehicle. A window opened as the armed guard within looked at him.

'You need to double your security,' Rico advised, 'and start patrols of the hills around the base.'

The guard stared at Rico for a long moment, then looked at his partner. Then they both smiled.

'Sir, there are more cameras, sensors, razor wire and seismic monitoring systems in place around Groom Lake than anywhere on earth. Even the coyotes have to ask permission to come in here.'

Rico held his temper in check once again.

'The same applies to Dugway, and two nights ago a pair of teenage hackers got inside the perimeter without anyone knowing. One of them lost his life as a result. Unless you want a similar situation here, and the questions that will arise when you both ignored what I just told you, I suggest you get on the damned case and get your people out on those hills!'

The guards did not argue further and hurried off as Rico, still under armed escort, turned to the men watching him.

'They're here, somewhere. I need to speak to the base commander.'

A guard gestured toward a long, low building nearby. Rico hurried toward it but his companion was held back under armed guard. Two more guards accompanied Rico to the building, one of them opening the door as Rico stepped inside.

Two men awaited him. One wore a suit and was a man that Rico recognised instantly, the Deputy Director of the CIA and his boss. The other wore camouflage fatigues and the stars of a General. Rico immediately snapped to attention, his salute briskly returned as he recalled the general's name as being Mackenzie.

'General,' Rico began, 'there may be a breach of security here. I need your men to begin a systematic search of the surrounding terrain.'

'We're already on it,' the general replied. 'I'm assembling two teams now and they'll begin a search at both main ingress points, but so far there are no indications of any breach of perimeter defences.'

'They know how to hack the system,' Rico insisted. 'They could be right here, right now, and they seem to know when classified operations are about to begin.'

Mackenzie's eyes narrowed.

'How do you know about this?' he asked.

Rico wasn't sure how to reply. Both the general and the DDCIA were watching him intently.

'Instinct, sir,' Rico replied finally. 'They showed up at Dugway at a sensitive moment, and data recovered from their site showed a presence in the United Kingdom a week or so prior at another, equally classified event. The odds of them accidentally showing up at two such rare occurences are staggeringly high. They must have known and that means someone must have talked.'

To his amazement, both McCain and the general seemed to sigh in relief.

'Did you understand what I just said?' Rico uttered in disbelief. 'Area 51 could have been compromised.'

'They're not here,' the general said.

Rico hesitated. 'How do you know it's a *they*, and not one person?'

Before the general could answer, a call came in. McCain picked up the phone and listened intently. Then he set the phone down and looked at Rico.

'Have you noticed that your men are being followed?' he asked.

Rico's nerve endings fired in unison. 'That's right.'

'Just seen heading down the 93 toward Groom Road, a convoy of vehicles driven by a known Russian sleeper cell. If you're quick enough, you might be able to cut them off.'

Rico barely heard the last as he whirled and dashed from the room. He knew that neither of the men he had spoken to were the base commander, and he wondered what the hell McCain would be doing here at Groom Lake ahead of him. Either way, he couldn't worry about any of that right now. Somehow, he'd got here before Kyle Trent and now he could finally intercept the kid and get him out of danger just as long as he could beat the Russians to him.

*

'The Russians might get to them first.'

General Mackenzie was concerned. Rico Savage was clearly an able officer but he did not have the resources right now to travel quickly enough to counter any threat to Kyle Trent's life. That, he figured, was probably what some folks in the service wanted right now.

'That's fine,' McCain replied. 'We just need them to be where we want them to be. If the Russians are there too, even better, we can just remove them from play at the same time. That will send a clear message to Moscow that we mean business, and it'll take the heat off of you and your family. This is how we're going to play things out, Scott. We turn every one of our enemies against each other, and let them lead us to the prize, okay?'

To his own surprise, Mackenzie nodded without question. There was no doubt in his mind that this truly was the only way.

'What about the safety of my field operatives, Warner and Lopez?'

McCain took a deep breath.

'They're not employed or contracted to us Scott,' he replied. 'Nor is Rico Savage, for that matter. We will do everything we can to protect them, but they're in this on their own account and we must prioritise our main misson, is that understood?'

Mackenzie nodded, no longer questioning the morality of the situation.

'I'll have the base guards follow Colonel Savage and his team.'

***

XLII

Ethan drove across the desert from Route 6 even as the sun was dipping below the mountain ranges to their right. The brilliant sky contrasted with the deeply bruised thunderheads soaring into the chilly heavens to their left, and Ethan could see faint flashes of lightning flickering amongst their towering heights.

'The place is called Brainwash Butte,' Kyle said from the rear seat of the car. 'It's as close as we can get on public land to the airbase and have a clear line of sight.'

Ethan knew from dead reckoning that they were at least twenty miles from the airbase, but with the clear desert air and the high peaks to observe from, it was likely that they would have a perfect view of the base from even this far out. Desert antelope dashed across the desert nearby, and Ethan had glimpsed one or two hawks wheeling on the last of the thermals spiralling up from the desert, but other than that there was absolutely no sign of life.

It took another hour of rough driving on ancient dirt tracks to make it to the foot of the hills, where the terrain was far too tough for anything but the best off-road vehicles to negotiate. Ethan pulled up, killed the engine and got out, grabbing the back packs and water canisters they'd bought before leaving Tonopah. The surrounding hills were now enshrouded in darkness, the first faint stars twinkling like jewels above them.

'Aren't the military going to be watching us?' Lopez asked as she slipped a backpack onto her shoulders. 'They're all over Groom Lake.'

Kyle shook his head as he hoisted two cameras from the trunk and checked them over.

'This base is run by the Department of Energy, not the Air Force. Sure, the security is tight, but they rely on disinterest rather than overt muscle to keep the public out. That said, if we wandered across the perimeter we'd be toast.'

Ethan had only had a few spare minutes to research this most mysterious of locations, and as a result his knowledge was sparse and his nerves on edge. This wasn't a place to get caught out for all kinds of reasons. If elements of the military were intent on killing them, high desert such as this was the perfect place to commit the crime. Hikers, tourists and other unwary travellers were often lost out here to rockfalls, dehydration, sunstroke, snakebites and other hazards that could easily be claimed to have taken their lives. That, of course, assumed that their bodies would ever be found. Nobody knew that they were out here, nobody travelled out here but for UFO fanatics and the Shoshone and Southern Paiute tribes whose land the base happened to have been built on. Whether they had been driven out or not Ethan was unsure, but three desiccated corpses could lay out here for decades and never be found.

Ethan covered their car with a camouflage net that he'd purchased in Tonopah, one more usually used to conceal nature hides, and then they set off for the heights before the last of the remaining light faded from the western sky. Kyle led the way, apparently having been here before some years ago with friends whom Ethan figured must have shared an equally unsatisfying social life.

The hillside was steeper than he had expected, large boulders blocking many of the easier routes to the top. He could see in the fading light the occasional sign of vehicle tracks but many of them looked old and faint, as though nobody had travelled up here for a very long time.

'This is the last time I agree to go wandering about in the wilderness,' Lopez complained behind him. 'You do realise that every time we do this, you've ended up getting us shot at?'

'You say it like it's my fault,' Ethan replied.

'I like to think they're shooting at *you*, and I'm just in the wrong place at the wrong time.'

'That's what happened to Greg,' Kyle pointed out.

'Whose side are you on?' Lopez uttered, apparently hurt.

Ethan said nothing as he climbed, following Kyle until they began to breach the summit. The sun had well and truly set by the time he saw a horizon before them again, the night sky glittering with a brilliant veil of stars so vivid it seemed he could reach up and pluck them with his hands.

'Best night skies in the world out here,' Kyle said as he saw Ethan looking up. 'And the best view of ET central you're ever going to get.'

As they crested the ridge so the deserts opened up before them in all their vastness, and at once Ethan could see a string of flickering lights nestled against the darkness of the mountains to the west.

The airbase looked surprisingly small from up here and so far away, but there was no doubting what it was. The runway was a long, thin line of lights while the buildings and hangars were illuminated by similar pin-prick lights. However, unlike a civilian airport there was no flood lighting of hangars and parking areas. The rest of the base was veiled in darkness and Ethan could see no movement of vehicles at all.

A rumble of thunder rattled the sky and the earth seemed to tremble beneath the blows. Ethan turned to see the thunderclouds looming over them, blocking out the stars as they advanced. A ripple of savage lightning illuminated their depths with vivid flashes of blue-white light that threatened the heavy weather that was to come. Ethan recalled Kyle mentioning that the Roswell event occurred during or after a major thunderstorm, and he guessed that the Hydra had brought them here to this airfield because of the significance of both the weather and the location of the airbase itself.

'We'd better get set up,' he said to Kyle. 'We'll need those covers for the cameras if it starts raining, and we're sitting ducks up here for lightning strikes.'

Kyle nodded as he started unpacking the new cameras they'd obtained.

'Don't worry, we can set up the cameras and observe from somewhere a little safer on the hillside.'

With Lopez, they spent the next half an hour setting up the cell phone cameras, pointing them in the direction of Tonopah Test Range so that they covered a vast panorama of sky both above and to the sides of the airbase. With ultra-violet, infra-red and optical cameras in play, Ethan figured that if anything came buzzing through the area they could hardly fail to miss it.

Kyle Trent ran a data cable to each of the three cell phones and linked it to a small dish that he set up to point down the hillside. Ethan watched as the kid switched everything on, the dish designed to send the data directly to his laptop computer and an SSD drive that would both display and store every second of footage that they recorded. That way, if the cameras were damaged Kyle would still have a record of what they had seen. At the same time, the satellite phone would pick up the feed and transmit it live onto the Internet.

With everything set up, they turned and made their way off Brainwashe Butte just as the sky crackled and a savage flare of lightning split the heavens with a crash so loud that it reverberated through Ethan's chest and he flinched instinctively. Lopez ducked and looked up at the turbulent sky above them, a roiling maelstrom of dark, tumbling clouds.

'I'd be amazed if anything was flying around through that.'

Ethan was about to reply when something caught his eye. As a distant fork of lighting twisted across the sky to the south and cast blue light across the desert wastes, he saw a plume of dust moving toward them. Ethan froze, his eyes fixed on the convoy of vehicles moving across the desert without headlights.

'We've got company.'

Kyle looked to the south and he panicked.

'They're here, they've come to shoot us, we have to get off the desert!'

'Take it easy,' Lopez replied. 'We can get out of here before they get to us, they're miles away.'

'They were miles away when they shot Greg,' Kyle complained, stumbling past her and taking off down the hillside. 'I'm not gonna become their next victim!'

'Kyle, wait!'

Lopez began running through the dark after Kyle. Ethan broke into a run to keep up with her and promptly bashed his knee against a boulder. He cursed, stumbling through the darkness and relying on the occasional flicker of lighting to illuminate the rocky hillside ahead of him.

Whoever was closing in on them would have IR cameras of their own, and though the hills currently shielded them from view as soon as they drove away from the site they would stick out like a beacon against the cold desert. Ethan knew that they had to get away from the cameras to draw attention away from them, but there were few places to hide out here and he didn't doubt for a moment that their enemy would kill them if they caught up with them.

Ethan hurried in pursuit of Lopez and heard a scuffle ahead as the fleet-footed former police officer caught Kyle Trent with ease. Kyle cried out as Lopez twisted one of his arms up behind his back and pinned him against a boulder.

'Ow, who's side are you on?'

'Yours,' Lopez insisted, 'and if you run now they'll catch you within minutes. They're in vehicles too, you know.'

Ethan jogged up to Lopez's side and placed a reassuring hand on Kyle's shoulder.

'Running isn't an option out here,' he said. 'We've got a few minutes before they arrive. We can plan an escape route into the hills to the east, sit tight there and see what happens.'

'But they'll *find* us,' Kyle insisted.

'Not if we're careful,' Ethan countered. 'Only if we're stupid and start panicking.'

Kyle looked at Ethan, and as another crack of thunder split the heavens he realised that there was no way he was going to survive on his own out here without them. He nodded, and Lopez released his arm.

Ethan turned to where he knew their vehicle was concealed somewhere in the darkness against the side of the hills.

'Let's get out of here before they arrive, and set up so we can see what those cameras of yours can see. Trust me, they won't catch us.'

Kyle sighed, and reluctantly began walking through the darkness. Ethan followed with Lopez, and then the night turned to brilliant day as white lights flared painfully all around them. Ethan threw his hands up to protect his eyes, Lopez and Kyle doing the same. There was no noise, no nothing but the searing light right in front of them.

A series of shadowy figures surrounded them, indiscernible against the brilliant white lights, and for a moment Ethan wondered whether the UFO encounter they'd been hoping for was going to be a lot closer than they had bargained for.

From the brilliant light, a single figure emerged and moved toward them.

***

XLIII

Ethan tried to see the object that was lighting them up, and then he heard boots running and the unmistakeable sound of weapons being cocked. Ethan squinted into the light as the figure moved through the ring of its companions, coming to stand within a metre of them. Ethan saw a broad, craggy face, pale skin and cold, black eyes.

'Ethan Warner,' the figure said in a Russian accent, 'Nicola Lopez and Kyle Trent. We meet at last.'

Vigor Vitesky stepped forward as the blinding lights of a row of vehicles behind him suddenly faded out and left them in absolute darkness. Ethan blinked, trying to get a look at the man confronting them. A flare of lighting danced across the horizon and Vigor's pale, emotionless visage glared at them in silence as Kyle staggered back and tucked himself between Ethan and Lopez.

'Y.., you're Russian,' Kyle stammered.

Vigor smiled, no warmth in his eyes as he stood with his hands behind his back.

'I was told that you were smart,' he uttered.

Thunder rolled across the deserts as though the gods were warring in the skies, and Ethan felt the first drops of rain on his skin.

'Who are you?' Ethan demanded. He could see that they were surrounded by armed men, and his only real hope was to appear unintimidated. 'Where is Sophie?'

'Mister Warner,' Vigor turned to him. 'What I want is only the very same thing that you want. We would very much like to share the technology that your clever young friend here has developed.'

'It's not for sale,' Kyle snapped, apparently recovering his courage. 'Not to Russia, anyway.'

Vigor raised an eyebrow.

'Perhaps to your capitalist overlords in Washington then?' he murmured. 'Oh, but wait, they killed your friend and are currently hunting you down like a dog. Are you sure you want to risk dealing with them?'

Kyle hesitated in his response, but Ethan stepped forward. He felt certain that the Dugway teams had not shot Greg, but this man before him radiated the kind of fanatical devotion to Mother Russia that would think nothing of taking innocent lives.

'How would you know anything about the death?' he demanded. 'And you've abducted an innocent girl! She's seven years old for Christ's sake.'

Vigor grinned.

'We made it our business to know,' he replied. 'But as for a missing girl? Mister Warner, Miss Lopez, I know much of what you have done over the years, just as I know that half the people placed under your protection have died. Kyle Trent is not safe here, in fact he's not safe anywhere in this country now. Kyle, Russia would welcome you with open arms if you were willing to come with us.'

Kyle almost laughed. 'Why the hell would I do that?'

'Because for the last seventy years or more your government has deliberately concealed from the American people the greatest secret of all time, the existence of other wordly beings that visit our planet. You, like so many others, are passionate about this revelatory knowledge because you believe that it will bring about a great change in the nature of humanity. So do I.'

Ethan peered at Vigor in silence, unsure of whether or not to believe him.

'Kyle,' Vigor entreated, 'this is not about Russia, or America, or any other country on earth. It is not about governments or nations. It is about the spirit of humanity, of who we are and where we come from. Knowing, for sure, that we are not alone in the universe and that there are other species out there who may befriend us, or attack us, is the one thing that might just finally bring us together as the one species, the one brotherhood that we have always been.'

Ethan saw that Kyle was listening intently, his idealistic fervor sparked by the Russian's impassioned entreaty.

'We are brothers in the same fight,' Vigor went on. 'The time for disclosure has come and you and I both know it, Kyle. The world is more educated than it has ever been, poverty is at its lowest level since records began. Despite all of the wars and the suffering we see on the news we know that life is getting better for people with each passing year, each passing decade. We have orbital telescopes due to be launched soon that are so powerful they will be able to image individual planets around other stars. How long do you think it will be before one of those planets reveals itself to have oxygen in its atmosphere, or signs of industrial or technological presence on its surface? We are living in an age of discovery like no other Kyle, and it's down to people like us to bring that knowledge to the people while we can.'

'At the point of a gun?' Ethan asked, gesturing around them.

Vigor smiled.

'It is your people who are doing the hunting,' he countered. 'It is your armed forces that are patrolling all around the globe, not ours. Russia is not policing the world, a service that no country has requested.'

'Thankfully,' Nicola shot back. 'The world would be in a hell of a mess if Moscow was the world's policeman. Queuing for bread, anyone?'

Vigor did not bite on Lopez's sarcasm, instead keeping his gaze fixed on Kyle.

'You and I are above politics and name calling. We both know that this is far more important than the petty wars of communism and capitalism. This is about the future of our human race. Imagine what will happen when the world finally knows that we are not alone! Do you want to bring that knowledge to the people, with the computer wizardry that you possess? Or would you rather let your government take you into custody, jail you, confiscate your work which they will then claim has nothing of defense significance or has been lost, and sit on the truth for another generation?'

'The people know,' Kyle replied. 'They don't believe the government's lies, they just don't know what to do about it.'

'Then take the inititative!' Vigor insisted. 'Take the chance, this *one* chance, to defy the government that hides secrets from its own people and let the world know that it was Kyle Trent who risked his life to reveal the truth!'

Ethan could see Kyle's eyes glowing with a faint light of delight, or radicalism. His fists were clenched and he was almost hopping about.

'He's right,' Kyle whispered. 'It's time.'

Lopez folded her arms and tilted her head as she peered at Vigor with a jaundiced eye. Another deafening crash of thunder split the heavens and the spots of rain began to fall more heavily, splattering against the dusty earth at their feet.

'And Kyle no doubt should make this announcement in Russia, of course, with Russian money behind him.'

'He will be safe there,' Vigor assured her, 'which is more than can be said for your experiences with your own government, no?'

'I've never heard anyone describe Russia as *safe* before,' Ethan murmured.

'We have a very different policy toward UFO events,' Vigor rallied. 'They are considered a topic of open discussion among the people. Such revelations as Kyle could provide would not cause the same rabid fears over national security as he is experiencing here in the United States. There is no Area 51 in Russia where he would be taken, no Guantanamo Bay where he would be hurled to die.'

'The Gulag?' Lopez offered. 'The Siberian Prisons? The…'

'All long closed,' Vigor cut her off. 'Kyle would be hailed a hero.'

'And a defector, a traitor to his own country,' Ethan added.

Vigor's forced smile slipped and he showed the first signs of agitation.

'Mister Warner, we stand here on the verge of the greatest discovery of all time and you, a man who has been responsible for more carnage and destruction in the name of your country than any agent I have ever encountered, is trying to prevent it.'

'My job is to keep Kyle safe,' Ethan shot back. 'I'm not the one surrounding him with guns.'

'The guns are a necessity in a country where Americans seem willing to shoot at one another just for the hell of it,' Vigor growled. 'The rest of the world is moving forward while you, the grand and great USA, seem to be slipping back into anarchy and lawlessness. I wouldn't be *without* a damned gun in this country!'

Kyle stepped toward the Russian.

'You can broadcast what we find?' he asked. 'It goes out to the world, to everyone, not just to Russia?'

Vigor nodded. 'Everyone, all people of all races. This is about humanity, not country.'

Ethan could not bring himself to argue with the Russian any longer. Although he did not trust Vigor, he knew that he could not prevent Kyle from leaving with the Russian if that was what he decided he wanted to do. Right now, all he was interested in was Sophie's safe return.

'We just want the girl back with her family,' Lopez snarled at Vigor. 'You two want to go play the X-Files together that's up to you but leave the girl out of it.'

'And me?' Kyle asked. 'What about my family?'

'They would be protected,' Vigor promised. 'We have people here who can ensure that. And you would be well cared for, until the furor over your revelations have died down. Then, I would imagine that you would return to your own country a hero too. Everybody wins.'

Vigor extended his hand toward Kyle. Kyle hesitated and glanced at Ethan and Lopez. Neither of them encouraged or hindered him in any way. Kyle took a breath, then reached out.

'Stand still with your hands on your head!'

The voice thundered out into the night and Ethan whirled as he saw American troops pour down the hillside nearby, laser sights sweeping the Russian gunmen as brilliant lights flashed into their eyes.

***

XLIV

The Russians leaped into action, their rifles trained on the Americans as they swarmed into positions on the hillside above them. Ethan and Lopez instantly moved slightly apart, forcing the various factions to pick two targets instead of one.

Kyle Trent jerked his hand away from Vigor's and ducked behind Ethan, his eyes wide with terror as he stared at the American troops now dominating the scene.

'Stand still with your hands on your head!' a soldier shouted.

The Russians looked at Vigor, their expressions taut, but they did not lower their weapons.

The US troops' laser sights were locked onto the Russians, who were now outnumbered two to one. Ethan knew that the convoy had been coming, but he hadn't realised that it was allied troops and he began to wonder how the hell they'd known Kyle was going to be here. More to the point, how had the Russians known?

Vigor Vitesky remained standing with his hands clasped before him. Ethan said nothing. The temptation to call out to the troops and inform them that he was working for the CIA was overwhelming but he figured it would be better to let them know later, not in front of Vigor and his goons.

'Drop the weapons now or we'll be forced to fire!'

Ethan could not tell who was speaking but clearly there was an officer somewhere among the men who was leading this whole parade. Vigor replied, his voice sounding almost meek compared to the American's.

'This is public land and we have the right to bear arms here,' he said simply. 'We are not trespassing.'

The reply came back, as uncompromising as ever.

'You're under arrest for the attempted murder of an American citizen and the suspected abduction of another! Either surrender now or I'll give these men the order to fire!'

Vigor frowned. 'Murder? Abduction? Nobody has committed any such crime! Where is the evidence?'

'I won't say it again!' the soldier bellowed back.

The Russians began shifting from foot to foot, their rifles held ready. Lightning flickered across the heavens and in the brilliant flash Ethan could see dozens of American troops confronting them. He could feel the charge in the air now more intently than ever. The Russians were unlikely to stand down and the Americans would open fire on all of them, and probably Ethan, Nicola and Kyle too just for good measure.

'Put your weapons down,' Ethan advised Vigor loudly enough for the troops to hear his voice. 'If you've done nothing wrong, you have nothing to fear.'

'We are innocent of any crime!' Vigor snapped and turned to Kyle. 'You trust these gun-crazed dogs more than you would trust us?'

Kyle wasn't sure what to say and cowered behind Ethan as the Americans held their position. Ethan knew that there was going to be a major incident if he didn't stand up and do something, and he had to find a way to turn Kyle away from the Russians.

'Is the victim of the alleged crime the family of General Mackenzie?' he called out to the American soldiers.

There was a long silence, and then the voice replied. 'What would you know about it?'

'We know the general,' Ethan replied. 'We heard about what happened. But we also heard that you guys shot an innocent teenager at Dugway two nights ago, so forgive us if we're a little reluctant to trust anyone right now.'

The silence of the troops deepened, the wind rumbling across the deserts and the tense crackling of energy through the tumbling clouds above. The rain began to fall more heavily, fat droplets splattering down all around them. Flashes of violent lightning forked across the horizon as from among the Americans a tall figure emerged. Wearing his uniform, General Mackenzie strode toward them without fear of the Russian guns.

'Scott?' Lopez uttered in amazement. 'What the hell's going on?

Mackenzie barely responded to Lopez, his eyes fixed on Kyle Trent. He walked to within a couple of metres of Ethan and studied the boy for a moment before speaking.

'Son, you're in a heap of trouble but I think I can help out if you'll come with us.'

Kyle shrank back from the towering officer and Ethan allowed him to move further behind him.

'I'm not sure that's such a good idea.'

There was something about the general that was different. That something had changed was obvious, and Ethan assumed that the failed hit on his family had altered his course, understandably enough. But now he was without the comraderly, affable air that had surrounded him when they had first met. His features were lined, serious, his bearing stiff and uncompromising.

'This isn't about us anymore,' Mackenzie said to Ethan. 'Either Kyle comes with us, or everything ends here for everyone.'

Ethan instantly knew that Mackenzie wasn't kidding around. The threat was clear: comply or die.

'What about Sophie?' Ethan asked.

Mackenzie's resolve stiffened further. 'We need to focus on Kyle.'

'What the hell happened to you?' Lopez uttered.

Mackenzie did not respond. He glanced at Vigor and called out to him.

'You and your men will be gone in the next sixty seconds, either by choice or at the hands of my troops. There are no other options.'

With that, he turned and strode away back into the darkness.

Ethan glanced across at Lopez, and he could see in her eyes that they had no plays left. There was nowhere to run out here, nowhere to hide. If they did not comply they would be shot, and even if they did play ball the American troops might be ordered to kill them anyway. Suddenly, the search for a kid with a clever idea had turned deadly serious and Ethan could not think of any way out of their situation.

'I *told* you this would happen,' Lopez snapped at him in a terse whisper.

Ethan looked at Vigor and he could see the resolution in the Russian's eyes. They did not trust the American troops one bit and none of them were showing any sign of backing down. In the next thirty seconds there was going to be a bloodbath and he knew that there was nothing he could do to prevent it.

'When I say get down,' he whispered to Kyle and Nicola, 'just drop flat on your faces and hope for the best.'

Lopez's whispered reply reached out to him from the darkness. 'Wow, thanks Einstein.'

'Ten seconds!' Mackenzie boomed.

Vigor's voice reached them from somewhere behind.

'This, Kyle, is the kind of government leadership that got your friend shot in the head.'

'They're going to kill us,' Kyle whimpered. 'I don't want to die.'

Ethan shook his head. Now he finally knew who had killed Greg.

'No details of the shooting were released to the public, Vigor,' he said without looking behind him at the Russian leader. 'How would you have known that Greg was shot in the head?'

A deep silence followed. Ethan turned to look at the Russian and saw the rage soaring through him at his mistake. Vigor opened his mouth to shout for his men to open fire and Ethan grabbed Kyle's head and shoved it down.

'Get down!'

Lopez dropped as Vigor screamed at his men. 'Now!'

Ethan saw a blaze of flash-bang grenades burst all around them, the darkness suddenly split with blinding light and smoke as a hail of bullets shattered the night air. Ethan saw the bursts of light flashing red behind his closed eyes as he hit the desert dust and heard the Americans return fire from the heights. Thick smoke from the flash-bang grenades clogged the night air and scalded his nostrils.

'This way!'

Ethan belly-crawled his way out of the line of fire with Kyle and Lopez right alongside him. Bullets seared the air inches above their heads as they crawled to the safety of the hillside and scrambled in among the rocks.

'Sophie,' Lopez said. 'The Russians have still got her!'

Ethan turned to Kyle, ducking and flinching as rounds zipped and ricocheted around them.

'Stay here and keep your head down!'

Kyle nodded, curling up into a ball with his hands over his head.

Ethan peered out from the rocks and saw the muzzle flares from Russian rifles as they returned fire against the American troops while retreating toward their vehicles. The Americans were descending from the heights, firing in short bursts, withering fire cutting down Vigor Vitesky's men as they scrambled for the cover of darkness and the protection of their vehicles.

'Wide and to the left!' Ethan yelled to Lopez.

She responded instantly, understanding his plan. Ethan knew that the Americans would not fire on the Russian vehicles for fear of hitting Vigor's hostage, and that was about the only thing preventing the American troops from laying waste to the Russian convoy.

Ethan broke from the hillside at a sprint and dashed out into the darkness, Lopez behind him as they ran across the deserts and arced around toward the Russian vehicles. If he could get Sophie out before the Russians could make good their escape, then Mackenzie's men could blast them all to hell.

The clatter of gunfire and the shouts of men in both American and Russian haunted the night as the storm raged overhead. The rain began falling in sheets, drenching his skin and surprisingly cold as he ran through the darkness. The Russians were to his right now, forced to focus their fire on the Americans to keep their heads down and unaware of Ethan and Lopez circling out wide and around them.

In a flash of lightning Ethan saw a small gathering of vehicles just ahead, two of them with drivers waiting for their comrades. The engines were running and Ethan could see that they had turned their tail to the gunfight to make their escape as fast as possible.

***

XLV

'Gun!'

The car door opened and Ethan hurled himself to the right and slammed his body against the side of the vehicle as a gunshot blast hurtled by at near point-blank range. In the flash of the weapon's discharge he saw Lopez running for the driver of the second vehicle. Ethan grabbed the shotgun by the stock with his right hand and folded his left arm over the muzzle and then hauled as hard as he could.

The driver tumbled out of the vehicle, desperate to hang on to the shotgun. Ethan stamped out at the inside of the man's right ankle with his right boot and the Russian squealed in pain as the bones snapped and he collapsed, releasing the shotgun.

Ethan turned the weapon over and with a grunt of effort smashed the butt into the injured Russian's face. The Russian fell silent as Ethan whirled and saw Lopez flicking the heel of her boot across the other driver's face in a valiant high-kick that sent the Russian sprawling across the desert dust.

Ethan peered into the vehicle and saw nobody inside. He cursed and hurried to the car that Lopez had under her control and saw her beckoning to someone inside. From within the car emerged Sophie, a stuffed toy clutched in one hand and a fearful expression on the other. About the only thing working in their favour was that she recognised them as the people who had visited her parents the previous day. Lopez's gentle coaxing got her out of the car, and Ethan felt a rush of relief as they turned to leave.

The clicking of a gun's mechanism brought them up short.

'Time for you to leave this mortal coil, Mister Warner.'

Vigor was standing before them, crouching out of sight of the gunfire as he held a pistol pointing at Ethan's belly. Ethan had the shotgun in his hands but he knew he would not be able to bring it to bear before the Russian fired.

'She's not going anywhere with you,' Lopez shot back.

A couple of American rounds zinged off the car's body work and they all flinched. Ethan put himself in front of Sophie and Lopez, the shotgun still in his grasp.

'You run, Vigor,' he said. 'That's your only play here.'

'Not without what I came for,' the Russian replied. 'If we can't take Kyle, then a girl who attracts alien abductors will be a perfect conciliatory prize.'

'Over my dead body,' Ethan snapped.

The Russian shrugged. 'So be it.'

The gunshot rang in Ethan's ears and time slowed down. He felt as though someone had slapped him gently in the guts, and despite himself he looked down.

For a moment he could see nothing unusual, and as he could feel nothing he thought for a moment that Vigor had missed the shot.

Then, he saw the ragged hole in his shirt and a dark, black stain that spread swiftly across his belly.

'Ethan?' Lopez yelped and rushed to his side.

Ethan was mildly surprised to feel no fear and no pain, but then his experience kicked in and he knew that it wasn't a good sign. He lifted the shotgun to try to take a shot at Vigor, and then the second bullet hit Ethan in the chest.

Ethan's legs crumpled beneath him and he sank to his knees.

Lopez screeched something that sounded like one of the cries of a bird of prey wheeling above the burning deserts and she launched herself at Vigor. The Russian turned the pistol but not quickly enough and Lopez crashed into him with her fists flying. Vigor smashed down onto the desert floor, the rain falling on them both as Lopez grabbed the Russian's head in both hands and smashed her forehead into the bridge of his nose.

Vigor's face collapsed into pulp as Lopez butted him again and again, and then the pistol fired twice more. Ethan's heart sank in his chest as he saw Lopez fall silent and still. The Russian rolled her off of him and struggled to his feet.

Ethan could not move. His limbs were numb and he realised that he was feeling suddenly cold while his belly and lap felt hot and damp. He slumped against the car, little Sophie crouched alongside him as Vigor looked down at Lopez's body with pure rage twisting his features. The Russian took aim another round into her limp body.

'Run,' Ethan whispered to Sophie, his mouth dry. 'Run away.'

Sophie stared at him for a moment, then shook her head and clutched him tighter.

Vigor turned and strode across to Ethan, lightning flaring in the sky and the rain washing down over his pallid face as streams of his own blood spilled down his chin and stained his shirt. He moved to stand over Ethan, jubilant in his pain as he aimed the pistol at Ethan's face.

'For Mother Russia,' he uttered, and squeezed the trigger.

The gunshot hit Vigor in the chest and hurled him backwards onto the desert floor. Ethan flinched, his heart fluttering weakly and his head feeling heavier with every laboured breath. He saw the Americans flock around the vehicle, saw Sophie surrounded by them and the fear in her eyes.

The soldiers took her gently and she looked at Ethan for help. Ethan nodded for her to go with them, and slowly she allowed herself to be drawn away. More Americans appeared, forming a protective circle around the vehicles as Kyle Trent appeared and he heard the teenager scream in horror and dash to their sides. Kyle was manacled but the troops did not stop him as he joined Ethan, his eyes fixed to Lopez.

'No,' he gasped, his tears spilling freely and mixing with the rain.

'She's gone,' Ethan whispered. 'It's over. Try to work with the Special Ops guys, it's the only play you have.'

As the American troops rushed through the swirling smoke in the wake of the battle, Ethan could just about see several bodies lying on the cold desert floor, each of them shredded by bullets, and he could hear cries of pain somewhere out in the darkness where another wounded Russian was dying.

From the darkness, General Mackenzie reached them and stood before Ethan, looking down at him. Ethan could see the pain in the general's eyes as he witnessed Ethan's and Nicola's fate.

'We were preserving the security of the United States of America.'

Ethan frowned at the general and gasped his reply, noting that no medic was coming to his aid. 'You sold out.'

Mackenzie lifted his chin in defiance. 'It's not as simple as that.'

'Yes, it is. You're working for the other side now.'

'I am always working for my country.'

'No,' Ethan insisted. 'I don't think that this is what our country wants, do you?'

'It's not like that,' Mackenzie growled, agitated. 'You haven't seen what I've seen.'

'And what's that?' Ethan challenged.

Mackenzie looked away and said nothing. Around them, the troops regrouped and their commanding officer, a robust looking man with dark hair, reported in.

'All suspects accounted for and both Trent and the girl are in our custody.'

'Good, Colonel Savage. Get your men up on that hill and confiscate those cameras and data.'

As the troops hurried away, Ethan saw Lopez roll over, clutching her side in pain. Kyle Trent almost screamed at the general as he pointed to Ethan and Lopez.

'Help them!'

Kyle stood with his laptop clasped to his chest as Mackenzie turned to confront him.

'That's not something I can do, I'm afraid. It's too late for them now. I'm sorry, Kyle, really I am.'

Kyle stared in horror at the general. 'Would you say that if it was your family dying here in the desert? And you wonder why people like me rebel against people like *you*!?'

Ethan saw the shock on the general's face, as though he had been physically slapped.

'There is far more at stake, Kyle, than you could possibly understand or know.'

'I don't want to know!' Kyle screeched. 'I want you to help Ethan and Nicola!'

General Mackenzie spoke softly despite the rain spilling down from the blackened heavens and the storms raging around them.

'Mister Trent, I understand that you do not wish to come with us, but I assure you that we have no intention of killing you. Far from it. Your talents are of immense use to us. You may think that our government is intent on hiding the truth from the people, and you're absolutely right. But it's the reasons *why* that you don't understand. Nor did I, until recently. Please believe me when I tell you that we're doing it for the right reasons. I can't explain them here and now, but if you'll come with me I promise that in return for the Hydra, I'll tell you everything that I can.'

Kyle hesitated and glanced at Ethan. This time, Ethan nodded weakly.

'It's okay, Kyle,' he whispered. 'They didn't shoot Greg, and I think you're being given a chance to escape two decades in jail. I'd take it if I were you.'

Kyle hesitated for a moment longer, looking at the laptop in his hands, and then he slowly held it out to the general. Mackenzie took it from him, and then rested his hand on Kyle's shoulder.

'Those Russians came after my family, son,' he said. 'So I know how you're feeling right now. Trust me, it's over. You're not going to be harmed and nor will your family.'

The fear that had enshrouded Kyle since Ethan had met him finally melted away and he turned reluctantly with the two soldiers guarding him and was led away. Mackenzie waited until they were gone, and then he turned to Ethan.

'I'm sorry this happened to you both,' he said softly.

'Yeah,' Ethan whispered, noting the troops hurriedly leaving the scene. 'You're a real hero.'

'You don't understand,' Mackenzie said as he turned to leave.

'Don't understand what?' Lopez asked, her voice barely a whisper.

Mackenzie turned his back to them and walked away into the darkness. With the last of his strength, Ethan dragged himself across the desert dust to Lopez's side.

'What, he's going to make us walk home?' Lopez uttered with contempt, then called after the general with the last of her indomitable spirit. 'You could just call us a cab y'know?'

There was no answer from the darkness. Ethan sighed.

'I told you this would happen,' Lopez murmured weakly. 'It's your fault.'

'I know,' Ethan replied.

He felt her hand clutch his and squeeze it gently as his eyes closed.

The sound of running footsteps rushing toward them made Ethan turn his head, and he saw Sophie Taggart dash to their side and throw her arms around them. For a moment he didn't understand, and then he saw the look in the girl's eyes, one of rage, as though she were protecting them from something else. Sophie directed her hatred up into the turbulent night sky above them, and screamed something at the night, and then the sound of her voice was snatched away.

A brilliant orb of white light burst from the blackness above them like a new born star, and Ethan felt a gust of heat wash down over them. The hairs on his arms rose up, as did those on his head, his scalp tingling as he squinted up into the flare of light. He could hear a humming noise that seemed to vibrate the very air around him, and he could see a faint ring of what looked like pulsing lights surrounding the central, painfully bright orb.

'Ethan?'

He heard Lopez's voice but when he tried to turn to her he could no longer move, his body either too weak or paralysed somehow. Panic ripped through his nervous system but no matter what he did he could not force himself to move, and then somehow he realised that he no longer cared anyway and he merely watched the lights above them as Sophie clutched them both and buried her face against his arm.

He tried to speak to Lopez but no sound came from his lips and he could not tell if she was awake. The blinding white light was surrounded by smaller, flickering lights in the form of a circle that glowed with vivid blues, yellows and reds. He could see the faint hint of reflections from what looked like a metallic surface and he figured the thing was maybe sixty or so feet across. The air hummed with intensity, and he realised that around the object the flashes of lightning in the sky above seemed twisted, as though viewed through the bottom of a glass.

The object descended closer to him, the air crackling with energy, and he saw a beam of light reach out slowly toward him. It crept closer, blue white in colour, shimmering with incandescent light and making his skin tingle as it drew closer.

The humming noise grew in intensity and then there was a final, shattering crash and a blinding beam of light and heat, and everything went black.

***

XLVI

Groom Lake, Nevada

Kyle Trent watched out of the airplane window as the Janet Flight 737 landed on the wide salt flats, rumbling down the asphalt runway. Out of the window he could see the rows of low buildings glinting in the sunlight, as famous as any in the world. He had looked at photographs and satellite images of this place all of his life, and now here he was. He could scarcely believe that he had just landed at Area 51 and this time, he'd been invited, just a few days after almost dying in the deserts outside Tonopah Test Range.

The aircraft taxied in, and as soon as it stopped two smartly dressed guards accompanied him to the exits. They were never rude or rough with him, in fact they had barely spoken to him since he had met them at McCarran Airport, but it was clear that he was to do everything that they said.

The hatch on the aircraft opened and Kyle was guided down the steps. At the bottom, waiting for him, was General Scott Mackenzie.

'Welcome to Homey Airport,' he said, using the base's official operating name. 'Did you do everything I requested?'

Kyle nodded, barely able to contain himself.

'I didn't bring anything with me,' he assured the general, 'and my parents think I've been hired by the army as an IT expert. They're just pleased I've got a paying job.'

Mackenzie nodded, satisfied, and he checked his watch before together they got into a vehicle and were driven across the base. There were no unauthorised vehicle movements at Area 51. All vehicular movements were booked and coordinated so that no person was ever anywhere they should not be. Hangar doors were routinely closed during known satellite fly-overs, and also when members of the public were detected observing the base from the distant Tikaboo Peak, the only place within ten miles from which the runway could be seen.

The jeep drove them to a low, non-descript building that shone in the bright sunlight. Kyle could see no other people on the base, as though it was just a giant model stuck out here in the desert with no actual staff. There was no trash, everything spotlessly clean and swept, and all windows on all buildings were smoked glass, concealing what was happening within.

The jeep pulled up and they got out. Mackenzie led them to the building and he waited for a few seconds and checked his watch. Moments later, the door clicked and he opened it and walked inside. Kyle followed, both excited and somewhat afraid, and the general closed the door behind him.

There was an elevator shaft, down which they travelled together, and then a corridor with bland looking office doors. At the end was a room, and the general led him into it and shut the door behind them.

The room was small, with no furniture, and there was another door that led further into the building. Mackenzie stood beside it with his hands behind his back and looked at Kyle.

'Kyle, beyond that door are some of the answers you've been looking for. I walked through it only days ago and my life changed forever. Things will never be the same again Kyle, and you'll understand why our government is trying to keep the UFO phenomenon a secret, why it works so hard to protect our people, all people, from what you've been trying to discover. The work you've done is hugely valuable to us, and in return we want you to work with us instead of against us. However, I cannot order you to go through that door. It has to be your choice.'

Kyle sucked in a deep breath. It seemed like the coming true of a dream that he'd held for as long as he could remember, since sitting fascinated as a child and watching endless re-runs of the *X–Files*. But there was something in Mackenzie's tone that cautioned him, and he looked at the general as he recalled a line from a movie he'd watched.

'Is it worth it?'

The general nodded without hesitation. 'It is, but not for any reason you'd have figured yet. The only way to know is to find out, but there's no going back afterward Kyle.'

Kyle nodded. He knew that this was it, the moment when he would finally discover what the whole UFO thing was about. He knew that there was no way he could walk out of this room now and never know, and besides, he had a job now. It sure beat flipping burgers.

Kyle walked toward the door, opened it, and without hesitation he walked inside.

The charge in the air hit him first. Electromagnetic energy hummed around him as though the air itself was alive and he saw the interior of a large building. For a moment his brain struggled to recalibrate itself as he was sure that the building they had originally entered was only small and low. He felt dizzy and his stomach flipped inside him as he staggered to one side and reached out for the wall to balance himself.

His fingers tingled as he touched the wall and he turned to see that there was no door through which he had come. Confused, he slowly dropped to one knee. His mind was spinning and he pinched his eyes between thumb and forefinger as he tried to clear his head.

He opened his eyes again and looked out across the vast space, which seemed to be some kind of aircraft hangar. Grey metal soared above him and he could see in the centre of the building a strange craft. It hovered without supports and seemed to be made from glossy black metal, triangular in shape. But, what was strangest about the object was that to Kyle it was both there and *not* there.

He squinted at it and could see pulsing lights flickering around its edges. There were figures moving around it that looked smaller than humans but it was as though he could see through them, despite the fact that they were as solid as he was.

Kyle got unsteadily to his feet, his legs feeling weak. His stomach was doing flips within him and he felt nauseous, vacant, as though he were witnessing something that was forbidden. He tried to move toward the craft but like a dream it seemed to be always too far away. None of the entities around it seemed to notice him. He tried to speak, to say something, but nothing came out of his lungs but a faint wheezing.

Then, slowly, the beings around the craft turned and looked at him.

Kyle's guts plunged as he saw their gazes, the big black eyes and the strange, pale skin. They stared at him and he realised that within their eyes there was no soul, nothing that he could determine as human. They seemed alive and yet they were not, intelligent and yet like machines, and one by one they started to move toward him.

Kyle recoiled, staggered back and away from them. Somehow he knew he had to stay clear, that they were dangerous in the same way that newborn animals knew that snakes, spiders and other predators were dangerous: it wasn't something that was learned, it was a primal fear burned into the DNA of every living thing.

Get away!

Kyle tried to flee but he could not move, his legs feeling as though they belonged to someone else. He reached out for something to hold on to, but there was nothing but air all around him and the walls of the hangar. He saw writing on the walls, strange shapes and patterns that looked just like ancient hieroglyphics.

He looked over his shoulder and the beings were right behind him, reaching out with their minds. Horror ripped through Kyle like lightning and he screamed out in terror as he tried to push them away, their long fingers reaching out for him.

***

XLVII

'Kyle!'

Kyle thrashed and twisted as he felt the beings touch him, physically, their probing fingers scratching against his skin.

'Kyle, you're okay!'

Kyle jerked and opened his eyes wide with panic, his breath sawing through his throat and churning in his lungs. He saw General Mackenzie looking down at him, two armed guards holding him firmly but gently against the floor. He blinked and saw that he was in a small room with no lights, a door open before him where Mackenzie had come through. Beyond was the room where he had started.

Kyle's mind flipped over and over upon itself, trying to calibrate what he had just witnessed.

'What…, I don't understand…' he stammered. 'What happened?'

For a moment he thought that he had fainted or something, passed out in shock. The guards helped him to his feet, checked their watches, and then left the way Kyle had come in. General Mackenzie waited until they were gone, and when the door was closed he turned to Kyle.

'Did you see them?'

Kyle felt queasy, and he nodded for fear that he would vomit in front of the general if he tried to speak.

'Good,' Mackenzie said. 'Did they see you?'

Again, another nod. Kyle's stomach settled a little and he spoke in a rough, raspy voice.

'What the *hell* was that?'

Mackenzie helped Kyle into a chair that was now present in the room, a glass of water on a table beside him. Kyle suddenly realised he was parched and he gulped the water down.

'That, Kyle, was what we're up against. We know how they travel. We know how to connect with them, albeit briefly and using large amounts of electromagnetic energy every time we do it, as you just found out. The energy tends to make us humans nauseous for a time. Put simply, we're not very well adapted for seeing or travelling through time itself. This is the nature of what we call the Disclosure Protocol: we can't just tell people about it because it absolutely has to be seen to be believed, to be understood at some basic level. But that human factor is only one aspect of why we try to keep this all so quiet.'

General Mackenzie sat down in the opposite chair, his eyes fixed on Kyle's.

'They're out there Kyle,' he said, 'and they're not friendly. They're not enemies, but they're not friendly. They don't understand us in the same way that we don't understand them.'

'Who are they?' Kyle asked, tears in his eyes for reasons that he could not understand.

Mackenzie sighed.

'They're *us*,' he replied. 'They're *us*, Kyle. That's why we see so many of them in our skies. They're here from elsewhere in time and we don't know why. That's why we can't tell anyone about this. We don't know what they're doing and we have absolutely no ability to stop them. That is our misson, Kyle; find out what they're doing and bring it to an end.'

Kyle frowned.

'I don't understand. You said that they're us?'

'Yes, they are,' Mackenzie replied. 'They're all that's left of us, Kyle, in the future.'

'The future?' Kyle uttered. 'Are you really saying that's what I just saw?'

Mackenzie spoke slowly and clearly.

'I don't fully understand this myself yet, Kyle, so bear with me. The reason that so much paranormal activity occurs on the 37th parallel is because of the amount of electromagnetic energy our planet creates at that latitude. It's as if it provides enough energy to breach the known laws of physics, albeit only when the conditions are right. These greys, they seem to use that energy to travel, or perhaps see, through time and the same energy allows us to see them. It seems that something catastrophic will happen in the near future to humanity. It will cause us to change direction dramatically, and the result is that we change ourselves in ways that we cannot reverse. We obtain or create tremendous technology but at the price of our souls, our humanity, who we are. The entities you encountered, that so many have encountered, are trying to go back in time and alter the path of our own history.'

Kyle struggled to understand.

'They're tinkering with our past? Why?'

'Because they're trying to save themselves, at *any* cost. Time, so I'm told, is an illusion Kyle. There is no present except for our own frame of reference. Everything else we see around us, from down the road to the edge of the visible universe, is the past. But time is flexible. It can bend, twist, distort and fold upon itself. We think that when we see ghosts it's evidence of natural fluctuations in time, brief images of the past projected onto the present. Our future selves have learned how to manipulate this flexibility and are attempting to alter human history. There are two hundred and thirty-three genes in the human body that are unknown in any other species of life on earth. Just think about that for a moment; *any other species* of life on earth. This isn't science fiction: you can read about it. We no longer believe that the presence of these genes is an accident or natural event. The genes express themselves from a point several million years ago in human evolution, when our lineage separated from earlier ancestors.'

Kyle began to understand. 'They messed with us all the way back then?'

'That's right, Kyle. It's not that we wouldn't have evolved anyway, that's not what they're changing. What's happened is that we should not be here *yet*.'

Kyle's mind went empty. He stared at the general for a long moment before he replied.

'They're trying to get us ahead of something, this apocalypse you mentioned?'

Mackenzie smiled and seemed relieved, as though some decision he had made had suddenly been vindicated.

'They're preparing us for something, something that doesn't end well for us the first time around. They're not humans, they're something that is made from us, something that survives us. Human like us don't make it, Kyle, we don't survive. All that's left is these things, these greys, and we need to find out what the hell happens to mankind so that we can put it right. That's all we have to work with. We can't do what they do, so we have to rely on their coming here to figure out our own future. This is our misson, Kyle, and now you're a part of it.'

Kyle nodded, but his expression was guarded. 'Ethan and Nicola could have been a part of it too. Is that how you treat people? Is that what I can expect to happen to me if I become a liability to you?'

General Mackenzie shook his head slowly.

'Ethan and Nicola were too close to the truth, and we absolutely have to keep the numbers down. They're both patriots and excellent investigators, but they're also both wildcards and the CIA didn't feel they should be included in all of this.'

'That didn't mean they had to die,' Kyle insisted. 'You could have helped them. Instead you took that girl Sophie away and left them to die in the desert.'

Mackenzie smiled.

'You just walked into a room where you saw another place in time,' he replied. 'That's something we're only just understanding ourselves and our efforts, based on the technology we've recovered, are unrealiable. We're not barbarians here, Kyle and we can't control everything. Sometimes it has to be left to others to decide who lives and who dies.'

'You sound like you're talking about gods.'

'I'm not talking about gods,' Mackenzie replied, 'but our ancestors thought that's who they were encountering and sometimes it's hard to tell the difference even today. What I can tell you is that everything you see, everything we are, is being manipulated on a daily basis. Second sight, déjà vu, visions, hauntings, presentience: they're all manifestations of the same things, of time looping on itself due to interference from these beings. What happened to you, Kyle, didn't happen to everyone involved. It's complicated, but you'll learn that not all histories remain the same. Our job is to try to figure out why before it's too late.'

'You're saying that timelines can be different for us?' Kyle asked. 'They can be altered?'

'Time is different for everyone, and that's natural,' Mackenzie said. 'But these beings, if you encounter them, can alter it further and do so with alarming frequency.'

Kyle thought for a moment. 'Sophie Taggart?'

'Safe, and she won't be experiencing any more abduction events,' Mackenzie confirmed. 'Creech Air Force base has installed an electromagnetic disruptor that hinders the greys' ability to appear. It protects the base, but also Indian Springs. It would appear that what works for the greys can also be made to work for us. Kyle, having seen what you have seen and heard what I've had to say, do you now understand why we keep this classified? Can I trust you to do the same?'

Kyle did not hesitate. 'Absolutely. Believe me, I'm glad you gave me the chance to be involved and I'll start work right now wherever you need me. I've only got one question.'

'Shoot.'

'What happened to Ethan and Nicola?'

***

XLVIII

Indian Springs, Nevada

The heat was probably the worse thing about being back in the United States. It was different to the heat of the Indian Ocean, dry and harsh, sweltering. Ethan drove with the car window open and tried not to think about their tropical home as he guided the hired Lincoln along the 95, heading north west out of Vegas.

To his right, Lopez leaned back in her seat with her sunglasses shielding her eyes. She seemed remarkably calm despite being back in the states, perhaps because their mission this time was to be unhindered by gunmen and the threat of death. Being paid merely to investigate and not get too involved seemed to suit her.

The desert stretched in every direction for endless miles, vanishing into a milky horizon of haze beneath the white flare of the Nevada sun. Indian Springs, Ethan had noted when he checked a local map, was just eighty kilometres south of Groom Lake, the home of the infamous Area 51 facility. Vegas was to the south east, and between each there was little more than scrub desert and lonely mountain ranges blue with distance. The terrain was spectacular but the same wherever one looked and Ethan found his mind wandering over his past, the conflicts in which he'd fought and the investigations he'd conducted with Lopez at the DIA. They had seen some tremendous things in those years, things that even now he could not explain to his family, or even to himself some days.

It was only after some time that he realised he'd had one of those moments where he had been driving on automatic pilot, his mind far away from the present. He couldn't really remember the past few miles of their journey, as though they had passed in a daze. There was also a vague numbness in his belly and chest, a sort of pain that made him shift in the driver's seat to try to get comfortable. The pain passed and he looked to his right.

Lopez was dozing on the passenger seat, and he realised that he too felt uncharacteristically tired. He figured it was down to the desert heat, which was so dry and draining compared to the ocean breezes of the islands they had made their home. Lopez stirred and dragged herself from her torpor.

'Man, I must've checked out there for a few minutes.'

Ethan smiled.

'Nicola, you were out for half an hour at least,' he said as he glanced at the digital clock on the car's instrument panel.

Even he was surprised at how long they'd been driving. Damn, these long straight roads and the seemingly static scenery sure played havoc with the mind. It wasn't any wonder that so many people claimed to have had strange experiences while driving alone out here.

'So, where are we headed?' Lopez asked.

For a moment, Ethan couldn't quite remember where they were going. He frowned, and then from somewhere in his memory he recalled Sophie and her parents.

'We're due at the home of Sophie Taggart, to figure out what's happening with these abductions, right?'

'Yeah, figures,' Lopez replied.

Alarm bells started ringing in Ethan's mind. Neither of them were on top form, both seemed somewhat confused and he was sure that they had left Vegas by ten that morning. They had been driving for about an hour and yet it was already half past twelve. Thoughts that they could be suffering from carbon monoxide poisoning from the engine compelled him to open his window.

The desert air gusted into the car, the air conditioning quickly overwhelmed. Ethan shut it off just in case, focussing on the long road that shimmered into the distance ahead. He blinked, felt a little more normal, but he was still on edge.

'Something's not right here,' Lopez said.

'I know what you mean, but I can't put my finger on it.'

'We left Vegas an hour ago.'

Ethan nodded, glanced across at Lopez and saw her staring into the distance, reliving their morning. As they drove, a road sign indicated the town of Indian Springs up ahead. They were only just arriving, and yet they had been on the road for almost three hours.

Ethan hit the brakes and the car slid to a halt on the dusty, silent road. He switched off the engine and checked his watch, Lopez doing the exact same thing alongside him.

'Missing time,' she uttered.

Ethan knew more than enough about how many abduction victims suffered from the phenomenon known as *missing time*. Returned from where they were taken, the only apparent evidence that they had been anywhere other than where they were being periods of time that could not be accounted for. Victims of the phenomenon had been taken while walking, driving and even when flying aircraft, each reaching their destination long after they should have arrived.

'You don't think that…,' Ethan began, scarcely able to believe that it might just have happened to them while investigating cases of abductions.

'Think back,' Lopez said, regaining control of her thoughts. 'Re-trace our steps. Where have we been, what have we done?'

Ethan thought back. They'd been at home, back on the island. Mackenzie had come to visit them and convinced them to investigate the abduction case of Sophie

Taggart and... something else. *Damn*, Ethan couldn't quite recall it, something else, something about a kid out of..., where was it?

'Vernon,' Lopez whispered. 'We were near Vernon.'

Ethan frowned, concentrating with his eyes closed, grasping at feint threads of thought that were drifting further from his reach it seemed with every passing second.

'Something to do with a shopping mall,' Ethan said.

'Yeah, and...,' Lopez squeezed her eyes shut for a moment and then hit the dashboard in frustration. 'Damn it Ethan, something's happened to us and I can't remember anything about it!'

Ethan slipped the Lincoln back into drive and eased away again, looking at the brutal landscape around them.

'All I can remember is lots of desert and roads,' he said, knowing how unhelpful that was. 'I can't tell one place from another out here.'

They drove to Indian Springs, and there met Sophie and her parents. Despite the traumas of their experiences, it seemed that the abductions had stopped and they watched Sophie playing happily with her brother in the garden for a while as her parents told them of how tough it had been, dealing with Sophie's fear of the night and of the strange beings she said came into her room. The staff at the local base had been very helpful though and, so far, things were looking up. Local law enforcement had told them to equip the room with video cameras in case it happened again, but it seemed as though things had settled down.

'It sounds like we're not needed,' Lopez smiled at Sophie's parents as she stood to leave. 'Which in this case is a good thing.'

'Yeah,' Sophie's father, David, agreed. 'If Sophie never has another experience again, it'll be too soon. Sorry to drag you guys all the way out here for nothing.'

'It's not a problem,' Ethan said as he shook David's hand. 'The biggest problem you'll have now is getting Sophie's toy down off the roof.'

The parents stared at him for a long moment. Ethan was caught off guard by their expresssions.

'What?'

The father shook his head, peering at Ethan in confusion.

'Sophie told us about the toy on the roof,' he said, 'but we hadn't told anyone else about it. How could you have known it was there?'

Ethan wasn't sure what to say. 'I don't know,' he replied. 'I just knew, somehow.'

'He probably saw it from a distance on the way in,' Lopez said as she stepped in with a disarming smile. 'Eyes of a hawk, this one, despite his age.'

Ethan and Lopez left the home and walked to the car.

'What was that?' he asked her.

'Well, you are getting on a bit.'

'I mean the toy,' Ethan nudged her. 'How the hell would I have known about that?'

'I don't know,' she replied. 'But we're called half way across the world to help a small child, and suddenly everything's fine and we feel like we're missing something, along with a couple of hours we don't recall.'

The pain in Ethan's chest swelled briefly again, and he rubbed the spot with one hand.

'What's up?' Nicola asked.

'I don't know, just a chest pain and my guts ache a little too.'

'I've had a damned headache ever since I woke up in the car,' Lopez confessed, rubbing her temples. 'Something's up, Ethan. We need to call Mackenzie.'

Ethan didn't hesitate. He pulled out his cell phone and dialled Mackenzie's number. The line answered and Ethan switched it to speaker as he listened in disbelief.

'This number has not been recognised. Please check your number and dial again.'

'You've got to be kidding me,' Lopez uttered.

Ethan shut the cell off and leaned on the Lincoln's roof, the metal hot to the touch.

'We've been cut out,' he said. 'Something's happened and we've…, I don't know. We're here, we know why we're here, but everyone else has either cut us off or doesn't need us anymore.'

They stood for some time in silence, staring across the deserts and wondering. Ethan wasn't sure what to do next. The most alien thing about the whole charade was the confusion, the sense that the world had somehow shifted around them and they were the only ones in the dark.

'Kinda makes you wish Jarvis was back,' Lopez said.

Ethan smiled in surprise at that. 'Wow, we really must be up to our necks in crap then.'

Lopez smiled back, but her eyes were haunted. 'We're on our own, Ethan. What do we do now?'

He sighed. Their best bet was to return to their idyllic life in the Cocos Islands and forget about everything that had happened. The trouble was that Ethan had the nagging feeling that that was precisely what someone wanted them to do. They had been the subject of some kind of mental brain wash or something, and yet they had not even left their car as far as they could recall.

'Mackenzie,' he said finally. 'He was the one that brought us all into this, and he's the one who can explain what happened. And there were some photographs, right? Someone was able to figure out when UFOs would appear and take pictures of them.'

'Sure,' Lopez replied. 'What if this time we got a little too close to the truth or something, and somebody had to get us off the case?'

'But then why drop us here? Why not take us back to the Cacos and leave us there? We might never have known.'

Lopez shook her head and shrugged. 'I don't know. All I do know right now is that somebody's been messin' with my head and I want some damned answers. Are you in?'

Ethan opened the car door.

'All in,' he replied. 'We find Mackenzie and *persuade* him to answer a few questions.'

'He might not even have been CIA,' Lopez said as she pulled out her cell phone and began searching the Internet. Moments later she smiled. 'Oh, well, at least they can't erase him from history. He's listed here as active United States Army.'

'Where's he based?' Ethan asked as they drove out of Indian Springs. One way or the other, he was determined to track Mackenzie down and get the answers they felt sure they deserved.

***

Sign up to Dean Crawford's Newsletter and get a FREE book!

www.deancrawfordbooks.com

ABOUT THE AUTHOR

Dean Crawford is the author of over twenty novels, including the internationally published series of thrillers featuring *Ethan Warner*, a former United States Marine now employed by a government agency tasked with investigating unusual scientific phenomena. The novels have been *Sunday Times* paperback best–sellers and have gained the interest of major Hollywood production studios. He is also the enthusiastic author of many independently published novels.

Printed in Great Britain
by Amazon